WARRIOR'S CAPTIVE

WARRIORS OF YEDAHN #4

EMMA ALISYN

SORA STARGAZER

HARD CANDIES PUBLISHING

STARGAZER
SCI-FI ROMANCE
*Alpha males. Fierce, sassy heroines.
High stakes adventure.*

Copyright © 2020 by Emma Alisyn

All rights reserved.

No part of this book may be reproduced in any form or by any electronic or mechanical means, including information storage and retrieval systems, without written permission from the author, except for the use of brief quotations in a book review.

Cover Design by Emma Alisyn

Editing by Brianne Smith

ACKNOWLEDGMENTS

Thank you to my Beta Readers! Your work on this story was invaluable.
Tiffany
Denise
Deborah
Rebecca
Joy

GLOSSARY

YADESHI WORDS

ADEKHAN: An honored warrior. One who proved his willingness in battle to die for his unit. They have high rank, usually command units and high social status. Are the strongest, the best trained. Takes years and many battles to attain the rank. An honorary title may, in some cases, be conferred for exceptional circumstances.

ADEKHYUN: Elder Adekhan. A step up, usually have political influence as well. Usually are teachers, weapons masters, etc.

AJA'EKO: Student of an Adekhan. Aja'eki (plural)

AN'BDAHN: Prince's concubine

BDAKHUN: Princess

DAHN: Prince

DAHT: debt that cant be repaid with money or something simple. Has to do with honor. Life debt, requires service, etc. Almost spiritual.

ENJA: mine

GAHWAH: spice coffee with nut milk

HAEEMAH: Goddess of Wisdom, Peace, Righteous War, Knowledge

JOKDAHT: rampage to avenge someone

KHAN: base word meaning warrior

KHETER: doctor

SHUJAHN: warrior, person with a warriors

spirit/heart even if they aren't formally trained. Term of respect to acknowledge a person's worth

S.I.A [Social Intervention Administration Institution in North American] responsible for social welfare of Low Tier citizens. Have strict employment and education guidelines and are also known for removing problem children from their homes to be rehabilitated in group youth homes. Determine housing, food, employment and education allowances.

YADOANA: Female youngling. Term of endearment.

YADA'AMI: Beloved mate.

V'DAHN(A): King/Queen

YETI: Yadeshi Earth Training Institute Facility where humans are trained to be Yadeshi style warriors, grunt soldiers, and skilled tech workers for ships. Human women are chosen from the recruits to mate warriors. Headquartered in Omaha, NE.

1

Tai'ri rubbed the phantom ache in his wrist. There was no scarring, the marks left from the once embedded manacles of his months' long imprisonment healed.

Physically healed.

"When a great evil has been done to you, you can still choose to move forward," *Bdakhun* Ibukay said.

The princess' narrow face and intent eyes reflected in the panoramic windows that gave the medical suite a one hundred and eighty degree view of Naidekai city at night. Fliers whizzed by; singles, doubles, and late night ground transports. Pedestrians traversed air walks between buildings, the city transparent below their feet nearly four hundred meters down.

Tai'ri turned. "I want *jokdaht*." He met her gaze head on, aware that a layer of his customary deference was forever burned away.

"*Jokdaht* would not be the wisest course," a deep, cultured voice said, its owner entering the suite through doors that shimmered open silently.

Vykhan, the *Bdakhun's* Head of Security, glided forward, a gray cloak moving around his body as if currents of air flowed underneath. Long black hair streaked with feathery silver was confined in a tight braid. He watched Tai'ri with calm, expressionless eyes. Not unfeeling, simply Silent.

Tai'ri had never met a warrior who displayed more mastery of his emotions than Vykhan. One day he hoped to be worthy of *Adekhyun* Numair's presence, but this was not that day—not until he achieved the same control. For now, he shoved his feelings and impulses inside a sealed silver box in his mind.

Feelings and impulses urging him to seek vengeance. Justice.

"Do you deny I have the right to hunt, to take vengeance?"

Tai'ri stuffed down his flash of anger, aborting his restless movements as emotions he always struggled to tame roiled. Even before Vykhan, his mother had taught him to allow his fiery bursts to flow through him. Over the years, he'd learned to contain himself enough that he could mimic a quiet, diffident mannered male.

"There are more important problems to resolve. You suffered." Vykhan shrugged. "Suffering is life."

"Vykhan," Ibukay interrupted, lips pressing

together. She sighed. "Maybe we should give him some time."

"Does the female have time?"

Ibukay winced. Vykhan never argued. Logic, he would say, was its own argument.

"What female?" Tai'ri asked. He'd been gone several months. He stiffened. "My sisters—my mother? Has something happened?"

Vykhan slashed a hand through the air. "Your family is well. Did you think I would not watch over them during your absence?"

Tai'ri grimaced. "No. Apologies."

The other male relented. "You have been through difficulty, and you are sane. I sense no permanent Disquiet in you. Some indulgence is allowed. If it were not for the circumstances, we would not trouble you at this time."

"I'm fit for duty, Vykhan." He scowled, then tried to smooth the expression.

Ibukay inhaled, then let the breath out in a heavy sigh. She lifted her gaze to the ceiling, a certain sign she was about to deliver bad news. "You know you weren't the only inhabitant of the pens."

"Yeah, I know. I heard others."

There had been other people, male and female, Yadeshi and alien, in the pens that imprisoned them all, awaiting sale to buyers on the dark market or worse. He'd infiltrated the traffickers' pod after months of investigation and had gotten caught in the web.

Months to break out and send a distress beacon, months of . . . rage rose in the back of his throat. He closed his eyes and allowed words to flow in a chant.

A voice rose in time with his, the chant clearing his mind and reclaiming his calm. He'd never be Silent—didn't have Vykhan's calling for it, but the *Adekhan* had trained every person on his team in the basic precepts and chants. Necessary in Tai'ri's line of work, when going undercover often meant becoming someone else. Which meant he must be able to clear his mind, wipe it clean.

Tai'ri opened his eyes, Vykhan and Ibukay falling silent once they saw his mind was present again. He nodded to indicate he was ready to resume the conversation. Vykhan eyed him with no condemnation, and the *Bdakhun* resumed speaking.

"There were several females. Human females," she said. "Several of them are pregnant."

Tai'ri stiffened, a hiss escaping his teeth. His incisors ached briefly, but remained tucked away. "My sister would offer them all care in her birthing center." He made the offer on Bey's behalf, knowing she would honor it. The mission of their family was to facilitate every female's desired birth experience.

"Her center is the best in Beysikai Province," Ibukay said. "I thank you for the offer, Tai'ri. We will communicate it to the females." Now she hesitated, exchanging a glance with Vykhan.

"How much do you recall of what was done to you?" Vykhan asked.

Tai'ri controlled his body's physiological response. Faint perspiration, a tremble of adrenaline through his limbs as his muscles tensed for battle. Ached for battle. He had to allow himself to be *rescued*. There had been no cleansing fight, no blood. Little honor.

"Wasn't conscious all the time." Something had been done. *The antiseptic scent of a low tech medical bay assaulted his nostrils as he woke after fumes released into his pen rendered him unconscious.*

Ibukay sighed and took a seat on the divan in the center of the room. Her shoulders slumped in an uncharacteristic display of weariness. A *Bdakhun*, youngest daughter of their Province ruler and trained to a level of poise and control at all times. Something troubled her.

Tai'ri approached, crouching in front of her. "What's wrong, *yadoana*? Don't trouble yourself for me."

He'd protected and obeyed this female since she was a small girl and Vykhan first recruited him. She was as dear to him as any of his blood sisters, though he'd never be familiar with her in a way that would disrespect her rank over him. He couldn't ignore her, or any female's, distress. Wasn't made like that.

She looked up, a sheen glittering in her eyes. Her cropped shoulder length hair was more tousled than usual, something he hadn't noticed until now, and her face was thinner.

Tai'ri's brows drew together. He glanced up at Vykhan. "Has she not been eating? Who's been caring for her?"

Vykhan gave him a look, and Tai'ri subsided.

"It's not his fault," she replied hotly. "And you know what a nag he is. We've been looking for you for months. We thought you were—" she stopped talking, composed herself and straightened her back. "Tai'ri . . . they took your seed."

The words made no sense. "What?"

"The times you told us you were unconscious and awoke in a med bay," Vykhan said, a flash of something akin to pity in his eyes. Not quite pity, because Haeemah's Precepts wouldn't allow it. Not when life was always to be celebrated. If one lived, there was hope. "That must have been when they operated on you. Your genetic material was extracted and used to impregnate at least one human woman. We don't think more than one. The others have undergone testing as well."

Tai'ri stilled, staring at him as if he was speaking an Earth language. Or hissing like one of the odd snake warriors. "I don't understand."

She reached out and took his hand, gaze soft with compassion. "You are the genetic father of an unborn halfling, Tai'ri. The mother is one of the females who was imprisoned in a pen near yours."

Vykhan was at his side in a flash. "Breathe."

Tai'ri didn't recall bending over, gasping as a powerful clamp seized his insides. Vykhan's chant slid through his mind like water through open fingers. He caught them, held on as the words settled into his gut.

Incandescent joy. Black, searing grief.

Rage.

The chant crashed through his mind, Vykhan initiating a mental link which he rarely did. Established during training, it enabled their *Adekhan* to guide them when mere words and demonstrations would not do. It only worked in proximity.

When Tai'ri returned to himself, he realized he was grasping Vykhan's hand, crushing it under the strength of his emotions. Vykhan said nothing, ignored what must have been searing pain as bones creaked.

"You have a few choices to make," Ibukay said from several feet away. She must have moved, or Vykhan must have moved her, when Tai'ri blanked. Her warriors were devoted to her, but each of them was dangerous when not in control. Despite Haeemah's Precepts of non-violence, they were all trained to kill. Because sometimes death was required to ensure peace and Silence.

"There is only one choice," Vykhan said.

"Vykhan." Steel in her tone, a warning.

"Does the female have a choice?" Vykhan asked pointedly.

"Yes, yes she does. She does not have to carry the child to full term."

Vykhan stood, facing their *Bdakhun*. "She is already full term. In human gestation she will give birth in four to six weeks."

Tai'ri straightened, feeling like an old warrior, but squared his shoulders and waited until the feeling of being repeatedly punched in the stomach resided.

"Has she . . . has she asked for an induction?" Technology had all but eradicated the need for such procedures centuries ago. But considering his family's generation's long calling, he understood more than most males about such things. "They're so small at this stage." So small. His baby *yadoana* had barely fit in the palm of his hand, half-formed, perfect limbs as fragile as brittle stems. Eyes that never opened. First tears never shed. A voice never raised in an angry cry.

She had been silent when she slipped into the world, and silent when she slipped away again.

A feral growl rumbled in his chest, but Tai'ri controlled himself immediately. There was no time for old grief. No time for the old, aching guilt. Normally, he had better control than this. What was wrong with him? This wasn't the first time a mission had cost him. He'd been tortured, beaten, enslaved . . . none of it had touched his heart until now.

"Tell me about the female," he said. He focused. Hadn't been able to save that child. He'd save this one, even from its own mother if that's what it took.

Ibukay spoke after a moment. "She's from Earth, a human. We don't know the circumstances of her abduction yet, she hasn't been willing to go into detail and I—I don't want to press her, or any of the others until they are ready."

"We need that intel," Tai'ri said. "We need to know how the traffickers are operating. They've changed methodology again, that was how I made a mistake."

"We will know in time. In the immediate present, the mental health of the aliens is more important. Especially while pregnant." Tai'ri nodded, and she continued. "She's young for a human, the tests we ran show her to be around thirty to thirty-five Earth years."

Tai'ri cringed.

"I know," Ibukay said. "She's young, but I'm told that's adult age."

"She has opted not to return to Earth at this time," Vykhan said. "We can place her in the shelter with the other females, but as we know the identity of the genetic father of her child, I thought you would wish to be informed so you can make more suitable arrangements. Naturally."

"Whatever he decides is the most suitable arrangement, Vykhan," Ibukay said, expression darkening. "You will not bully him into doing what you think is right."

Vykhan was unmoved. "I know what this means to you, Tai'ri."

He shook his head. "Not my choice. It's hers."

"The human female is in no condition to make these kinds of decisions."

"Vykhan," Ibukay growled.

"This is a second chance," Vykhan said, gaze unwavering.

Tai'ri rubbed his sore stomach, the words another verbal knife. A chance to redeem himself for the pain he'd caused in the past. A chance to replace the life lost.

"I won't coerce her. But if she keeps the child, they'll have a home with me. If she wants to birth the child and give it away, I will take my son or daughter. That's my right, no matter how they were conceived."

Ibukay nodded. "That much we can give you, even if she decides to induce birth now. The child is developed enough that it would survive. But I don't think that's the choice she will make. I've spoken with her some."

"May I see her?"

"I already asked, and she agreed to a meeting if you wished it."

"You will have four months of leave," Vykhan said. "That will give you time to acclimate your female and child to their new home. There are—"

A beep sounded, first on Vykhan's comm unit and then a split second later on Ibukay's. The *Bdakhun* glanced at the incoming message and cursed. She whirled, Vykhan at her heels.

The doors shimmered open, letting in the blaring sound of the med bay alarm. Tai'ri knew that sound, knew it in his bones. Someone was dying.

He ran after them, propelled by instinct.

One look at Ibukay's face and he knew.

A human woman lay pale in a bed surrounded by the normally silent tech and medics who, with calm urgency, tried to stabilize her.

"You can't be here," someone told him. Tai'ri snarled.

Ibukay glanced at the medic, who subsided and then snapped, "Don't get in the way," muttering something under her breath about 'royals'.

Tai'ri gazed at the female on the table. Tangled dark hair, her tawny brown skin too pale. And under the sheet, a swollen belly.

"She's seizing again." Someone cursed. "I don't understand these vitals. Where are the downloads? I can't do my job without data!"

"Fetal tones dropping," another medic said in a monotone.

"We should have put her in a tube. Why are we providing manual care?"

"You can't tube a gravid alien, newbie. Who authorized residents on this floor? Get out."

"Order an emergency surgical birth. And get me those downloads!"

Tai'ri stepped forward, not thinking, not even feeling, propelled by a fierce need to *do* something after months of being able to do nothing. The marks on his arms flared to life as he seized the female's wrist.

"Oh shit," someone said. "What the fuck is he doing here? Wait, wait, what are you *doing*?"

His marks split, flaring to life. He didn't question it. Perhaps they recognized his blood in the child, nestled inside this female and about to leave the world before he even had a chance to hold this one in his arms. Not again. Never again.

"Well, fuck me, it's stabilizing. Blood pressure dropping back to its baseline."

"*She*, you fish bait. We can't call aliens 'it' anymore, remember your sensitivity training?"

"I didn't know the marks could do that with an alien."

"Oh, Goddess. Where have you been? Why do you think . . ."

Tai'ri tuned their bickering out, his grip on the female unbreakable. It could not be a bond, not quite, because mate bonds required consent and intention. But perhaps the marks recognized the need for healing and acted in response.

He held her wrist long after the newly formed marks had slithered up her slender arms and settled into grayish blue strokes onto her skin. Her skin lost the gray tinge—not a good color for humans, he recalled—and her strained breathing and thrashing eased.

Her eyes opened once, dark and fathomless, then closed.

"The baby?" he asked.

"Heart tones normal," a medic said. "You saved their lives. Congrats."

"That's the father," someone whispered in a hushed tone. "He initiated a bond."

"Great. We can finally fill out the damn forms then."

Tai'ri let go of her finally, stumbling back. Vykhan caught him, wrapping an arm around his shoulders.

"Well done," he murmured, releasing him once Tai'ri was certain his knees would not collapse.

When she woke, they would speak. But staring down at the bed, at the sleeping, vulnerable female, he knew he could not coerce her into making the decision that was already made in his heart.

2

A CELL WAS A CELL NO MATTER HOW THEY prettied it up. Vivian wanted out. She was so sick of having no choices, of behaving and doing what she was told, fitting in where she was told.

Of course the only time she had rebelled had landed her . . . here.

Her parents would be so proud of their only child —and would inform her she had learned a valuable lesson.

"When will I be discharged?" she asked.

It hardly mattered she had nowhere to go—she just wanted the choice *to go* given back to her. Anger curled in her gut, but anger was useless. The princess had insisted Vivian's decisions would be respected. Even if she chose to—she rubbed at her lower lip, flinching away from the thought.

"Well, we need to discuss your situation first," the

doctor said. They called them something else here, but Vivian's translator must be a basic model.

The doctor sat at the edge of Vivian's bed, dark hair slicked back, a white lab coat covering her black skin suit. A datapad dangled from her fingers and her eyes were trying, and failing, to be kind. Her slate blue skin matched the warmth of her voice, which was to say, there was no warmth.

The doctor's bedside manner was lacking.

"I've spoken with Princess Ibukay," Vivian said. "Can you clarify the chain of authority here?"

Movement inside, maybe responding to her spike of anxiety. If she looked down, she'd see a tiny protrusion outlined against her taut skin. She tried to imagine what the person attached to that tiny protrusion was thinking or feeling, but remembered it was too small to have thoughts . . . correct? They'd shown her an image. The image had closed eyes, two of them. A nose she recognized. A tiny bow mouth.

So . . . no tentacles. But the Yadeshi didn't have tentacles, just blue skin and blue eyes of all shades and silky hair even her cousins would envy. And blue skin. They redefined the pedestrian term blue.

They were also all tattooed, or the limited personnel she had seen.

"The *Bdakhun* has no authority over our medical care," the doctor said. "And she is biased. She prefers a single outcome, and that isn't really fair to you, is it?"

Vivian rubbed her arms and the strange markings

the . . . doctor? . . . had informed her were placed on her skin to save her life. She couldn't imagine medical technology that was imprinted into one's skin, but she was, after all, a long way from Kansas. If it was only medical tech, why did all the Yadeshi have them, unless they were tech to ward off disease and perhaps aging?

"Run everything by me again, please," Vivian said, stalling for more time to think.

She didn't like the doctor, recognized her tone and mannerisms from years of dealing with state officials who came into her classroom to assess her students' progress, and Vivian's performance. They came with carrots, and sticks, and agendas that had agendas.

The baby kicked, telling her to pay attention.

"Certainly," the doctor said. "We've reviewed the results of your mental and physical health diagnostics, and all indications are that the extent of trauma you have endured—"

"I'm fine," Vivian said. "Everyone on Earth has trauma. Especially Mid Tiers, though I surmise Low Tiers have it worse."

That was what her parents had always said. Be grateful they were Mid Tiers. Afforded a higher class of education and occupational opportunities, assigned slightly higher quality living standards. Her entire life she had been a coward and never chafed against the rules. She completed her allotted advanced education, been awarded a certification and position in a neighborhood Education Center as a Primary Grades Facilitator.

If she occasionally colored outside the lines by bringing the students old world paperbacks—which were not on the approved reading lists—to read, administration indulgently looked the other way because her students exhibited exemplary behavior and average assessment scores. Exactly the outcome the state desired; docile and dumb. Over time she had fooled herself into thinking that she was trying to make a difference by introducing different books. She could no longer afford to indulge herself in an illusion of her bravery. If she couldn't advocate for her own freedom, for her students, how could she advocate for this baby?

"It's my professional opinion we should proceed with an induction to alleviate the stress on your health. Your seizure concerns me."

Vivian frowned. "You said these markings took care of it."

"They did, but after reviewing information regarding human gestation, we've realized that your seizure was the result of—"

"I understand." Eclampsia. A condition that never would have been untreated if she had been in standard medical care. But of course, nothing about being imprisoned in a slave pen was standard.

"Would it not be a relief to release yourself of this burden?" the doctor asked. "You aren't currently in a mental or financial position to properly care for an infant who may have unique needs due to its genetic profile. On a planet that is alien to you. You should return home, Vivian."

Vivian flinched. This was the first time the doctor had simply come out and said it, though she'd been skirting around the issue. And no, this pregnancy hadn't been by choice. Vivian reached for the glass of water at her bedside, took a sip to ease her dry throat. She didn't recall the circumstances of her insemination other than it had been completely medical, while she was unconscious. There had been no pain. She had not even realized she was pregnant for months. That didn't make it any less a rape, though.

"I'm not prepared to make that decision yet," Vivian said. "Ibukay said there was some place I could go out of here, to settle and think. When will she return?"

The doctor's mouth tightened, and she straightened on the stool. "I am the lead on your case, and as such all decisions—"

"Are mine," Vivian said, though her heart rate spiked.

They *should* be hers, but what legal rights did she have? It wasn't as if her own government didn't frequently step in and assert its authority over what should be personal matters. And even if she had legal rights, who would enforce them?

"Where is Ibukay? I would like to see her now."

"You're becoming hysterical." The doctor rose. "We can administer a—"

"No." She struggled to keep her voice modulated, her expression pleasant and non-confrontational. "No drugs. I prefer not to be administered any drugs, please."

No choice. Never any choice. Her mother would say to go along, swallow the indignity and powerlessness to avoid the wrong kind of attention. Move forward. Forget she was kidnapped and impregnated and her choices taken, forget this doctor who clearly disliked Vivian trying to exert agency. . .

"Vivian, your blood pressure is spiking."

"Where is Ibukay?" She reined herself in, softening her voice to something less demanding. "Please, may I see her?"

"Vivian?" a familiar voice said. "I'm here. I'm so sorry I didn't return yesterday."

Princess Ibukay glided forward through doors that shimmered closed behind her, glancing at the doctor. She was a beautiful woman, short silky hair in a shade of bright blue that would have horrified Vivian's mother, tiny jewels traveling up one ear lobe and dangling from the other. Tall, slender, rich blueberry skin and matching dark eyes with spiky, jewel tipped lashes.

"The doctor was suggesting I induce and place the baby into state care." The doctor hadn't said as much but Vivian wasn't stupid, she could read between the lines.

"I'm concerned about your state of mind and—"

"The circumstances surrounding a birth quite often aren't ideal," Ibukay interjected. "But that hardly calls for such drastic measures when we already have support mechanisms in place." Ibukay bared her teeth in a shark like smile. "*Kheter*, thank you for your time, I'd like to speak with Vivian alone."

Ah. That was the word.

The *kheter* slapped her datapad in her open palm. "The medical care of human patients falls under my authority. With all due respect, *Bdakhun,* you don't have the qualifications to—"

"Is that what you think?" was the soft reply. Ibukay continued to look at the woman, and moments later the doors shimmered open again, a man stepping through.

He fixed his emotionless gaze on Vivian as he spoke to the doctor. "Dismissed."

"I don't think so." The datapad slapped against the doctor's palm, a crack of sound that caused Vivian to flinch again. The baby kicked. "This female is not fit to give birth and be in possession of a Yadeshi child."

"Excuse me," Vivian said, struggling to breathe. "You can't just—"

"There are laws that—"

She couldn't breathe. They couldn't do this to her. "Ibukay," she gasped. The doctor frowned and moved forward, then froze when the man looked at her.

"Get out," he said softly.

She left the room. Vivian's panic resided.

"I don't like that female," Ibukay told him. "She has an agenda and I'm not certain what. I don't want her alone with any of the pregnant women."

His eyes narrowed. "What does she want?"

"That *is* the question, isn't it? Maybe she's just a bitch."

That word translated easily enough. Vivian wondered briefly who had programmed her unit.

"Perhaps."

The pair returned their attention to Vivian. Ibukay approached, snagging the stool abandoned by the *kheter* and pulled it up to Vivian's side, taking her hand.

"How do you feel? I am sorry I haven't been back to see you since yesterday."

Vivian lowered her head, her long dark hair covering her face. "There are others, aren't there?"

"Yes."

"It's fine. I know I'm not your only concern."

Ibukay hesitated. "No, but you are unique to us, for reasons."

"I don't understand."

The princess glanced back at her bodyguard. "During our last conversation, I told you that we knew the identity of the genetic father of your baby, and that he was also a prisoner."

"Yes. Does he—did you tell him about me and the

baby?" Did she want him to know? He'd be one more person whose opinions would be thrown into the ring of her messed up life.

"We did, and he would like to meet you." Ibukay glanced away, casually, but Vivian's eyes narrowed. She was hiding something. "He would like to discuss the situation with you and come to a decision together on the best course."

Vivian withdrew her hand from Ibukay's. "There is no together. I'm the one having a baby."

"Half of the genetic material is his," the bodyguard now said. "It is true you are the mother, and that carries significant weight. Do you believe he has a right to determine the fate of his relationship with his child?"

"You don't have to stay on Yedahn," Ibukay said softly. "Don't let Vykhan try to bully you and Tai'ri. He will. He does it from a place of love, but sometimes that just makes it worse. I've been with him for decades."

Vivian's attention caught on the new name. "Tai'ri . . . that's the father?"

"Yes," Vykhan said. "And you should know that the reason he was imprisoned with you is that he is an agent working on behalf of the *Bdakhun*, a warrior under my command who was on assignment to infiltrate the trafficking ring that took you. He suffered greatly, as have you. Despite this, he has insisted we allow you . . . choice. I cannot say I agree with him fully, but it is his right to proceed as he sees fit."

All hope that she would be allowed to choose the outcome of this pregnancy dissipated. This was personal for them. This baby was theirs, or they thought of it that way. Her. Him. Not it. No tentacles, remember?

"I sense your turmoil," the man, Vykhan, said.

Well, *that* was unsettling. Vivian looked up, meeting his gaze. He smiled a little, proof enough she'd failed in keeping all the resentment from her expression.

"A little turmoil is to be expected in the circumstances," she said.

He inclined his head. "Of course. Let me choose different words. We understand this is a difficult time for you. We can empathize with the wrongs you have endured and our only intent is to ensure the best possible outcome for yourself and your child."

"Whatever you decide to do, I'll support you, Vivian," Ibukay said, with a look at Vykhan. "Even if you decide to leave Yedahn and return to Earth with the baby."

Vivian stiffened. "Would I have to live on a YETI base?" The Yadeshi-Earth Treaty Initiative bases were tighter than a government budget, and once on it would be hard to leave.

She pitied the poor, mostly Low Tier, recruits to the training facilities. Who but a Low Tier would want to become a soldier or grunt tech? And, of course, compatible human women were also encouraged to form relationships with the Yadeshi men.

"It might afford you and your child some protection," Vykhan said. "Unless you trust your government and choose to chance living on civilian grounds."

Ha ha ha HA. Trust her government. Vivian kept her laugh on the inside, especially since the laugh was really closer to tears.

"No, I—" What option did she have? "What does Mr. Tai'ri want?"

Ibukay rose. "For now, just to meet you." She held Vivian's gaze. "He is very upset at what was done to you. He feels responsible, that he failed his assignment."

"I think you will be pleased when you meet him," Vykhan said, "and if you are not pleased, then we will continue this discussion."

Vivian nodded.

3

After making her way at a snail-paced waddle through the campus, Vivian realized the unease slithering down her spine wasn't because the hospital was situated in the sky rather than on the ground like a reasonable medical facility should be.

She paused, ostensibly for the purpose of checking the directions on her comm, and looked around. Absently, her hands cupped underneath her uterus, bracing the muscles to relieve some of the pressure on her back.

Over there was the same couple she'd seen in the waiting area on the floor of her suite. Nondescript, a man in what seemed to be business casual here—bodycon pants, high-collared sleeveless shirt—and a woman next to him in a loose tunic over leggings, and molded flats. The man wore a messenger bag slung over his back and the woman held her arm in front of her face, a holo-tablet at reading distance springing from her wrist unit, like any self-respecting whale reader.

Never leave home without it.

Except Vivian *was* an avid reader, and if she was obsessed enough to bring her tablet with her, she'd also be taking the time while standing around waiting to . . . read. The woman didn't even glance at the screen, her still arm betraying the kind of muscle control normal people didn't bother with. They didn't speak to each other, or interact in any way. Even long-time couples comfortable with silence would make a comment here and there.

Several times Vivian allowed her gaze to connect with the woman's, who would then casually look away. Maybe she was curious.

That had to be it. Vivian didn't see any other human women, though Ibukay had assured her there were enough humans on Yedahn—and other aliens—that Vivian walking around would draw notice but not comment.

By the time she descended several levels to the location of the first transportation hub, the itch between her shoulders was morphing into full blown alarm. There again. The same couple.

There were six other hubs on this level, all leading to different parts of the city.

Vivian was about to swipe her pass when she heard a voice call out.

"Vivian! Security, stop that human."

Her hand jerked up, and she swiped the pass, about to push through the entry. It flashed red.

"Please remain and await instructions," a computerized voice requested politely.

Vivian turned, heart sinking. She'd hoped never to see the *kheter* again.

She strode towards Vivian, long limbs slender in her medical skinsuit. Like praying mantis legs. "Vivian, I'm glad I caught you. I was on rounds and missed your discharge. For some reason the paperwork wasn't routed through me."

The *kheter's* attempt at a pleasant wide smile looked incongruous as usual. It didn't reach her staring, unblinking eyes.

"Perhaps we could step to the side, Vivian."

Why did she keep saying Vivian's name? Some psychological attempt to create rapport?

"Ms. Huang, please," Vivian said politely, evading the outstretched arm.

The wide smile faltered. "What?"

"I prefer to be addressed by my family name. Ms. Huang. Forgive me. We don't know each other well enough for personal names." Even government officials addressed the lowest tier adult citizens by their last name. Using a first name without permission was a subtle condescension.

"Of . . . course. Ms. Huang. I wanted to talk to you

before you were discharged, please excuse me for taking up your time. Come with me."

The *kheter* spoke with casual authority, as if she expected Vivian to automatically follow along. It was a neat trick, but Vivian was no child.

"Please excuse me," Vivian said. "I prefer to remain here. I have a few moments before I must depart."

The false smile faded. "Ms. Huang, I'm concerned. You've taken advice from the *Bdakhun*, who is well intentioned, but as she is a royal she is hardly in touch with the realities of day-to-day life."

Vivian remained silent, refusing to be drawn into what was probably intended to be a conversational trap.

The *kheter's* brow drew down. "I'd like you to reconsider your birth options. I have a surgical suite and am prepared to quickly and painlessly remove the fetus and place it immediately into the care of a well situated Yadeshi couple. You could even meet them, if you like."

Vivian wondered if Ibukay knew the doctor was part of the trafficking circle. There was literally no other reason, once Vivian put all the behavior clues together, why she would be so insistent on taking custody of Vivian and the baby.

"I appreciate the offer," Vivian said. "Ibukay is expecting me to check in shortly, and if I miss the check in she will send security. I don't want to waste their time like that when I'm clearly in no danger."

Vivian spoke slowly, emphasizing key words, hoping the subtext of her meaning was clear without conveying overt threat. Criminal behavior would not go unpunished.

Despite her relative assurance that she was safe in such a public locale, and she had her comm on to signal Ibukay as needed, sweat broke out on her chest as a wave of anxious heat flooded her. She hadn't processed the memories of her kidnapping, mostly because they were shrouded by whatever drug she'd been given to induce unconsciousness. She wasn't ready to process them now. Was there any point in adding more trauma to her already tired mind?

But she'd promised herself she would begin to practice bravery, to protect herself and her ... responsibility. What would a woman with courage now do? She didn't have to *be* brave, she only had to go through the motions. The actions of being brave would yield the same results.

"You look flushed, Vivian. Why don't you come with me and I'll order you a nutrient enhanced beverage and you can sit and rest? Security, requesting an escort—"

"No!" Vivian rarely raised her voice, but she did it now. A woman with courage would forcefully advocate for herself, resist. Would bring attention to the situation and hope a bystander would intervene. And be prepared to use force if no one stepped up to help.

She shunted aside a lifetime of training to remain

composed, to not draw attention, to be *polite* because any resistance would give the government an excuse—and instead channeled her anger at having her wishes pushed aside like she was nothing. Like she wasn't even a person.

Vivian took a step away from the *kheter*.

"I'm not going with you." The marks on her skin began to pulse in time with her increasing heartbeat. They warmed, but she focused on her adversary. "I've been discharged from medical care, and you have no legal right to detain me." She didn't know whether that was true, but she was guessing. *"Bdakhun* Ibukay and her Head of Security, Vykhan, have given me strict instructions and I intend to follow them. If you plan to interfere—"

"Vivian, I don't understand why you're so hostile. You are clearly experiencing a post traumatic episode." She furrowed her brow. "I'm only trying to help you."

She reached out and took Vivian's wrist—

—and jumped back, exclaiming in shock as she cradled her burned hand. The jolt of energy that flared from Vivian's marks heated her skin enough she thought it might burn. Could . . . were the marks *hissing*? That low buzz of sound had to be in her head but the *kheter* stared at the uncoiling, burning tattoos wide-eyed.

"What are they doing?" Vivian asked, keeping her voice calm. Hissing tattoos wasn't the worst thing she'd been through in the last several months. She eyed the *kheter* stonily. As long as they weren't trying to kill her, she could deal with them later.

"That's not possible," the Yadeshi woman said. Fury enveloped her expression, and she straightened, the false demeanor of helpful professional fading. "You're coming with me."

Vivian whirled and began to walk, fast, pushing her body into something approximating a run. She looked around frantically. Anything, anyone that could help her. The same couple from before were watching her and casually began following.

Too fast. Too fast to be a coincidence. Were they plain clothes security? Something more sinister?

Ibukay had said she was safe. Ibukay had promised.

Not just Ibukay. *Him.*

He had promised.

She brushed aside the nonsense image that rose in her mind like a memory. It felt real, but there was no time to process the softening warmth emanating from her tattoos when she thought of him. The sense of peace and possibility. As if this man represented a possible future path she had yet to take the first step towards.

"Security," she heard the *kheter* snap in a low, restrained tone. It wouldn't do to appear to be kidnapping an unwilling person when kidnapping an unwilling person. Until they were out of the way of witnesses, facades must be maintained.

If she hadn't thought she'd wanted her baby before this, she now knew she did. The flare of protectiveness shocked Vivian. She held her swaying uterus to keep the precious bundle inside from sloshing around too much.

The couple was gaining ground. Vivian cursed herself, then punched the face of her comm unit.

"Help! I need help, please." She should have done that already, but evidently panic was not congruous with practical thinking.

She shrieked as a form clad in black from head to toe, face masked, snapped into existence in front of her. It was no holo—it swept her into its arms and turned to shield her from her pursuers.

"Got you, *yadoana*," it murmured. Not it, he. As if gender wasn't obvious since the jumpsuit left nothing to the imagination. "Abort the distress signal."

Her one glimpse before he'd wrapped her in an oddly protective embrace revealed honed muscles and broad shoulders, a warrior's physique.

"Who are you? I'm not aborting the signal."

"The *Bdakhun* sent me," he replied calmly, then nodded to indicate several more black clad figures popping into existence. "And them."

"Teleportation?" Her voice trembled.

"Hardly. Basic cloaking tech." His voice hardened. "We were watching for something like this."

She shivered. The chill in his voice left no room for

imagining what would happen to the doctor. "I think she was trying to medically kidnap me."

"We'll find out why."

"That doesn't require a leap of logic considering the circumstances. Who are you?"

And why did she feel none of her now customary panic in his arms? Embarrassment at the necessity of being rescued and carried, but he felt . . . familiar.

"Your shield," he said.

Tai'ri escorted Vivian to one of the waystations for trafficked people founded by Ibukay years ago, as the *kheter* was escorted to a location for questioning.

"Thank you," Vivian said once he left her at the front desk.

She turned somber dark eyes on him, studying Tai'ri with an intensity that caused his insides to clench. She couldn't know who he was, that they had shared, in some vein, a harrowing experience together. That they now shared even more.

He kept his gaze trained on her face, though he ached to reach out and cradle her—them. His chest tightened at the thought that she likely, and understandably, didn't share his hesitant joy. The possibility of a newfound matebond, the presence soon of a new child. On the heels of his hope always came guilt—his redemption came at the expense of her abuse. To think of this as a second chance felt selfish, even exploitative.

At every step in this journey he'd rein in his impulses, his instinct to claim, to offer everything that was his to give. Let her come to him, let her choose.

Questions swirled behind her gaze, but she wouldn't ask. Even tired, scared and confused, a gentle dignity cloaked her. In her quiet voice was a steely strength.

"You're welcome," he murmured after that long moment of considering his response, then left.

Each step his jaw ground. Hated leaving her, but there was no choice.

The first time Ibukay had tried to circumvent the law by placing aliens into private housing, she'd caused an uproar. By law all aliens must check into a waystation and remain there until they were processed.

The solution had been to build and staff her own waystations throughout the city, making her the de facto sponsor of each inhabitant. So far, the solution had worked, since most individuals chose to immediately return to their home world. Those who didn't were found alternate worlds or allowed to apply for employment and transition into Yadeshi society.

The marks on his arms crawled, almost leaping off his skin. The brief moment he'd held her in his arms, he fought a vicious battle to force himself to let go.

This was his bondmate. His child.

But even if his own ethics hadn't already dictated

it, he was ordered to leave her until their meeting. She must come to him of her own free will. It could never, ever, be said that Ibukay facilitated the forced bonding of an alien female to one of her warriors as a goddamn perk. Her funding, her support, would evaporate.

What he was allowed to do was join the team assigned to guard her, cloaked in the shadows, waiting for any lurking enemies to reveal themselves.

"That was quick," Ibukay's voice said in his ear.

"They are either bold or foolish," Vykhan said, "to show their hand so soon."

"Has the couple been IDed yet?" Tai'ri asked.

"Mercenaries," Vykhan said.

"I'm en route," Tai'ri said. "Vivian's secure."

"We've tripled security around the building," Ibukay assured him for the third time.

Another decision they'd gone back and forth over. The *kheter* would soon reveal in whose interest she was acting, and they would know if she was in any way tied to the traffickers. They'd allowed the *kheter* to speak with Vivian to see what she would say and after it was clear the intent was to shuttle Vivian back into medical custody whether the human female liked it or not—

Tai'ri reminded himself not killing the *kheter* was the right choice.

"Better to lessen security and wait for the enemy to reveal themselves," Vykhan said coolly. He'd made his opinion known, and Ibukay had vetoed.

"I won't risk their safety," the *Bdakhun* said. "We'll wait it out and use one of our operatives as bait."

"None of them will be the bait that the human female is," Vykhan replied. "They would have expended considerable resources in breeding her. That level of expense means they have a buyer for her, and the infant. There would be consequences, not only financial, if they fail to deliver."

"I know all of that, Vykhan," Ibukay growled. "In case that's the reason why you felt the need to restate the obvious."

Tai'ri frowned. She sounded at the end of her patience. "*Bdakhun*, when did you last rest? Can't function if you don't sleep and eat."

"You go sleep and eat," she retorted. "You aren't supposed to even be on duty, and you need to prepare for your meeting with Vivian."

"I concur," Vykhan said. "Tai'ri, sign off and see to your bondmate. She must agree to come with you or our hands are tied."

Anticipation surged, and Tai'ri obeyed, veering off from the team and heading home. He had a few hours to meditate, stuff the whirling mass of emotions inside his mind where it would not affect his female, and change into his civilian skin.

4

VIVIAN RECALLED THE DISCUSSIONS AT THE DINNER table where her parents would browse through the profiles of single Mid Tier professionals, filter for compatible genetic, lineage, and financial status, and discuss the circumstances in which she would apply for legal cohabitation and conception of her first child.

And here she was pregnant on an alien planet, about to meet her infant's father for the first time.

It wasn't ideal.

It certainly wasn't boring.

Excitement, she now understood, was vastly overrated.

She'd been just fanciful enough growing up to daydream about meeting an intelligent, free thinking (but not in front of her parents), modern man with a few social connections in the upper Mid or lower High Tiers. Just enough that perhaps their children could ease, through social influence and judiciously applied bribes, into a better quality of life. Crossing Tiers wasn't impossible, it just took the right combination of circumstances, and careful attention to whom one bred with.

She doubted her genetic profile was in any way, shape, or form a match for the father of this baby.

That wouldn't bother her, because all those dreams were dust now, except that she still yearned, despite everything, for . . . kindness, if not love. Contentment. A man who would like her hidden personality and not the government sanctioned one.

A husband, not just a legal partner.

Vivian smiled bitterly, wondering at her own emotional health that she was even capable of desiring love after her experience in the pens, and glanced at the comm unit secured around her wrist. Before her escort to the halfway house where staff provided a room and clothing along with a New Visitor orientation tablet, Ibukay had placed the thin metal cuff on her and activated its instructions for operation. Evidently it would serve as a homing beacon, link to Ibukay and Vykhan during her transition, as well as provide her with GPS and other data she would need to navigate this new city.

New, and strange. And quiet.

There was no vehicle traffic on the ground level, for one. Only pedestrians. She craned her neck to look above her head, amazed at the transports flitting high above. She assumed there was some mechanism to control traffic; no one crashed.

But down here, people on foot competed with nothing faster than a stray mammal on two legs that hopped and sometimes flew short distances between buildings.

"Mommy, there's an alien," a high-pitched voice said as a woman walked by with a poppy skinned child in tow. "I want to talk to it!"

"It's a she, *yadoana,* don't be discourteous."

People glanced at her, some stared. Vivian didn't blame them, there was no particular hostility in any of the looks. So far she'd seen several aliens, but only a handful of humans, and those only in passing.

The unit on her wrist intoned instructions into her aural unit and she adjusted her course; the restaurant where she would meet the baby daddy was only a minute away on foot. She waddled along, and when she approached, was greeted with a pleasant beep alerting her she'd arrived.

Outside the cafe was a bench. Vivian lowered herself onto it, tired and a little dizzy from her walk. She'd exited the transport too far from the meeting place, wanting to explore. That had been a mistake, but then this was the first time she'd experienced a long walk while pregnant. She had not understood how draining it would be, especially since she was undernourished from months of confinement. A staff *kheter* had prescribed her several supplements, and she was to eat six small meals a day and one nutrient shake to replace lost calories, fat, and protein.

She closed her eyes and enjoyed the sun on her face. So quiet here. No loud arguing, no creak of old-world buses painstakingly repaired over and over. No fumes.

Was this what freedom felt like? A quiet afternoon walk where no government officials stopped you to randomly check your business? Sitting on a bench and enjoying the fresh air?

Her comm unit beeped. *Incoming,* it intoned.

Opening her eyes, she tilted her wrist as she had been shown to accept the communication. Ibukay's face sprang into view in the palm of her hand.

"You made it," the princess said in a cheerful tone, then frowned. "You look a little pale, Vivian. I think. It's a bit difficult to tell. Reign is browner than you."

Who was Reign? "I wanted to walk and overestimated my endurance. I'm sitting now."

"Well, take your time when out and about and don't forget you can activate your distress beacon if you need help. And there are public med links."

Vivian had seen the symbols, brightly colored and indicating a distressed individual could receive basic first aid and request transport to a facility. She'd studied this city's emergency protocols before leaving this afternoon.

"I only wanted to wish you good luck for your meeting with Tai'ri, and comm me if you need anything. And remember, nothing will happen unless you give consent. You are in control here."

Vivian wasn't certain she believed that, but Ibukay seemed sincere. "Mr. Vykhan seems intent on Tai'ri and I coming to an understanding."

"Mister." Ibukay snorted. "Vykhan thinks he knows what's best for everyone, but his intentions are good."

Intent was the tiny, niggling line that separated him from the *kheter* at the facility. That woman had made it clear she thought Vivian shouldn't be allowed to choose what happened to her and the baby—Vykhan also had strong opinions about what should happen, but at least he was willing to give her an illusion of choice. She wasn't locked up.

Inside her, the baby moved. Somersaults had slowed over the last several days, probably because it was growing. Pressure low in her groin, like a tiny leg flexing for room. Vivian winced.

"Thank you, *Bdakhun*," Vivian said. "I'm sure everything will go well."

Ibukay signed off soon after—she had to be busy as a province royal and also with her anti-trafficking platform. But she still made time for Vivian. Of course, Vivian's baby was special to them.

She let her eyes drift closed again, a wash of tiredness coming over her. A nap would be fabulous, but first she had to get this meetup out of the way and learn if the princess and crew really meant what they said when they insisted everything was Vivian's decision.

"You well?" a deep, calm voice asked.

Vivian opened her eyes.

The gentle afternoon faded, a shock running up both her arms as the urgent . . . *hushed tones of a voice she barely understood bounced off the walls around her. Standing over her, a man with skin a shade deeper than blue flame, fierce determination in his eyes.*

"Live," he whispered. "You both are mine. I won't give you up."

A stark statement of possession, one that somehow didn't stoke poisonous memories of her captivity, but instead offered hope.

Vivian jerked her mind back into the present, shaken enough by the surge of emotion that she remained mute, and simply stared.

He didn't seem to mind, crouching with an air of unending patience.

He was the kind of man her parents would instantly dislike—not hate, hate was too impolite a term, and her parents frowned on strong emotion. Mid Tier's did not do well to allow strong emotions to creep into their lives, not when emotions led to forbidden things like wanting to live life according to your own terms, and then you walked yourself right into your own kidnapping. She wondered if they would feel vindicated that they were right, despite her arguments against assimilation. When she gathered the nerve to reach out to them, she would find out.

The man watched her silently with an intent gaze, head tilted, perhaps waiting for her to maybe stop staring and say something. But since he appeared to be in no hurry, she took her time studying him.

Shoulder length hair with a deep lapis sheen to it. The cut was ragged, deliberately so because who used manual shears to cut their hair anymore? A skin toned t-shirt of some soft material stretched over broad shoulders and clearly defined arms. His pants were a loose fit, and tucked into flexible looking boots. Strands of multicolored beads wrapped around each of his wrists. He reminded her of something—pictures she had seen once about old Earth cultures. Skater grunge, maybe.

She stopped judging him by his clothing and instead looked into his eyes. Calm, a bright, saturated blue as striking as his hair, and slightly upturned at the tips. His face looked a hair too sharp, as if he hadn't eaten well in a few weeks, despite the muscle defined by the clingy shirt.

"Tai'ri?" she asked, ignoring his previous question. Ibukay had said his name often enough she knew the syllables. Tie-rhee, a gentle roll on the 'r' her tongue executed well enough.

No one had approached her on her excursion—these people seemed to have a deeply ingrained sense of personal privacy. It made no sense someone would randomly approach her now, so this had to be him.

"Yeah," he said. His hands rested on the tops of his thighs, fingers long, and still. But as she observed him, they flexed. "Vivian." He seemed to be testing out the syllables of her name.

"Yes." She corrected his pronunciation, and he said it again, perfectly.

His voice shivered through her, sparking a sense of familiarity. She had not particularly liked Vykhan's complete lack of emotion, though she appreciated his calm. This man was also calm, but with waves underneath. Expression flickered on the edge of his face, there and gone.

"Thanks for agreeing to meet with me," he said, then stood. "You want to go in? It's less open." His gaze roved their surroundings, tension in his stiff shoulders. She realized that as soon as he'd stood, he'd lost some of his stillness, brimming with hoarded energy.

So he felt the eyes too.

Her comm beeped insistently. Vivian tilted her wrist.

"Tai'ri!" Ibukay exclaimed. "You made it. Have you two had a chance to—"

"*Bdakhun*, we'll speak later," Tai'ri said, gently but firmly, then pressed his thumb against Vivian's comm. It flickered off, and he spoke three words her unit didn't translate.

"What did you do to it?" Vivian asked.

"Set it to privacy mode. It'll reset to regular functionality in two hours."

It was a little presumptuous, but she understood why he did it. "Fine, but ask next time, please."

He nodded. "Sure. You want to go in now?"

Tai'ri wasn't upset by her quiet rebuke. Vivian relaxed and nodded, pushing to her feet. His hand shot out to take her elbow, hesitated, but when she didn't pull away, he continued the assist.

"Thank you," she murmured, wondering why nothing in her flinched. She hadn't liked the doctor exams, preferred no one but Ibukay touched her. But this stranger . . . was it because his sperm had fertilized her egg? Maybe her subconscious already felt a kinship with him, and coded him as 'safe.' Tai'ri's fingers felt strange on her arm, but he didn't linger. He helped her to her feet, waited until she was steady, and then released his hold.

"Welcome." He smiled at her, though his eyes remained grave. "Let's get you fed."

Somehow, the statement sounded like so much more than an invitation for lunch.

5

Predictably, Vykhan and Ibukay had argued.

"You will have to move quickly to seal the bond," Vykhan had told Tai'ri bluntly.

Ibukay's exasperated glance conveyed the depth of her annoyance. "No, Tai'ri. Slowly, gently. Allow her to take the lead."

The only way to escape the argument had been to sign off the comm, banishing their holo images. Neither was wrong. The marks were laid but quiescent, in a half state. They'd offer Vivian some healing benefits, the nanotech in the ink working to eliminate any antibodies that might react poorly when introduced to his . . . genetic material.

But to seal the bond, the marks required a far more primal claiming.

Wasn't the right time. She must feel alone, frightened, and tired as heavy as she was with child. He could use those facts to his advantage—he was trained in manipulation. But that wasn't the foundation he wanted with his child's mother and hopefully, his bondmate.

However, small gentle touches, and brief skin contact to slowly stoke the marks and her internal fire . . . he was not an unattractive male. Females never found him wanting. Now, when it mattered the most, he'd use every tool in his arsenal to gently woo his alien mate.

"You have a preference?" he asked, indicating different tables. She shook her head, so he chose something that gave them both a view of the windows and entrances.

He'd hoped she'd seem less fragile once awake. Strange now, speaking to the living, breathing female. Intelligence and emotion in her eyes, wariness in her body language. She reached up and flicked the strands of her long dark hair out of her face, and glanced up at him. Odd for a species to be so . . . plant colored. Soil colored hair, tree bark eyes, and herbal tea skin. Except for her lips—deep pink, reminding him of his mother's favorite velvety blooms.

She was lovely. Strange, but lovely. In another time, another place, he might have seen her walking and followed, offered her his name. Though he chose his lovers with care and didn't flit from female to female, he wasn't celibate. Also true that he hadn't had a long-term relationship since that first, disastrous one during his youth.

As they sat, a server approached. He liked the low tech service, one of the reasons he'd chosen this location.

Tai'ri reached for her elbow to help her settle into the seat but lowered his hand when she jerked.

"Every time you touch me there's a spark," she murmured. "Like static electricity."

He played with the beads on the wrist of the offending hand, the familiar weight of the bracelets a comfort. His eldest sister's son was a bead blower and gifted the family with new strands every year. Tai'ri chose not to tell her why there was a spark. He doubted she would like the explanation.

"It's dark in here," she said.

Tai'ri frowned, but waited until the server had set down the paper menus and glasses of water. Sunlight streamed in through the wall length window, bathing the walls in warm color.

"Do you have standard vision?"

She blinked. "What?"

"Is your vision normal? Can you see color, distant objects?"

"20/20, you mean? Of course." She stared at him, a little baffled at the random choice of subject. "They don't do standard vision correction on young adults here?"

"Poor vision is not a vulnerability Yadeshi suffer from."

"How do you know about it then?"

"Yedahn has a small but healthy alien population. Increasing in the last century since we've begun to actively recruit—"

"Grunt labor?" She looked down at her hands, folded on top of the table. "I noticed that the training programs all offered by YETI are for menial tech positions and . . . breeding."

He frowned. "Not breeding."

"What would you call it when you encourage human women to mate and have children with your people? And give them financial incentives to do so?"

"Genetic diversity. We're a small planet, and we're at a stagnant population growth."

"Why not encourage your own people to have babies?"

"It's not that simple."

"The Yadeshi drive to increase genetic diversity and its alien population—in order to staff the war cruisers that protect your scientific expeditions—is one of the reasons we're in this predicament. It created an appetite among segments of your populace. You have a demand, but limited supply, and it's created a black market."

Tai'ri blinked. "You've done some thinking about this." This was going to be tricky. Intelligent people were harder to distract. He wanted her settled in somewhat before he revealed the truth of the marks.

"I'm an educator. I can read, research, and come to conclusions." She looked at her arms with a strange expression. "Though I'm realizing I was researching the wrong questions."

He braced himself for the inevitable question about the marks, and felt relief when she didn't follow up that line of inquiry.

"My child has an intelligent mother." He winced internally, realizing how patronizing that sounded.

She looked away. "I suppose we have more personal things to talk about right now."

He wanted to reach across the table and take one of her hands, comfort her, but he knew the touch would be premature. "We can talk about whatever you want, Vivian."

"No, it's fine. I'm stalling, and that doesn't do anyone any good."

The server returned, and they ordered. Vivian couldn't read the menu so he spent a few minutes explaining drinks and dishes to her, including the ingredients labeled as potential allergens to non Yadeshi. As the server left, pain flashed across her face, and she grimaced.

"What's wrong?" Tai'ri asked, tensing.

"Nothing. The baby kicked in my groin."

"That can't be comfortable."

Her lips twitched. "Nothing about this is comfortable."

Damn. "Sorry, Vivian. Should have. . ." What? Done his job better? Not gotten caught because of outdated intel?

"I'm told it wasn't your fault. You were harmed as well." She picked up her glass and took a sip of water.

"No, I didn't do this to us," he said, keeping his voice low, soothing, measured. "But I still owe you an apology for my failure. Did the *Bdakhun* tell you the duties I perform for her?"

Vivian hesitated. "She said you're one of her upper level bodyguards."

"Of sorts. I don't deal with matters of her personal security. I handle information."

"You're a spy."

Tai'ri grinned. It was brief, but real. "Not like in the vids." His job was more dangerous, bloodier, and the consequences literally involved death, and now, life. "You should drink."

She stiffened, face paling, and he cursed himself. "They made me eat during my imprisonment," she said.

He remembered. *Subject Alpha Two Zeta Toro Lao: Mandatory nourishment has commenced. Consume all assigned food and beverage, or intervention will be required.*

He had tested it once. 'Intervention' was four masked, silent orderlies who fought him with the ruthlessness of military grade war bots, literally forcing the food and drink down his throat. If she had resisted even once. . .

His stomach clenched. Needed to punch something. Draw blood. "Can't imagine what you're going through. I don't compare what happened to me with what happened to you."

Tai'ri took a few deep, even breaths, chanting one of the prayers for Silence Vykhan taught all of his subordinates. In moments, the training kicked in and he recovered his equilibrium, banking rage yet again.

"I do." She met his gaze again. "It . . . helps. It helps to tell myself we're in this together." She paused, looked down and began to run her fingers through the moisture drops on the table top. "Is that what you want? To be in this together?"

Tai'ri watched the micro expressions in her face, assessing the inflections in her tone. It was what he was trained to do. Trained to read, and to manipulate. But he didn't want to manipulate her. Didn't want to use the data his mind was collecting about her emotions and mental state and exploit it to guide her to make the decision that benefited him the most.

"Do you want honesty, or neutrality?" he asked.

Her finger paused, and she looked up at him through her lashes. The look punched him in the gut. "Honesty."

The server brought their food, and he waited until she began to eat, clenching words behind his mouth.

He wanted to fuss, it was his nature to fuss. A mother, sisters, aunts, cousins . . . he'd taken care of them all and they always allowed it. The females of his family expected pampering as their right.

"I want this child. It's half mine, and I want it." He pressed his hands against the table top, the only lapse in control he allowed himself. She couldn't handle the torrent inside him right now—and shouldn't have to. "I'd like my child's mother to co-parent with me. My childhood was happy. My family—if they knew, they would want to meet you, and they would welcome you both."

Ibukay had sent him an extensive file on Vivian. The data they had managed to scrape from Earth government files, and Vivian's own words. She was educated, thoughtful, and responsible. No reason to think she wouldn't be a good mother.

"How do you envision this co-parenting taking place?" she asked. "Because I have to decide if I want you in my life, and I have to know if our visions of life going forward coincide."

"Just tell me what you want." It was a barely restrained demand. "I can give you whatever you want."

Vivian smiled a little. "I doubt that. And that's not even required. I just need certain assurances."

He wanted to lunge across the table. Not shake her, but gather this fragile female trying desperately to negotiate her way through a strange situation, into his arms. His instinct to protect, to shield, to make her decisions, strangled him. For a moment his palms flexed against the table, recalling the phantom weight of a tiny, silent baby before he lowered her into her mother's arms.

Tai'ri took a deep breath and released the feelings. They did him no good. "Tell me what assurances you need."

"One, that any choices I make, even if you don't agree with them, will be honored."

Tai'ri relaxed. "Insofar as your decisions are not governed by law, that's fine. I'd ask you accept my input."

She hesitated.

"Trust is hard," he continued quietly. "You feel you're alone. I get it. But do you understand that if we had intended you any harm, or . . . not intended to honor your will, we wouldn't even be sitting here? We have the medical skill—we could have taken the child and left you living. Or not."

She flinched, a shudder running through her entire body. Tai'ri's jaw clenched. Even that small distress bothered him, was a tiny dagger in his gut, but he needed her to understand she had nothing to fear from him.

"Forgive me. I could have chosen gentler words."

"No. I'm not a child. Plain speaking is good enough."

He inclined his head. "What else?"

"That's the biggest one. Everything else is more or less a variation." Her expression hardened subtly. "Just don't ever lie to me."

Tai'ri smiled at her. "Sure. I can promise you that. Now let me tell you what I can offer you."

"The sales pitch." Humor warmed her voice momentarily, and she resumed eating, which pleased him.

"If you say so. You know who I work for."

"Yes. My parents would be thrilled. You'd be considered High Tier on my planet."

Whatever that meant. He'd have to look it up. "I own a home here in the city, suitable for a child. I have family here as well. My family owns a birthing center."

"We would get the family discount?" Her voice was dry.

"Yes." He didn't understand. Was there something wrong with that in Earthen culture? "Would you like to see it? They have daily tours."

She stared at him, eyes wide and inscrutable. Would his child have her eyes, or his? The medical facility hadn't provided him with any data or images because Vivian had not legally acknowledged his paternity. He didn't know if that was deliberate, or if no one had told her she must do so.

"I haven't even thought about the birth," she said, looking over his shoulder. "I haven't even thought past today."

"There's time. And if you allow it, I'll help you."

6

"This is Vivian," Tai'ri told the woman he'd introduced as his older sister Abeyya. "She's from Earth. We're having a child in . . . " he turned to Vivian inquiringly. "Eight weeks?"

"Four to eight," she murmured.

The Yadeshi woman stared at Tai'ri but recovered quickly, the shock on her expression smoothing into a warm smile.

"I'm glad to meet you, Vivian," Abeyya said. "Are you here for an introduction to the family?" She looked at Tai'ri. "Daobah is on duty today."

"Our younger sister," Tai'ri told Vivian. "Doula. Everyone in the family spends a few years here in training before branching out."

It took her translator a moment to process the word doula, it must not be quite the same thing here as it was on Earth.

"I told Vivian you'd give us a tour." He tilted his head. "Viv?"

His shortening of her name to something like a casual endearment took her aback . . . but didn't bother her. She didn't think he was trying to be emotionally manipulative. No, perhaps he was just comfortable since he was on his home turf, so to speak.

"That's fine," Vivian said. "I don't think I should delay making some kind of decision." No matter how tempting delay was.

Abeyya nodded. "Where have you been receiving care? Have you begun looking at options?"

Vivian took a deep breath, placing her hand on top of her rounded stomach. Tai'ri nudged his sister's shoulder. "I think just a tour for now, Bey."

The facility was impressive, designed to be a cross between a well-appointed home and a spa. Abeyya spoke in low soothing tones about the different birth experiences they offered, including options for pain relief if desired.

Eventually they were led to an office that was more like a living room with low couches and side tables. Abeyya arranged for refreshments as she invited them to seat themselves.

"So," she said when she returned with a tray of small finger foods and what looked like tea. "Tell me what you think, Vivian. I know you said you haven't had time to think much about what kind of birth you'd like, but if you'd like to begin thinking about that now, I'm happy to answer any questions."

Vivian sighed, glancing down at the warm colored floors. Of course Abeyya would have questions, but Vivian doubted the woman was stupid. She would realize there was something not quite right about the dynamics between Vivian and Tai'ri and the fact that her brother had just . . . turned up after a several months long absence with a pregnant alien woman in tow.

But she didn't know how much Tai'ri had told his sister, or what he was allowed to. She gave him a sidelong glance. "You can . . . tell her whatever you're allowed to."

Vivian hadn't realized how tense his shoulders were until she said those words. She rubbed a hand over her eyes, sighing. She reminded herself that this situation wasn't all about her. There were other people, and other feelings, involved. And Tai'ri didn't seem like he would try to talk her into anything she didn't want to do.

But Tai'ri looked down at his discreet comm unit, a sleeker model than hers. He glanced at Vivian.

"I have to take this comm. Vivian, will you be comfortable here for a few moments?"

She realized he hadn't taken a comm the entire time they had been together so far and appreciated his courtesy. She nodded. "Go ahead."

There was a long moment of silence, and then

Abeyya said, "Tai'ri didn't tell us much about what happened. You were there with him?"

He hadn't actually told Abeyya anything, and she wasn't sure what she was allowed to say. Ibukay had asked her not to discuss her experience with anyone but Tai'ri for now, for her safety and the safety of operatives currently in the field.

"Yes. I didn't know he was there, I never saw anyone. I was taken . . . a year ago, I suppose."

"I see. And there were genetic tests done on your baby?"

She nodded. "That's how they found Tai'ri."

Abeyya leaned forward, reaching for Vivian's hand, squeezing gently. "My compassion, Vivian. May I ask if you want to raise this child?"

The question was delivered with such a lack of judgement that Vivian didn't bristle, and felt she could be honest. "I don't know. I didn't choose to become pregnant."

"No, you didn't. If you wanted to turn over custody of the child to Tai'ri and walk away, no one would blame you."

Yadeshi culture must be vastly different from human culture then. Of course, on Earth accidental pregnancy was all but unheard of with state mandated contraceptives for every adult after puberty. No one was having a child without a legal filing of parental and financial responsibility.

"I think I would blame me." She stared at her

hands. Her parents had treasured her, been conscientious in her upbringing even if they lacked imagination and affection. "I realized that Tai'ri is innocent, too. He's as much a victim as I am. And if he is, this baby certainly is."

"Motherhood is an irrevocable commitment."

She looked up. "And I'll still be a mother whether I walk away or not. I don't think I've bonded with the baby."

"That's not unexpected, Vivian. You've been in a highly stressful situation. Be gentle on yourself. Give yourself time to begin your healing process. Do you want to return home?"

Vivian felt the urge to stand up and pace the floor —but it would have taken too much energy to get to her feet. She processed a sharp pang of guilt.

"No, I don't. If I took the baby, I would have to live on a YETI base, and I don't want that. I want to be free. It's bad enough that if I stay here—"

She cut herself off. She was talking to the man's sister, after all. But Abeyya simply tilted her head in silent encouragement.

"There's a shelter I can live in until I've—Ibukay said I'd have to demonstrate I wasn't a drain on planetary resources in order to receive resident status."

Abeyya's lips twitched. "I don't think those are the official words."

"No, I'm paraphrasing. That was the gist of it."

Tai'ri's sister leaned forward and refilled Vivian's

cup. "Did they tell you that if you are a parent of a Yadeshi child, it grants you temporary status?"

"Yes. And Tai'ri said the program on Earth isn't meant to be a breeding program." She snorted.

"Ah, yes. Well, that program is one of many ideas the planetary council has had regarding our population, military, and genetic diversity concerns."

She could return to Earth with the baby, and that would be a whole host of issues. She could return without . . . but even though she hadn't bonded with the child inside her yet, some part of her rebelled at the thought. Maybe it was the tiny feet snuggled under her ribs, and the fact that this was the only person who had kept her company for the last several months. Maybe it was because looking into Tai'ri's eyes, and Abeyya's eyes, she could envision her own child's innocent gaze. Silky black hair and . . . blue skin? Lavender? What did a half human, half Yadeshi baby look like? Her captors had done things to her for months before the day she believed she'd been inseminated. Shots, procedures, testing . . . she'd realized some time ago all of that must have been fertility treatments.

The universe had conspired to bring this child into existence. Evil people had conspired. The least she could do to repay their kindness was raise the baby and ensure he or she never fell into their hands. It was the only revenge she could ever have the power to exact. Depriving them of a profit.

The doors opened manually, and Vivian met

Tai'ri's gaze as he entered. "Sorry for leaving you so long. Did you two—" he made a motion with his wrist, the beads tinkling "—female talk?"

Vivian's eyes narrowed.

"We talked, I'm not certain what gender has to do with it," Abeyya said. "Vivian has a lot to think about."

"I'm keeping the baby," Vivian said abruptly. "I want to raise it."

Tai'ri stared at her, tilting his head, and the fierce expression that crossed his face might have scared her if she didn't already know in her bones that this man would never hurt a hair on her head. If she didn't already know, despite his and Abeyya's careful restraint, that they both wanted this baby and were just waiting for an all clear from Vivian.

"That's good," he said, a little hoarse. His voice smoothed back into its easy tenor as he continued to speak. "I appreciate the sacrifice you're making, Viv." He inhaled silently, and as he exhaled it was as if he were shaking weight off his shoulders. "You and our child can come home with me, if you're ready to discuss it."

"I don't know if I want to move in with you." Which she hoped didn't sound as foolish to them as it did to her. She had nowhere else to go besides the shelter where the other human trafficking victims were currently residing. She couldn't raise a baby there. How would she even begin to support herself? And was she planning on staying on Yedahn forever?

She still didn't know the answer to any of those questions.

Vivian covered her face with her hands, a familiar crashing wave growing out of her attempts to think rationally. Chanting caught her attention, a low rhythmic murmur of words her translator struggled to convert to Earth Standard. She was going to have to learn to speak the language manually.

Hands rubbed circles on her lower back, exerting just enough pressure to grab her attention and make her wince, but not enough for pain. She leaned into the massage, mind returning to present time.

Abeyya watched with concern in her eyes, still on her couch. It was Tai'ri with the soft chant and soothing hands. His words faded into silence.

"What is that?" Vivian asked. "The chanting. It has the cadence of an old world Gregorian monks."

"I don't know *Gregorian monks*," he said as his hand stilled, pulling away slowly.

"I think I should learn."

"That's a good idea," Abeyya said. "It's an excellent stress reduction technique, even if those among Haeemah's acolytes are aghast at the thought of Her hymns used for something so mundane."

Tai'ri straightened, but didn't move away. Vivian glanced down, watching the fingers of his left hand play with the beaded bracelets on his right.

"Vykhan doesn't share that opinion, or he never would have taught us."

Abeyya shrugged. "Vivian, I can send you a digital file with more information on the center as well as how to register. We have midwives on staff, as I don't think you have your own? No. Tai'ri, you should take her to see your house before she makes a decision on living arrangements."

He glanced at Vivian inquiringly, and she nodded.

"Good idea," he said. "If you like it, then maybe . . ."

He didn't follow the statement up, but Vivian understood. Then perhaps she would agree to live with him for . . . however long the invitation was open. She sighed, rubbing at her itching belly. They still had a lot to discuss. And she just wanted to curl up on a flat surface with something dense and chocolate and a good book and just relax.

"We'll see," she said. "Moving in together is a big step, even if the circumstances are a little dramatic." Tai'ri's mouth quirked. "Is there—I think I'd like to take a walk, have some time alone for a few minutes."

The panic didn't return, but she needed quiet and some time alone to think. To process the day and decide, before she stepped foot in Tai'ri's house, what she would say and do if she did or did not decide to move in with him.

Tai'ri hesitated. "There are gardens here in the center."

"They're lovely. That's not what I'm in the mood

for." She pushed to her feet, shifting the weight of the baby with a grimace. Her back *ached*.

Abeyya picked up the expression. "Do you have a support band, Vivian?" She stood. "Just one moment, we have several here, I'll get you one."

"I don't like the idea of you walking alone outside," Tai'ri said once his sister left the room. He stood, putting an arm's length between them as if he was bracing for her reaction to his statement.

She stiffened. Was this how it would be? Now that he had a toe in the door, he would start issuing directives?

"*Bdakhun* Ibukay trusted me to make my way to the cafe by my little self."

The look in his eyes said he was weighing his response. "I'm not questioning your capability, Vivian. You're a pregnant alien—suicidal people might allow their curiosity to overtake their manners."

"Really? You seem to be a very insular people. I saw a few looks when I was walking, but for the most part I was politely ignored."

"You can hardly call a space faring species with outposts on several major worlds insular." He didn't move, settling into stubborn stillness. "The *Bdakhun* would have had you under surveillance, possibly even assigned a covert guard to you. Until we form a legal arrangement, she will limit what she tells me regarding any arrangements made on your behalf."

That was good to know. But recalling Vykhan's

mien, Vivian doubted he would be any great respecter of her privacy over her safety. He already openly considered her Tai'ri's business.

"What are you afraid of? I'm not safe here, am I?"

He shoved his hands into the pockets of his pants, and was silent a long, brooding moment.

"Fine. Give me your comm, I'll input my code."

7

Abeyya gave Tai'ri a look when Vivian mentioned his protest against her taking a walk outside alone. He escorted her to the front doors, again with that sense of contained, coiled energy, and let her go without another word.

Vivian needed to feel in control. The space to take a walk alone helped preserve that illusion. The unit on her wrist wasn't exactly a prison, but it was close enough. Why had Ibukay assigned her a guard? Because of her connection to Tai'ri, or because of the risk she could be recaptured?

Walking in a slow waddle, she passed a shop with a display of colorful papers, rolls of fibers and trays of glittering polished stones and beads. A crafting shop?

Her eyes widened as a pleased smile curved her lips. The one skilled hobby she had cultivated at home, and here by chance she had stumbled on the Yadeshi version. Her fingers itched to touch and sort as she stopped to appreciate the intricate window display.

Growing up she had always expected an alien planet would be *alien*. But so much was familiar. It seemed as if civilization developed more or less along the same lines when dealing with species that were, for all intents and purposes, of a similar genetic profile.

The Yadeshi weren't all that different. Their coloring, and some internal differences in their organs. Muscle density, and the tattoos, of course.

She rubbed hers as she stared in the shop window, debating whether there was any point in going inside when she had nowhere to store purchases even if she had credits for them. But it couldn't hurt to look, could it?

Her nails dug into the itching tattoos. They rested against her skin with an ever present subtle hum, as if aware and waiting. Waiting for what? Or maybe that was just the tech she felt. It had to be tech—no one had mentioned magic.

The buzzing intensified, and she looked down at her arms in irritation. She couldn't live like—

A sharp sting struck her upper arm. Vivian exclaimed and swatted, but when she examined the pain point, there was nothing there. No insect. Just the smallest, rapidly swelling red mark.

That was odd. Unless the tattoos were causing her

nerve synapses to randomly fire off. If it happened again, she would ask Tai'ri. Or a *kheter*, if she ever let one near her for the remainder of this pregnancy.

About to enter the craft shop, Vivian paused. Her vision clouded, ears filling with cotton. If she didn't find somewhere to sit, now, she would fall. She braced her back against the glass door, waiting for the dizziness to pass. When it didn't, she touched her comm unit then spoke Tai'ri's code.

"Vivian?" His voice was clear, sharp with concern but not panicked.

"I—something's wrong. I'm about to pass out." She looked around for help, saw a figure approaching at a fast, casual walk. It could be a jogger, but her instincts screamed. "There's someone coming. It doesn't feel right."

The shop door opened just as darkness closed over her head.

She was only out for a moment. An unfamiliar face peered at her, speaking in a high, alarmed pitch. Great, her translator was on the fritz.

Then Tai'ri was there.

"You were following me," she slurred. "No way you could have got here so fast."

That was the last thing she said before darkness claimed her again.

Tai'ri cradled Vivian's weight in his arms, eating ground to return to the security of the center. His team, the guards assigned to Vivian, were already canvassing the area to find her attacker.

He *knew* it wasn't dizziness due to her condition. She'd been fine just a moment before, and then suddenly, out. As soon as he'd broken cover, sprinting towards her, the male on the sidewalk switched directions and crossed the street. Maybe innocent, but just as he ordered his team to detain him, a transport landed and the male jumped in. A smooth extraction, which took under thirty seconds.

The timing told him one thing.

He burst through the front doors, barely waiting for them to open. The receptionist gave him a startled look. She must have signaled to Bey, because his sister met him halfway down the hall leading to the intake rooms.

"Tai'ri! What happened?" Her voice was startled, eyes wide, but she turned on her heel and led him to an open room. They were all stocked with medical supplies and equipment needed to take care of minor emergencies. "Get her on the table."

Tai'ri laid Vivian down, watching as Abeyya ran a scanner over her.

"Hit. Went unconscious three minutes later."

His marks reacted to the cold fury snaking through him, sparking and slithering on his skin. They revealed his inner turmoil even if none of it showed on his face.

"Pulse and breathing are normal," Abeyya said. "I'm detecting an abnormality in her blood. One moment."

"They're gone," Banujani, the lead for Vivian's team, reported, her brisk voice cool in his ear unit. "No DNA trace."

"How did they know I was bringing Vivian here today? We checked her for trackers." The question was rhetorical. He cursed himself. He'd let the enemy get the drop on him, too distracted by Vivian.

Vykhan's voice came onto the private comm line; Vivian's unit would have sent an automatic distress signal and alerted him.

"They would have had agents posted in all the places it's likely you would take her. It is no leap of logic to assume you would come to your sister's birthing facility sooner or later."

Tai'ri refrained from snarling with impatience, or saying he already *knew* all of that. "Fools. After capturing their *kheter,* they must know we're aware of their plans."

"They are not fools. They've invested too heavily in the child's production to take the loss."

"I'll get with Evvek and check the chatter on the darksphere," Tai'ri said. He might technically be off duty, but this was still his team despite the monumental fuck up that had led to his capture, and they would still follow his orders. "Find the client."

"Belay that," Vykhan said. "Tai'ri, Banujani can recon."

Tai'ri reminded himself Vykhan deserved his respect and obedience. "This is my bondmate, my child. I want in on the hunt. I know you're searching for the leader of the cell that imprisoned us."

"We continue to have this conversation. My thoughts on the matter have not changed."

"I have served the *Bdakhun* and you well for three decades. Have I not earned the right?"

There was a long moment of silence. "The quality of your service is not in question. You are emotionally involved. You cannot be trusted to make the decisions necessary—"

Tai'ri exhaled and forced his voice to remain emotionless. "Vakshit, Vykhan, and you know it. I can be whoever I need to be to get the job done. I'm trained to be whoever I need to be."

"And right now," was the soft, but not yet dangerous reply, "you are a male infuriated by the danger to his mate. Every instinct in you is crying out to protect your loved one, to exact vengeance. To kill, destroy, with no thought to subtlety or consequences."

"Don't trust me?"

A longer, colder, silence. "Very well. Your sole task is to find the most recent broker arranging for the sale of females like your mate. The broker will be the weak link that breaks and leads to the head of the supply chain."

"Agreed."

"Alert me when your female wakes," Vykhan said, then went silent as he left the comm line.

8

Vivian fought a haze of unnatural sleep, the surface under her back firm. The air was an ambient temperature for once; normally they keep the cells chilled. It was harder to fight back when you were freezing.

How many times was it this week? How many times she'd inhaled the odorless gas and then woke with a lingering antiseptic scent in her nostrils, a burn in her throat and small, neat bandages covering needle pricks on her veins.

"You're safe, Viv," a smooth, masculine voice said.

That wasn't right; her captors never spoke to her.

But it was a familiar voice. Her arms itched even as her back relaxed, tension draining away. She knew that voice, recalled steady eyes set in a handsome face. He would never hurt her. He had saved her.

Vivian frowned. Wait . . . what?

"Vivian?"

Something in the voice warned her all was not well. Anger and stress were emotions her ears had become attuned to hear.

Eyes opening, the veil of drug-induced sleep fell away, and she knew she wasn't in a cell, wasn't being subjected to—

Turning her head, she jerked involuntarily. "Get that away!" She shoved the narrow tray away from her bedside and it clattered to the floor.

"Vivian," Tai'ri said, grabbing her hand. "You're safe. You know where you are?"

She tugged her hand, and he released her. "I know where I am."

The small room was one of the intake chambers Abeyya had shown her, where they placed mothers with appointments who preferred to wait in privacy rather than in the common area.

"Did you do something to me when I was unconscious?" She bared her teeth at him.

His expression hardened but his voice remained gentle. "No. No one will do anything to you while you aren't awake to give consent."

"Then what is that stuff for?"

The door opened and Abeyya entered, pausing as she surveyed the mess of vials, needles, and other instruments. She crossed the room, touching a wall panel. It slid open, and she extracted supplies to clean the mess.

"She flailed as she was waking," Tai'ri murmured to his sister.

"I don't need you to cover for me." Vivian's voice was sharp. "I knocked it down. And I will again if anyone ever comes near me with that stuff." Tears scored her eyes. She swiped at them, furious.

"All right, Viv. It's all right."

Abeyya disposed of the mess and turned to Vivian. "Please pardon me. I should have kept the supplies put away until you woke." She gave her brother an oblique look.

"What happened?" Vivian asked.

The looks between the siblings changed.

"I don't want to alarm you. We performed a basic diagnostic. There is a substance in your bloodstream we believe is a sedative. A strong one. I did inject you with a general counter agent. I deemed it important to get you awake. I apologize if this is not what you would have preferred."

Vivian waved a hand. She wasn't going to complain that they acted without her consent in order to wake her up. As long as that was the only thing they had done, then she had no reason to not trust them.

Tai'ri hovered with his hands in his pockets again, shoulders slightly hunched as he eyed her. It was odd to see such a tall, muscular warrior seem so apprehensive of her reactions. But then, she had something he wanted and evidently he wasn't willing to coerce her into giving it to him.

"I don't understand," Vivian said. She glanced at her arm. "I felt a bug bite on my upper arm. A sting."

Tai'ri's expression went cold. "That's likely how you were injected. A dart."

Her heart rate sped up, and not just in reaction to the sudden air of menace emanating from him. "Do you think the traffickers were trying to reclaim me?"

"It can be nothing else. Normal people don't walk around with projectile tranquilizers."

"Then they didn't know you were following me."

He gave her a look. "I'm an operative, Viv. No one knows I'm there unless I want them to." He stopped, wariness flashing across his expression.

Probably because he'd just admitted to stealth following her . . . when she'd requested some time alone.

But the assault vindicated his initial concerns about her walking alone in his first place, and he'd been kind enough not to say 'I told you so'."

Vivian sighed. "Are you going to tell Ibukay?"

"We spoke." His voice was grim.

Vivian looked between Tai'ri and Abeyya. "Should we even stay here? If the traffickers know I'm sitting here like a duck . . ."

Tai'ri frowned. "A duck? . . . fowl. I don't understand."

"It's an Earth saying. I guess it loses meaning in the translation."

"We have security," Abeyya said. "Our mothers

sometimes come here to birth in complicated circumstances. Besides, Tai'ri oversaw the fabrication of our system here himself."

"Vykhan advised me on it," he added. "It's secure here for now." His comm pinged. "Accept."

"Vivian, are you well?" Ibukay's form sprang into existence, the image so dense Vivian thought the *Bdakhun* was really present. Yes, Tai'ri's tech was way better than hers.

Vivian nodded. Ibukay visibly relaxed though her mouth remained tight. "Tell me what happened," she ordered.

By the end of the explanation, Vykhan flashed into existence, standing at the *Bdakhun's* shoulder. He watched Tai'ri, who stood with one arm braced against the door as if he was silently talking himself down from a flare of temper.

"We anticipated this," Vykhan said. "It is good that they showed their hand so soon. Tai'ri."

Tai'ri turned, then began toying with his beaded bracelet. After a moment, his familiar calm, if slightly wary expression, settled over his face. "She's more valuable to them because of the baby. The price they'll both command . . . " his calm broke, and he whirled, slamming his fist into the wall.

Vivian jerked. Violent outbursts in public on Earth were ruthlessly curtailed.

"We will take precautions," Ibukay said, then sighed. "Extra precautions. Tai'ri, I'm assigning you solely to Vivian until the threat assessments are lowered."

Tai'ri leaned his forehead against the wall. "You need me."

The *Bdakhun* frowned. "I'll take someone from B circle to fill your vacancy. I have a new team member in mind, anyway."

Vykhan narrowed his eyes slightly. "I have not heard of this."

She avoided his glare. "Because you're not going to like it," she muttered. "Her. We'll talk about Reign later."

He glanced at Tai'ri. "You will take Vivian back to your home. It is the most secure location for her other than the palace, and I assume she does not wish to reside there. I will have her belongings brought from the shelter."

"Your pardon," Vivian said. "I haven't yet decided if moving in with Tai'ri is the step I want to take at this time."

Vykhan pinned her with his wintry stare. "Is your first duty, and priority, to see to the safety of yourself and your child?"

"Of course."

"Then it is reasonable that you stay with Tai'ri. Not only is he trained, highly skilled and willing, but he has access to resources and a security system you will not find anywhere else but the palace." He gave her a toothy smile. "Or my domicile. I would be honored to host you."

Not *likely*. Vivian just barely managed to suppress her recoil.

"And here," Abeyya murmured. "But we don't have long-term stay facilities. Vivian, I don't think the *Adekhan* means to imply this is a permanent arrangement, or that your consent is not a factor." She pitched her voice to a soothing tone. "But at least until the baby is born it may be the most convenient, and not just for safety reasons. His home is quite comfortable, and in a good location."

Tai'ri finally turned away from his wall, calm exerted over his expression. He watched her silently.

Vivian knew her anger was irrational, so waited until she could speak calmly to reply. What else could she do, in any case? They were right. And she didn't want to live in the shelter, no matter how clean, well-stocked, and tastefully decorated it was. A shelter was a shelter. She ached for a *home*.

And a man, a voice whispered. *A family.*

But not like this. Not now.

She closed her eyes. If not now, then when? This was the reality she'd been dealt. She could either rail against it, or navigate her way to a compromise she could live with.

The baby shifted, spending a happy, uncomfortable moment stretching little arms and legs before settling back down. Vivian's back ached. Her feet felt hot and tight and her belly itched. And she had to pee.

"Have I exhausted all my options?" Vivian asked carefully, opening her eyes. "I'm aware of Tai'ri's generous offer, and I'm grateful to you as well, *Bdakhun*. I'm only concerned that I haven't had time to properly reflect on all the avenues that may be available to me."

"What avenues?" Vykhan's tone didn't change from its flat baritone.

Vivian's shoulders prickled. It was as if he was so certain of her cooperation or capitulation that he couldn't even be bothered to feel annoyance or anger that she was pushing back.

"You are an alien illegally on this planet," he continued. "You have gone through none of the required channels to secure permits to remain here. Your situation is unique so there are precedents in place to remedy a breach in procedure. However, because you are carrying a child who is one of us, and you have a well-placed sponsor, such permissions that are required may be expedited."

He paused, as if to give her time to come to the correct conclusions.

"Furthermore, your presence presents risk to our people. Doubtless the traffickers will attempt to retrieve you again, as you represent a significant investment of time and resources. Attempts to retrieve you might place others in danger. We cannot have you wandering about the planet unsupervised. In short, either you accept Tai'ri's offer or you must return to Earth where you will no longer be our problem."

She took several short, ragged breaths. None of the others gainsaid him, which meant they all agreed, even if none of them might have phrased it like that. So, Vykhan was to be the battering ram, then?

The dressing down hurt and forced home the fact that she was here on sufferance and had no real rights. No legal representation. It was the choice of one purgatory or the other, and resentment swelled. They were so certain what she should choose. Vivian opened her mouth, about to inform them she would board the next ship to Earth, when Tai'ri interjected.

"Viv, all I care about is your safety." He crossed the distance between them and crouched partway down so they were at eye level. "Let me keep you and our baby safe until we have the threat under control and then I swear to you on this child's life, I will do everything I can to help you build the life that you want. On your terms."

She held his gaze, observed the tightness of his mouth and how he held himself so contained that he'd even stopped fiddling with the beads. She wondered if this was how he expressed fear. She didn't doubt he cared—it would have been all too easy for him to walk away from the entire situation. Could she take a child away from its father, a father who *wanted* it?

She would have to hold her own with these people,

have to insist on making her own decisions, but in the circumstances it would be foolish to try to head out into the wilderness of a strange planet just to assuage her need to feel independent.

"Fine, all this discussion is water torture." She stopped short, feeling her cheeks heat up at her rudeness. "Excuse me, my temper is a little short."

"Understandably," Ibukay said. "So it's settled? Excellent."

"We have already dispatched backup," Vykhan said. "ETA one quarter mark."

Because he had assumed she would comply. For a moment, Vivian hated him. All of them.

9

"It's from the Olathian period that swept the Province about two hundred years ago," Tai'ri said, placing his palm on the door plate. "The wealthy went through a phase where the higher your status, the more floors you built onto your home. Don't know why."

He'd been chattering the entire trip from the center. Like a tourist guide. And now he was discussing, in depth, the architecture of his house.

The door slid open rather than shimmering, and Tai'ri stepped aside and gestured for her to precede him.

It hit her. "Stairs."

He must have heard the dismay in her voice. "When I renovated it, I had the living quarters all moved to the first two levels. Third and fourth levels are guest suites, offices, and a studio."

That caught her attention. "A studio? An art studio?"

The door slid shut behind him. "I don't use it much. My mother always insisted we learn something of the gentler pursuits but . . ." he shrugged.

Vivian turned her attention to the house. Walking up from the outside it had looked like a stack of haphazardly placed white boxes, with cut outs for sheets of glass. He'd filled the windows with plants, and two of the levels boasted balconies.

Inside, light poured from the ceiling. More white walls, blonde wood floors.

"Would you like to see your room first, or the kitchen?"

"The bathroom, please, actually."

He grinned. "Sure. You have an ensuite, but I'll show you where all the bathrooms are just in case."

"That's probably for the best."

Vivian all but pushed him out of the way to enter the first guest bathroom.

When she emerged, Tai'ri wasn't waiting. She paused, but an inset light flashed yellow on the wall and Tai'ri's voice sounded.

"I'm in the kitchen, Viv. House, show Vivian to the kitchen."

She followed the yellow flashing light to the kitchen/living room combo. More light, soft colors, clean lines. Tai'ri stood at a center island, chopping. He indicated a couch with his chin.

"Sit, put your feet up. Do you want a fruit smoothie or juice? My sister Daobah ordered groceries, Bey had you a nutrition plan drawn up. Kitchen's fully stocked."

Vivian glanced at the couch he'd indicated and found absolutely no reason to protest that directive. She lowered herself onto the soft cushions with a sigh.

"The house program is familiarizing itself with your voiceprint," he said. "Try it out. Ask the couch to recline."

"Couch, recline fifty percent, please." The couch obeyed, smoothly lowering her back while lifting her legs. Vivian moaned. "They don't have these at the shelter."

"They don't have me either," he said, voice deep.

She opened her eyes and looked at him, but his expression was neutral. "Do you normally cook for yourself?"

"Yeah. I've used meal services, but it relaxes me."

"Your job is stressful," she murmured, then mentally kicked herself. "That sounded silly."

"Nothing you could say would sound silly. And yes, it's stressful, but . . . " he shrugged. "Ibukay is third in the royal line after her parents, and she'll never rule, but the Province is better for having her. I'm proud to serve."

Her eyes drifted closed. "Smoothie."

When she awoke, it couldn't have been from a long doze. Tai'ri was standing over her, a glass of thick pink liquid in his hand, expression inscrutable. The tattoos on her arms shifted, awakening as if sensing her emotions, then settled back into their static doze.

"Oh, sorry," Vivian said, realizing she was staring at him, and asked the couch to incline.

He set the glass down on a side table. She was comfortable, the couch nestling the small of her back, the light from the fading afternoon sun streaming through the windows from the balcony doors. The quiet, open and soothing decor lulled her into a sense of safety.

"Sleep," he said softly.

Vivian picked up the glass and took a long swallow, then closed her eyes, imagining the weighted warmth of her favorite blanket covering her. As she drifted off, she realized that in her mind, the formerly red blanket was now the same color as Tai'ri's eyes.

"I told you your dissatisfaction would lead you to trouble," her mother said. Nadine Huang tabbed through the latest file of prospects sent by the matchmaker, and refused to look at Vivian. "Who will marry you now?"

"I feel empty," Vivian said.

Her mother flicked her extended stomach a glance. "Not so empty now, are you, girl?"

"Nadine," her father murmured, and set bowls of

steaming oxtail stew and dumplings on the table. He returned moments later with an apple pie.

Vivian put her hands over her belly, feeling the baby shift and kick.

"She's not very nice, is she?" the baby asked.

"We must respect our elders," Vivian informed the child. "Or else we will go to jail."

Her mother clicked her teeth. "Kidnapped and impregnated. What will I tell my sisters?"

"That they wish they were so lucky," her father retorted. "Those old biddies. Tai'ri is very rich, isn't he? And not bad looking."

"Oh, Tai'ri isn't—" Vivian began, but stopped, confused. Tai'ri was the father. But she didn't remember having sex. How could she forget the conception of her own baby?

The doorbell rang, interrupting the brewing argument. Her mother got up to answer. "What's the meaning of this?" she demanded.

Vivian's hand jerked, and she looked up to see government officials storm the condo.

"Vivian Huang?" a black clad agent demanded. "You're under arrest. Independent thought is illegal under Section—"

"Don't worry about the Section," another agent interrupted. "It doesn't matter. Ms. Huang, we're returning you to the lab."

The words struck chills down her spine. "The lab?"

"You ran away, and that was a big no no. You hurt their feelings."

They lunged at her, grabbing her arms and dragging her out of the condo as her mother folded her arms and shook her head. Her father began ranting in his native patois, but there was nothing anyone could do.

They dragged her out of the condo and into a cold, white box. A narrow bed was shoved into one corner.

Vivian began to struggle. "No! I won't go back."

A white-coated figure turned, and the kheter's cold stare met Vivian's. "It's time to have the baby, Vivian. Don't worry. We'll give it a good home. Halflings are delicacies, after all. You're in no position to roast it yourself; you should leave cooking to the professionals and stick to being a disobedient daughter."

The agents wrestled her towards the bed and Vivian screamed.

She jerked awake, her thin blouse soaked with her sweat. The nightmare played through her head, her heartbeat loud in her ears. She forced her fingers to unclench; her entire body trembled. She stilled, realizing she felt no movement inside, and held her breath. Moments later, the sluggish kick of a partially sleeping baby, snug inside her womb.

Everything was quiet, the light streaming in from the ceiling now from the twin moons, and not the sun. Tai'ri must have decided to let her sleep on the couch rather than waking her. Pushing to her feet, she walked on unsteady legs to the wide balcony doors and stepped out, looking up at a starry sky so different, and yet so similar to the one she'd known. Any sky was a blessing—at one point she'd despaired of ever seeing clouds again, or feeling a fresh breeze on her skin.

Her throat closed as tears pricked her eyes. It was ridiculous; just a nightmare. She was safe here. The *kheter* couldn't touch her or take the baby. And her parents would never be so . . . well, her mother *could,* but probably not to Vivian's face.

Closing her eyes, she willed away the burgeoning headache, knowing her growing dizziness was from a lack of appetite earlier this evening as much as it was from stress. She grabbed the railing, inhaling lungfuls of air.

"Vivian?"

She screamed, jerking. Strong arms wrapped around her shoulders and pulled her back from the balcony.

"It's fine, you're fine," Tai'ri said. But he didn't let her go, his hold inescapable.

Her teeth chattered from the shock. "I didn't hear you approach."

"I'm sorry." He spoke in low, soothing tones. "I was alerted that you were outside. Your vitals are showing signs of stress."

"Of course they're showing signs of stress!" Was he an idiot? "You startled me."

"I'm sorry."

"Then let me go!"

"Vivian, take a deep breath. I'll let you go when I know you're calm."

Her surge of rage found a target. "You don't get to tell me how to feel. You don't get to tell me how to react! Now let. Me. Go!"

"Do I need to seal the balcony off, Vivian?"

His steely tone, the tension in his still body, pierced her welling panic. "You think—you think I'm going to . . ." she couldn't say the words.

Tai'ri said nothing.

"I would *never*." She took several breaths, closing her eyes and forcing her body to relax. He wasn't going to budge until he was certain she wasn't a danger to herself. To his baby.

Just when she thought she was calm, she burst into tears.

"Oh, fuck," he swore. "Alright. Alright, Viv." Tai'ri lifted her into his arms and strode back inside towards the couch, sitting down with her in his lap.

"I'm sorry," she said, struggling to calm the sobs. "I don't know what's wrong with me."

"Yeah, I'm not touching that one," he said with a chuckle. But worry was under the humor. "Nothing is wrong with you. Cry if you need to, *yadoana*."

He murmured as she cried, the same rhythmic syllables he'd spoken in Abeyya's office. After a time the low chant leached away the worst of her stormy emotions and as she focused more and more on his words, found herself calming.

Tai'ri continued the chant until well after she'd stopped crying, and even when he was done, she didn't move off his lap.

In fact, she realized she was leaning against a very naked chest. If she were less emotionally exhausted, she might have blushed. But as she shifted in his arms, she only noticed how well formed he was. Silky skin, strong, sculpted muscles. She must have awakened him from his own sleep.

"I should learn that chant," she said. "It seems to work well on hysterical women."

She felt lips brush the top of her head. "If you think that was hysterical, you should have seen my oldest sister during *her* third trimester. Wouldn't use the word hysterical, though. Not to her face."

Here was a man unfazed by messy emotions, uncaring of the mess she was making on his bare skin. Who spoke matter-of-factly about her outburst, sparing her pride. Willing to hold her and let her rage. Even if it was just his baby he cared for, he didn't have to do this.

"Haeemah is a goddess of knowledge and self-mastery," he said. "Her Precepts teach us to master our emotions and past traumas and achieve Silence. When Silent you are completely yourself, your actions governed purely by truth and logic and not by one's darker nature. The chants help you to focus, allow emotion to flow through you until you are able to be yourself again."

"Teach me the chant," she said.

She had guards, in theory. Almost a week in Tai'ri's home having not seen nor heard from one, it was difficult for Vivian to accept their presence. She supposed that made them professionals. It wasn't like on the vids, after all, where they would be hovering at her sides in slick business suits, bristling with weapons and attitude.

After a mid-morning snack, and bored for now with the mosaic she was working on, Vivian decided that if Tai'ri was going to pay for guards, she should take advantage. A walk around the block would provide some exercise, fresh air and sunlight, and also test the limits of her invisible perimeter. She assumed that if she wandered too far, Tai'ri would inform her.

Leaving the house, the support band snug under her uterus, Vivian slowly made her way down the block. If they had any objections, they would—

"Ms. Huang."

The disembodied voice came from her comm, and didn't startle Vivian too badly. Her heart rate leaped for a moment, then she responded. "Yes?"

"Is there something I can help you with?" A female voice, neutral and brisk, but not unkind.

"Who is this?" Vivian asked.

"Banujani, Ms. Huang. I'm daytime point."

"You can call me Vivian, Banujani." She paused, looking around. During the five-minute walk, the residential block had given way to a small, circular shopping district situated like a cul-de-sac to support the community. There were several businesses including a cafe, a small grocer, what looked like an office of some kind, and a salon. "And no, I don't need anything. I just wanted a walk."

"Please wait. I'll accompany you."

Vivian turned. A tall woman with a smooth, indigo scalp and serious eyes approached. She wore the same loose, nondescript dark trousers Tai'ri often wore, tucked into flexible boots, and a long-sleeved shirt that molded to her torso tightly enough Vivian saw the delineation of firm muscles in her arms, shoulders and abs.

The woman approached, her lips spread in a wide smile. Vivid green metal glittered up one earlobe and dripped from the other. "Viv! You made it!"

"Um, hello," Vivian said. She wasn't much of an actress, but she understood that while the guard was with her, they'd pretend to be friends.

"Did you want tea?" Banujani asked.

"Tea would be lovely." Vivian frowned slightly, then sighed and held up her comm. "Tai'ri said I could wave this thing over a terminal and it would debit his account?"

"Yup."

Banujani steered them towards the cafe. Vivian

only knew it was a cafe because she spent a part of each day learning the local dialect manually from a program loaded into a learning tablet the safehouse had allowed her to keep.

"You should be able to access the list of foods approved for your physiology as well," the guard continued in a lowered voice.

They placed orders at a kiosk and chose a table. Vivian hadn't had any particular purpose when emerging from the house, had just wanted to get out.

Banujani lounged in her chair, eyes constantly roving, foot tapping on the floor as if there was an invisible tune running through her head. Or maybe she drank a lot of coffee. Or whatever passed for coffee here. She hadn't yet gotten her hands on beans.

"This has to be rather boring," Vivian said, apology in her voice.

The woman's gaze swung back towards her. "Boring is good. We want boring."

"Of course." Vivian almost blushed. "I should know better."

Banujani nodded. "Feeling boredom means you're acclimating. That's good."

She'd needed this. Another layer to help her return to normal. A new normal. She was healing. She didn't wake in the middle of the night disoriented anymore. She smiled when she thought of her baby. She would never forget how the child had been conceived, but it was becoming easier to have small pockets of time where everything felt hum drum. Domestic. As if they were just another new age mixed species couple planning for their first child.

"So," Vivian said, determined to emerge just a little more out of her self-imposed shell, "tell me something funny about Tai'ri."

Banujani glanced at her, then grinned and tugged on one of her multitude of earrings. "Yeah? Okay, I've got a story for you."

10

Sitting and waiting was the worst. When that happened, Tai'ri distracted himself with minor tasks—administrative work or training. But this mission was personal. He hovered beside Evvek, eyes trained on the monitor.

"Cover is solid," Evvek muttered, red-tipped cabled hair draped down his back.

The data analyst made up for the ruthless blandness of his work environment with yellow skin pants and nothing else, displaying a honed physique. He'd left his arms where the bonding tattoos were placed alone, but every other inch of his body was inked in swirling alien designs. Script, symbols, all revealing Evvek's fascination with off planet cultures.

"Should have hits by now." He rattled off a string of commands, switching to manual after a time, and then his fingers flew across the boards.

"Up the bid again," Tai'ri demanded.

Evvek's head snapped up, his tri-colored gaze irritated. "Slow down, *aja'eko*. If you look too eager, you'll scare the suppliers. This has to be done carefully."

Tai'ri ground his jaw against a reply and nodded. He refused to prove Vykhan right about his lack of objectivity for this hunt.

If today his job was to wait and hover, then he'd wait and hover.

He'd left Vivian with Banujani and come to this hidden satellite office in the city. Their equipment was unregistered, and in front a real currency exchange conducted brisk daily business.

"Wait, wait." Evvek hunched over, fingers swiping. "I've got an offer."

"What is it?"

Tai'ri's insides clenched as he struggled with anger. Evvek had crafted a careful profile for Tai'ri of a bored, wealthy male from a two-generation merchant family looking for 'off-planet' pets for his new menagerie. Female, proven breeders, of good health and trainable. Evvek sprinkled a host of other coded language guaranteed to attract the right brokers—those who traded in alien females of compatible species for sex and breeding purposes.

Tai'ri reminded himself that wasn't always the fate of these females. Several times Ibukay's teams had busted households who kept the aliens for household labor or even as party entertainment. The females weren't always abused. If it had happened to Vivian, she might have gone to a household where she'd be relatively well treated.

He told himself these lies to stymy the flood of images and thoughts that spiraled into the darkest waking nightmares of what might have happened to his mate and child had they not been rescued. What might yet happen to them if Tai'ri failed.

He'd slit his own wrists before he allowed them to be recaptured. He'd prefer to slit the enemy's, though.

Tai'ri realized Evvek's silence was odd. "What?"

Evvek cleared his throat, then spoke quietly. "The offer is for a young, gravid human female. Class B."

Class B. Perfect health, above average attractiveness and above average intelligence, deemed able to perform a multitude of common tasks and of biddable temperament. The only better classification was A, and that was reserved for rare or dangerous to acquire species. Humans weren't especially dangerous to obtain, and their attractiveness often hit and miss.

"How much?" Tai'ri forced himself to ask.

"They're willing to split the infant from the mother. Price depends on the package."

Tai'ri whirled, grabbing the back of a chair. When he realized he was in danger of splintering the wood, he let go and closed his eyes, and began the chant.

It took ten minutes, but he regained his calm. Maybe Vykhan was right.

"You good?" Evvek asked. He leaned back in his

seat, studying Tai'ri. "Listen, no one blames you if you need to sit this one out. It's close to home. They're targeting your mate, and that vakshit would drive me crazy, and I'm the sanest person here. Only Vykhan has that Silence mastered. The rest of us are normal."

"No." Tai'ri pushed the breath to utter cogent words out of constricting lungs. How did people survive with this much rage bottled up, for long periods of time? "We identify this broker, use him to identify his suppliers. I will destroy them all. Slowly. I will see this through until their ashes decorate my mantle."

"Macabre, but if that's what soothes you. You memorized your cover?"

Tai'ri stared at him.

Evvek rolled his eyes. "Just asking. Alright, take a seat in the booth, I'm loading backgrounds now. Ordering audio/visual prelim."

Tai'ri slipped into the narrow booth in the corner, outfitted with tech that allowed Evvek to project any impenetrable background image he chose. Tai'ri, recalling the brief, would be lounging on a divan in a half open robe, the picture of a successful, indolent male bored with what legal and morally acceptable avenues of entertainment had to offer.

Tai'ri sprawled in the cold seat, and waited for the comm line to open. The screen remained black, but a voice sounded.

"Greetings, CityNightLord. I received your request for a viewing." Not a Yadeshi voice, but accented with something he couldn't quite put his finger on. Yet, anyway.

Tai'ri jerked a shoulder, expression bored, and let his gaze wander. He spoke in a high, slightly nasal tenor. "I prefer to know who I am dealing with. I prefer long-term relationships. Only brokers who understand the value of my attention will receive my business."

"We pride ourselves on flawless service. I understand you are inquiring about our latest acquisition."

"If it meets with my quality standards. I refuse to waste my time on inferior merchandise."

"We cater to clients with refined palates."

Tai'ri lifted a brow. "We'll see, I suppose. The last time a broker promised me superior service I was delivered a hag. I had to fumigate after it died. Do you have any idea how expensive it is to replace genuine Lonorian silks? They absorb *any* scent. I'm still recovering." He shuddered, tilting his head back in despair to stare at the ceiling.

"We have a guarantee," was the smooth reply. "If you are unhappy with any of our merchandise, we offer a replacement of even higher value, no questions asked."

Tai'ri lowered his head, allowing distaste and anger to show on his face. "Fine. But I won't pay full offer on the first transaction. You will have to prove yourselves."

"I'm confident we can come to an arrangement."

The smooth, oiled voice grated on Tai'ri's nerves.

His hand tightened. "When will you have your next showing?"

"I can arrange a showing at your convenience. However, the alien you were interested in is still in processing. We spend several weeks training, grooming, and ensuring our merchandise is in the best health and fully understands its new role."

"Very well. If you don't have that one ready, in the meantime I will go to—"

"We can arrange for the showing early, CityNight-Lord. We're impressed with your credentials and are eager to serve you."

Which meant the trafficker had managed to hack into the fake persona Evvek had created, and was salivating. To them, Tai'ri was a rich mark, willing to spend recklessly and aggrieved at the lack of quality on the market at present. Also someone with an impeccable public record, low profile but influential in certain circles.

"Fine. Transmit the details as soon as you have them." Tai'ri signed off. "Comm, connect Banujani." Insects traveled up and down his spine and he grit his teeth. Everything in him urged him to go to Vivian, ensure she was safe. But the best thing he could do was continue to hunt down their enemies, and trust his team to protect her.

They would give their lives for her, Tai'ri was certain of it.

"Sir," Banujani said.

"Vivian?"

"Perimeter is secure, everything is quiet. Vivian recently retired for a nap."

"Remain vigilant. Someone's coming for her. I'll brief you fully when I return."

"Copy."

Tai'ri left the virtual closet. Evvek looked up. "He's biting. Says he'll message with a time for a showing sometime this week."

Tai'ri stiffened. "How can he arrange a showing that soon when Vivian is safe at home?"

"We just *think* she's the one being targeted."

"Unless he has other females he can put in her place until he has her."

Evvek shrugged. "Doesn't even have to be that. Just marketing. Advertise something sweet to get nibbles, then reel the clients in with your real stock. Hope they don't notice the lights are a little dim. They guarantee good health for at least ninety days, after all."

Tai'ri grimaced. They were talking about people, but it didn't help to focus on that. The thought that other females were still enslaved chilled him. It was so much more personal now, even though it had always been personal.

But now . . . it hit him home in the gut in a way it hadn't before.

He didn't need *more* motivation to take down the broker and his supplier, but motivation kept getting rammed down his throat.

Vivian roused, feeling eyes on her even in her sleep. She shifted on the couch, wincing a little at her sore hips, and looked up. Tai'ri leaned against the kitchen island, arms crossed over his chest as he watched her.

She didn't quite know how to greet him. He wasn't her husband or cohabitation partner. Or even her boyfriend. But he was even closer than that, the father of her child. A stranger, and yet after a week of living in the same home . . . not really a stranger.

"Good evening," she said, settling on the simplest greeting. "Have you been here long?"

"No."

She'd learned over the days to gauge his moods. Though he was always kind, gentle, some evenings the gentleness was edged with something she couldn't quite define. As if he held back a maelstrom. He didn't frighten her but it would be foolish to ignore that suppressed darkness.

Tonight, he stared at her unblinking, his stillness predatory. Her heart rate increased, and she licked her bottom lip, hesitating. "Is something wrong?"

He finally blinked, then straightened. "No. You took a walk today."

"Yes."

"You haven't left the house in a week."

"Am I a prisoner?"

"No."

"Then is there a problem?"

He shook his head and pushed away from the counter, approaching to crouch at her feet. "No. The exercise is good for you."

Her back tensed. She didn't have the energy for this. Something was wrong, but if he didn't want to share, that was his prerogative. "I agree. I think I'll go to bed now."

"You're tired? I thought we could go out to eat?"

"You're hardly in the mood for it," she snapped. "And spending an evening walking on eggshells around you isn't my idea of recreation."

Tai'ri furrowed his brow. "Why would you crush eggshells at my feet?"

"What do you—oh." The translator must be borking again. She really needed to learn the language manually. "No, what I meant was, I can tell something is bothering you, and I don't have the energy to watch my words."

His expression cleared. "You don't have to watch your words." He paused. "I—it's hard to separate from work some days. Today was rough for reasons."

Ah. Vivian relaxed, and even felt a little embarrassed. Of course. And he certainly wasn't used to having to come home and shed his work skin for the sake of another person.

"I see. I'm sorry."

He reached up, brushed her bottom lip with his thumb, gaze unflinching. Her mouth opened lightly as she inhaled, the moment stretching between them.

"I'll be more careful about not bringing work home with me." His voice was soft, an impossibly gentle caress . . . but the darkness lurked, now warmed with heat.

"I—I'm sorry." She kept apologizing, and she didn't even know what for. All she knew was that sometimes, when he looked at her like this, her breath caught in her throat and she forgot *why* she was supposed to feel broken.

He stood. "If you're sorry, then come to dinner with me."

Vivian nodded. "Let me change into something less loungy, though."

"You look fine, but I'll wait."

Vivian eyed the shoes with something close to despair. She'd misplaced her slip-ons somehow and hadn't yet figured out how to get House to locate them. These alternatives were lovely, and totally impractical. Someone had thought adorning heeled booties with little hooks and laces was a good idea. She couldn't bend forward enough to even reach her calves, much less her feet.

The first day she'd spent in Tai'ri's home, a flood of packages had arrived with selections of shoes, clothing, undergarments, cosmetics. Everything in her size and suitable for late stage pregnancy. She wondered if he had just picked a pre-assembled wardrobe package because everything was ruthlessly matchy, and with pieces she'd never need to wear—like business attire and formal wear.

A light tap on her door gained her attention. "Come in."

Tai'ri entered and stopped, surveying her as she sat on the edge of her bed. He didn't often come in her room.

He shoved his hands in his pockets. "Figured you'd be awhile since my sisters always like to fiddle, but I was hoping against hope."

"I'm dressed." The coral colored maxi dress was a comfortable fabric, but pretty enough for a restaurant. She'd brushed her hair back in a pony tail and slipped beaded earrings into her lobes. "It's just the shoes."

"That's easy." He strode forward and knelt at her feet, taking a bootie in one hand and her ankle in the other. "My mother used to go barefoot when she was carrying her babies. Said it was simpler." His touch was light, fingers cool against her ankle. Her foot jerked.

"That tickles," she said, clearing her throat when he looked up quizzically. Her skin tingled where he touched hers, and the marks on her arms crawled.

"Sorry." He didn't sound sorry. He stroked the top of her foot with a single fingertip; it felt like a caress, but innocent enough for deniability. Then he said, "You have lovely feet."

Well, definitely *not* deniability then.

Vivian took a few seconds to make sure her voice was even. "Thank you. They're just feet."

Tai'ri's gaze brushed her face for a second, inscrutable, but then he put the shoes on her feet and fastened them.

He stood. "These are stupid shoes for a pregnant female. Weren't there any flats in the stuff Bey ordered?"

"I lost them."

"Hmm." He eyed her. "We'll get you some slip-ons while we're out. Do you know what you want to eat?"

"Food."

"Funny." He slipped his hands back in his pockets, giving her a half-amused look. "What kind of food?"

She smiled at him. He'd changed out of his all black work clothing and was now his dressed down, slightly disheveled self. The broody aura completely gone. This was the companion she could let herself enjoy getting to know some more over dinner and an evening stroll.

"Surprise me," she said.

11

"We'll go to the art district," Tai'ri told her as they stepped into a two-person transport. He programmed the destination. "*Bdakhun* Ibukay prefers it, so we already have security set up all over."

"What kind of security?"

"Surveillance, safe rooms. Stuff."

"Sounds like a vid."

The trip was quick and quiet, the sort of companionable silence Vivian appreciated because it meant she didn't have to struggle to find conversation. Outside of the classroom, she'd never been a chatty woman. But the last week he'd spent as much time with her as he could, and they'd talked. About their lives, their goals. They'd crammed weeks of getting to know you conversations into a matter of days while cooking together, or watching the sun set on the balcony, and Vivian had learned Tai'ri was an intelligent, empathetic man with a dry sense of humor and deep well of personal responsibility.

Someone she would have truly liked in normal circumstances; she liked him now.

The transport set down on a rooftop pavilion. They exited, Tai'ri taking her arm in one of the casually courteous gestures she'd come to expect as second nature to him.

"Can we walk and eat, is that done here?" she asked. The rooftop pavilion led into a building of open-air shops and restaurants. She saw plenty of shiny, and wanted to chase all of it down.

"Yeah, but as soon as you're tired, let me know."

One of the restaurants offered a brisk walk up and go service, and Vivian found herself with the equivalent of Beysikai province walking tacos. A recyclable container filled with some sort of savory grain, chopped marinated meat, vegetables and two complementary sauces. She ate it with a fork, walking slowly.

"Shoes," Tai'ri said suddenly. His hands full of his own meal, he pointed his chin to a shop three doors down.

She hesitated, vaguely uncomfortable. Receiving the first delivery of clothes had felt like a necessity—she couldn't walk around naked, after all. Him buying dinner was reasonable on a date. And, again, she had no income. But him buying her shoes . . . it felt so married. Which they weren't.

"I think what I have on is fine," she said.

"Nah, worst design ever. Too many hooks." He finished his meal and slipped the remains into a receptacle in the wall.

It was better to just be blunt. "I can't pay you back, Tai'ri."

He stopped, looking down at her with narrowed eyes. "Did I ask you to, Vivian?"

Vivian pressed her lips tight against a retort that would be less than polite.

Sighing, he took her hand. "It's my privilege, alright? I have plenty of money and not a lot of ways to spend it. No time. If buying you things makes me happy, you owe me that much, right?"

She opened her mouth, shut it, looking up at his too innocent expression. "I know what you're doing."

"Good. Now let's go get practical shoes. If you trip and twist your ankle, you could also hurt the baby."

"You make getting your way sound so reasonable."

Slipping her arm in the crook of his elbow, he wisely refrained from a reply since she was going along with him now, anyway. Smart.

Allowing him to buy her a pair of shoes didn't mean she would indulge herself, however. She spent a bare minimum of time browsing and chose the most neutral, serviceable option possible even though he kept pointing to expensive, colorful wisps of footwear, and held her ground.

In the end he compromised, perhaps recognizing

when to give ground. They left the shop with a pair of navy flats, and a pair of coral to match her dress.

They strolled, Tai'ri pausing at a vendor with a display of beaded earrings. Vivian said nothing only because a different booth caught her eye—a colorful display of craft paper, watercolors, and other art supplies. A few items had come in the same delivery as her clothing, but she wanted *more*. She waddled over, eyes wide, fingers twitching.

Let him ooh and ahh over jewelry. He'd soon learn the way to her heart was colored pencils.

She glanced over her shoulder, saw him haggling with the vendor. His head whipped around and he met her gaze, then relaxed and smiled. She rolled her eyes and waved a hand, then turned back to consider three different shades of green pencils.

The vendor hovered. She pointed. "What is the difference in brands? Besides the price."

He launched into his spiel and Vivian listened intently, glancing absently over her shoulder again. She frowned. Tai'ri was gone.

"I'll be back," she told the vendor, uneasy. Maybe he'd just slipped away to find a restroom. She was a big girl, after all, and there were plenty of people around. There was no need to be nervous.

But she backtracked, craning her head to try to spot a tall blue man in a sea of tall blue men.

She'd discuss this with him and let him know exactly how she felt, in no uncertain terms.

Vivian realized she'd backtracked all the way past the shoe shop when she stopped, frustrated, and decided to grab a seat on a nearby bench and wait for *him* to find *her*.

Fuming at how inconsiderate he was, she smoothed her expression and continued to scan the crowd and not look like an angry badger, composing a suitable, but polite, diatribe in her mind. She was really going to let him have it—

"Vivian?"

Vivian froze. She would never forget that cool, brisk, slightly superior tone—and had never wanted to hear it again.

She whipped her head around. The *kheter* stood several feet away, staring at Vivian. She wore a simple jumpsuit, her hair back in a sleek bun.

"Are you lost, Vivian? I'm happy to offer assistance." She moved forward.

"I'm fine." Vivian didn't bother to blunt her sharp tone. "I don't need help."

The *kheter* smiled. "It's fate that we met here, isn't it? I've been meaning to apologize for some time now."

"Weren't you arrested?"

The false smile faded a notch. "I was not."

Where was Tai'ri? He'd been gone way too long now. Vivian felt beads of sweat on her upper lip, her breath coming in short, fast puffs. Oh, no. Not here. She couldn't do this here. It would give the *kheter* all the ammunition she needed.

Besides the fact that Vivian didn't believe in these kinds of coincidences.

She pushed to her feet, nausea roiling in her belly.

"Why don't you come with me, Vivian?"

Such a soft, insidious voice. One in a long line of soft, emotionless, insidious voices. She would never be taken again. *Never*.

The *kheter* reached her, an arm outstretched. Fingers wrapped around Vivian's left wrist.

Never again. She swung, seeing nothing but a hated face, her fist connecting with a slender jaw. Pain burst in her knuckles even as her vision blurred.

Never again.

Tai'ri eyed two different sets of dangling earrings, the unhewn stones a match for the color of Vivian's dress. But one included gold beads and little stars, while the other was simpler. He glanced at his mate several stalls down, intently studying green pencils that looked the exact same. It *did* occur to him that if she wanted art supplies, he should buy her art supplies. He wanted to see the earrings in her lobes though. Nothing sexier on a female.

Well. No reason why he couldn't buy both pairs, then buy her art supplies.

"I'll take them both," he said, just as his comm beeped. Tai'ri answered immediately.

"Tai'ri," Vykhan said. "We've spotted the *kheter* in the plaza."

His blood went cold, the mellow warmth inside evaporating. "She's in custody."

"Demonstrably not."

"You wanted to see where she'd scurry off to."

"I did. There was also some doubt as to her intentions when she encountered Vivian. We need more in order to justify detaining her. It seems no coincidence she happens to be in the same location as you and your mate, so I suspect we will soon have that justification." Satisfaction in Vykhan's tone, quickly banished. Satisfaction wasn't Silent after all.

"Vivian's being tracked."

"Bold of them to attempt an extraction with you present. Bold is vexing. I feel we have not been firm enough with these insects."

Tai'ri scanned the crowd and began to walk casually towards Vivian.

"No," Vykhan said. "Stay back."

Outrage, hot and immediate, welled up. "Vivian isn't bait."

"She is in no danger. Draw the *kheter* out now so we may eliminate the ultimate threat all the sooner."

"*Fuck,*" he swore under his breath, knowing Vykhan was right. "Fuck." But because Vykhan had not ordered him to comply, he obeyed. Unhappily.

He knew how to slip into the shadows so completely none would see him. Tai'ri did so, and waited, seeing the moment Vivian realized he was missing, and the moment when her faint irritation turned to unease, and then alarm mixed with anger. Haeemah's Mercy, it twisted his heart when she finally sat down, trying desperately to maintain calm.

"Can't do this, Vykhan," he said. "I can't do this to her."

"Wait," was the sharp reply. "Our prey approaches."

A split second later he saw, because now he was no longer staring so hard at Vivian's face.

The evening was ruined. The *kheter* would pay.

Calm settled over Tai'ri as he moved, approaching on silent feet, listened to the brief conversation. When the female reached out and grabbed Vivian's arm, he shot forward—then halted.

Vivian hauled back between one moment and the next, and landed a solid blow on the *kheter's* jaw, the crunch of knuckles on bone causing him to wince. His fierce mate made a deep sound of pain, but it was the *kheter* who stumbled back, crying out.

Tai'ri moved up behind the traitor, slipping fingers around her neck. "You should have stayed away," he whispered into his enemy's ear, pressing down. She crumpled, and Tai'ri let her drop to the ground.

People around them cried out, several starting forward but Tai'ri pinned the bolder ones with a look and a snarl, then flicked his wrist so the official insignia of his rank flashed out in front of his chest like a shield.

The civilians stopped, then backed away. There was not a person in the province who did not know the insignia of the royal guard.

"Sir," Banujani said, appearing in the crowd as Tai'ri stepped over the *kheter* and slid an arm around Vivian's shoulders. She stared at nothing, body stiff as he examined her knuckles.

"That was a mean jab," Banujani muttered. "Be careful."

She said nothing else as she hefted the unconscious *kheter* over her shoulder and jogged off. Tai'ri would take Vivian home, tend to her hand, and then slip away after his mate was asleep to watch the *kheter's* second interrogation. And perhaps participate.

"I'm sorry, Vivian," he said in her ear.

"I'm not a child, I can take care of myself," she said, body still stiff, "but I realized how unsafe I feel when you aren't with me."

He choked down anger; at himself, at Vykhan, at the people who'd done this to her. He almost started to lie to her, but couldn't.

"Vykhan ordered me to stay back when we saw the *kheter* approach. We wanted to see what she would do once she made contact. But I swear, you were never in danger."

She looked up at him, studied his face, her eyes impassive. "You were using me as bait."

This time he did swear, low and vicious. "Yes. I won't do it again. I don't care who orders me."

Vivian shook her head. "No . . . I understand. But if you could warn me next time, that would be helpful."

He couldn't help himself. She stood with such quiet dignity, though her mouth was tighter than normal, the look in her eyes strained. But she wasn't going to cry, or yell at him, or blame him for not protecting her. She simply offered to cooperate next time.

There wouldn't be a next time, damnit. Tai'ri lowered his head, uncaring of any witnesses, and kissed her. He kept his desire in check, his need to claim her. For now this small touch was enough to reassure himself she was alive, well, breathing. The child in her was safe and at peace.

After a moment her lips opened under his and she made a small noise, her small hand reaching up to cup his face briefly. He wanted to curl his hands in her hair, yank her head back and plunder, but this wasn't the time for it, and that she'd let him have this much was a precious gift.

So sweet, her soft lips. Tai'ri drew away slowly. "I'm sorry," he repeated. "Do you want to go home?"

She shook her head after a moment. "If the immediate danger is over, I think I'd like to stay for a little while longer."

He caressed her cheekbone with his thumb. "Anything you want. Anything."

"So, you've got a natural mean right hook," Banujani said, scanning their surroundings as they enjoyed the early evening air and low hum of voices at the cafe.

Vivian had needed the walk when she woke from her late afternoon nap, relieved to be told that the neighborhood cul-de-sac shopping center wasn't off limits now due to last evening's adventure.

Vivian clutched her teacup—with her left hand. The right still ached. "It was shameful behavior. Violence doesn't solve anything." Despite Tai'ri's rather savage satisfaction he'd unsuccessfully muted while tending to her hand last night.

"She underestimated you, *yada'ami*," he'd said. "Probably because you're so short."

"Hey," she'd said.

He'd laughed and put away his first aid supplies. "I like your height. You fit perfectly in my arms."

Vivian's cheeks warmed thinking about the look in his eyes, and she had to make herself pay attention to Banujani.

Banujani shrugged. "I'm unofficially an acolyte of Haeemah. All into the nonviolence shit. You know what She teaches? Never instigate violence, but if defending yourself, others, or property, throw down. Put the enemy in the grave. That way lies ultimate peace."

Vivian stared at her skeptically. Banujani grinned.

"It's the Precepts Tai'ri follows too, you know. You should let me train you."

"Absolutely not. That was a one-time occurrence, and I feel terrible." And sick to her stomach. Worse than crushing a bug, and the icky noises the exoskeletons made under foot or broom.

Banujani's smile disappeared, and she speared Vivian with an intense look. "What were you thinking when you punched her?"

Vivian inhaled. The same feeling hit her again, the complete, utter refusal to be anyone's victim again.

"Exactly," Banujani said softly. "Remember your why. Harmony and Silence is the goal, but you can't have either without violence. That's why we train, to know when is the time for peace and when is the time for blood."

"I'll . . . think about it."

Banujani smirked. "You should have seen the look on Tai'ri's face. He was all set to save you and then *crack*. You saved yourself."

"He apologized for leaving me. Vykhan told him to."

"It was a strategic decision. You were in no real danger." Banujani smiled again, catlike. "Demonstrably."

Vivian hesitated. "Vykhan is rather focused, isn't he? Determined he is right."

She tilted her head. "He trained all of us. He's been with the *Bdakhun* forever."

"I see." There wasn't much she could say. They didn't know each other well enough for Vivian to express her concerns about Vykhan's ruthlessness. Or the ruthlessness she sensed under the calm exterior. "But he's on our side, you're certain of it?"

Banujani's eyes widened. "I am very certain. And glad of it."

"That's good." She lifted her tea cup. "I think I'd like one for the road."

"No problem." Banujani pushed back from the table and rose. "How about one of those sandwiches? You didn't touch your lunch."

Vivian stared at her. "Are you all monitoring me that closely?"

The guard's gaze slid away from Vivian. "Not quite—" she stiffened, gaze going flat.

Vivian dropped the tea cup and used the chair arms to push to her feet. "What's wrong?"

"Comm line is down. There's a store room in the cafe. Opposite the restroom. Head there now, lock yourself in. Don't run, but move quickly."

12

SHE DIDN'T HAVE TO BE TOLD TWICE, RESPONDING to the quiet authority in Banujani's curt instructions. Vivian moved as fast as she was able, fear and urgency a bitter venom in her throat. Suddenly she was glad, very very glad, of Banujani's presence. But if the comm line was dead, what had happened to the rest of the team?

The guard was a weight at her back as they moved towards shelter. It occurred to Vivian that that weight, that shield, meant Banujani might be harmed on Vivian's behalf.

Horror slithered through her, enough that she almost tripped on her own feet, as if her body was following two sets of instructions. One to flee, and the other to halt.

A laser stream burned a hole into the whitewashed stone wall as she approached the door.

"Duck under a table!" Banujani rasped.

Vivian heard the whine of a laser weapon and dropped with cumbersome slowness to her knees, wincing as she jarred her uterus, and crawled under a table as nearby patrons began to realize something was wrong.

Stone shattered, startled yells and then screaming. Vivian crouched under the closest table, then shouldered the pedestal base to tip it over for cover. She'd seen that in a vid somewhere.

Despite knowing it was stupid, she lifted her head just enough to peek over the rim of the metal table and glanced around frantically. She saw none of the enemy, which only meant they were cloaked, or hiding in buildings. People ran, half crouching as they ducked. Oblong light shimmered in front of Banujani, taking the brunt of the multiple streams of enemy fire.

She was magnificent.

The guard handled her first weapon with the ease of experience, and innate skill. She withdrew a second weapon, firing so quickly Vivian perceived her hands to be moving almost in a blur. Five streams of fire decreased to three. All around them flower pots, trees, outdoor furniture and walls blew apart, smoking.

Several people screamed, high-pitched moans of pain, falling to the ground.

"Can't shoot worth crap," Banujani ground out. "They're hitting civilians."

Vivian realized the guard wasn't talking to her. She

must have a device streaming the incident. Which meant even if the team was down, backup would arrive soon.

A voice projected through the air. **"We will continue to fire on civilians until the human woman comes to us."**

Vivian froze, jaw loosening in shock. As she inhaled, for one mad moment she considered it. People were hurt, dying . . . but she had a baby curled inside her.

"Don't even think about it," Banujani warned.

The guard's shield flickered. She began to back up slowly, then reached down and grabbed Vivian's arm. The shield just barely covered them both.

"Your body shield is at thirty percent integrity. Release the human, and we will allow you to walk away with your life."

Banujani snorted. "Why do they all watch the same bad vids?" She raised her voice. "We all know how this goes. You want the human, come get the human." She kicked open the cafe door with her heel and backed them both inside.

"Is . . . that the most effective taunt?"

The guard laughed softly, but Vivian heard the grim edge. "Comm is down, I don't know if my distress signal got through, they've got a dampener. Temporary if we're lucky. Long term would attract too much attention. Shield is holding, but it wasn't designed to take sustained fire from multiple weapons for a long period of time." She began grabbing tables and chairs, pulling them in front of the entrance.

"Then what was it made for?"

Banujani glanced at her, expression quizzical. "Short bursts, protracted fight. Or short bursts, short fight. We aren't supposed to be in pitched battles or sieges. We're not cavalry. We're spies and assassins."

"They must have spent a lot of money capturing me." She wrapped her arms around herself. Well, rested them on the shelf of her uterus. "Why are they attacking in public like this?"

"Terror tactics. They'll count on the media reporting on it. If the *Bdakhun* looks bad, like she's in a petty private war that harms civilians for a pet cause, it feeds into their agenda to quash her funding. Get to the storeroom." Banujani crouched, staying out of sight as she approached the large front windows and yanked on a cord. "Manual blinds. Shit. This district is too prissy for security shields on the windows." She sneered. "Okay, so I'm going to lure them away from here. We've planned for this. You've got your comm, it'll work short range despite the dampener. You stay in that storeroom until you get the all clear. I mean it. Barricade and stay put."

"How are you going to convince them to follow after you?"

Banujani pressed a button on her wrist unit and instead of a shield snapping into place, a petite, brown skinned, dark eyed human woman settled over Banujani's skin. The woman stared at Vivian with a calm expression and slightly wild eyes.

"You had a decoy holo of me configured."

Holo Vivian grinned, teeth a savage slash of white. "Fresh out of R&D. They'll learn the hard way that neither of us is prey. Come on."

Banujani rose, stalking toward Vivian with a grace she never hoped to possess, and escorted her to the storeroom.

Vivian froze, staring inside. It was a medium sized gray box, shelves lining the walls stocked neatly with supplies. A vent in the ceiling. Lights flickering on as soon as the door slid open.

Her breath caught in her chest. "I can't lock myself in here."

"Vivian—"

She whirled, tried to barrel past Banujani. Bile in her throat, and a haze over her vision. "It's a cell! No, I'll go with you."

Banujani grabbed her shoulders. "My shield is going to give out under the fire I'll be taking. We planned for covert scenarios, not direct assaults, and it was a sloppy mistake Vykhan is going to kick our asses for."

"I don't care about Vykhan!"

"If you are taken or killed, I will offer my life to Haeemah for my failure. And then Tai'ri will offer his."

Vivian stared into the cold, almost cruel expression on her own face, stunned into momentary clarity.

"You're strong," Banujani said gently. "Stronger than you know. Get in that storeroom, *yadoana*. Wait for instructions."

Vivian took a deep breath, nodded. "Will you open a comm line so I can hear you?"

Banujani hesitated, then nodded. "But no matter what you hear, you stay put."

Vivian nodded, stepped into the storeroom and barricaded herself in. "Banujani?" she whispered.

"I'm here," her voice said through Vivian's wrist unit.

Vivian settled into a corner and began mentally designing embroidery patterns as she listened to the battle waging outside.

The *kheter's* second, real, interrogation had revealed her role as a limited piece on a larger gaming board, consistent with the pattern of this particular trafficking cell. Her job was to identify potential targets and if possible, get them in place for extraction. She was paid a bounty per head. She knew nothing except for one address, the location of her handler, which changed every three months.

It was a break, and Vykhan had ordered a new branch of their investigation to begin to comb through medical facility records for patients and personnel. Before this, no one had even imagined the traffickers would recruit from among those whose oaths were to heal.

"Fuck," Evvek muttered, eyes on his datapad. It looked like a youngling's game, though Evvek was clearly an adult, hunched over it with his gaze trained on the screen. No one blinked, people passing by without a second glance.

They sat on a park bench across from a nine-story building, commercial shops on the bottom four floors, single and double occupancy flats on floors five through nine.

The cloaking technology Evvek had developed was out of R&D and functional for portable use. The slim unit on Tai'ri's wrist appeared to be a simple comm unit, but in actuality held the illusion surrounding him that he was a slender, nondescript office drone. A lunch container on his lap and a messenger bag added depth to the illusion as he sipped iced chai, one of the Earth drinks Vivian had introduced him to.

"What's wrong?" he asked, deceptively calm. "You need to hurry, Evvek."

They had to move quickly, not knowing if the *kheter's* capture would cause her handler to flee. She was supposed to report in weekly, and had missed her check in call by a single day.

Sometimes the timing just fucking sucked.

His team were on standby, Adyat coordinating,

waiting as Evvek attempted to remotely bypass the security of their target. Preliminary scouting confirmed the handler had left his unit that morning, and Corann had orders to track at a distance and report back.

The rest of them needed to get in, search the unit, and get out without alerting the handler to their entry, if he hadn't fled yet. Better to put him under surveillance, and use him as another fishing line to climb another rung in the ladder.

"Slippery bugger," Evvek muttered. "Don't think you're gonna catch me like—fuck me. *Nooooooooo nonononono . . .* vakshit. Okay, okay, wait . . . hmm."

"Evvek. Not inspiring confidence."

"Traps, and traps entrapped in traps. Someone doesn't want their security bypassed. The goddess damned nerve. Everyone thinks they're fancy shit, these days."

"Just tell me you can bypass the—"

"Yeah, yeah. Fuck. Okay, we're clear. Let's go, I can't hold this for long without it sending out an alert."

Tai'ri stood, slinging his bag over his shoulder and tossing the remains of his lunch into a nearby recycler.

Several tense minutes later they strolled down the hallway leading to the flat. One entire side of the building was transparent, each floor open to view by anyone walking below. It was a feature for the residents: step outside one's apartment and sip a morning beverage while watching the city below. It supposedly made up for the lack of rooftop greenspace or individual balconies, one of the reasons why these units were so affordable.

A couple exited the lift moments later, holding hands as they approached, chatting. The female was as short as Vivian, and dressed in slacks that swung playfully around her ankles and a blouse that tied right above her waist. Her shoulder length hair was artfully mussed, her makeup subtle and tasteful.

Holding her hand was a taller, lean male in a collared business casual shirt and slender trousers, his feet encased in delicate rope sandals. They looked young, soft, oblivious to the dark undercurrents of the city.

Evvek ignored them and stepped forward, placing a round disc next to the security panel. The panel flickered green, and the door slid open. He sneered. "No one is ever as good as they think."

He stepped forward, but the business casual male touched Evvek's shoulder and went first, Tai'ri on his heels.

And swore as the air erupted into a shriek of sound and flame.

"What vakshit places manual booby traps?" Evvek groaned, emerging from cover. He'd dived behind a couch as the others returned fire, dismantling the drones.

Tai'ri processed the ringing in his ears as Adyat's voice demanded status. The remains of three hand constructed aerial drones littered the floor along with the furniture the team had dived behind for cover.

"Cancel backup, Adyat," Tai'ri said. "We're good."

Ebwenna and Dayan completed a perfunctory scan for serious injuries and then gloved up to begin packing up the remains of the drones, looking as cheerful as if they'd just come from a lunch date. Being under fire agreed with their temperaments. Tai'ri had watched remotely one time as Ebwenna slipped through a crowd to assassinate a target with a single stroke to a femoral artery, then chatted with the completely oblivious bystanders while sipping a beverage.

Evvek kicked the threshold of the projectile scarred door. "It's safe to say the occupant of this apartment won't be coming back."

"Then we'd better make the search good," Tai'ri said. Evvek scowled but they began tossing the unit.

Adyat's voice came through the comm again. "Sir, Corann lost the target. She reports diversionary tactics were utilized, and the target was extracted in the fight."

Tai'ri swore. "Find me something, Evvek. How the fuck did they know we were coming?"

"They didn't," Evvek said, rich satisfaction in his voice. "These units come with built in study centers." As he spoke, a section of a long, nondescript wall slid open to reveal a datasphere unit on an inset desk.

Evvek reached underneath the desk and pulled out a folding chair. "The handler must have called for an extraction once the booby trap alerted him, and he made Corann. But he wasn't expecting us or he would have taken this unit."

"Unless he wiped it."

"We're about to find out."

"We shouldn't do this here," Dayan said. "They could send people to torch the unit. I'm uninterested in a firefight today, I'd like my manicure to last at least two weeks."

"Can you uninstall the unit?" Tai'ri asked.

Evvek gave him a withering look. "Really? Just step away, it probably has a self-destruct."

"This should be interesting," Ebwenna murmured, then wandered into the kitchen. "I wonder if there's coffee."

Back to waiting at the hidden office, Evvek and the other techs combed through the darksphere console they'd extracted, finally assigning Tai'ri a low-level task that would normally go to a drone, just to prevent him from hovering. He accepted the task because it was that or pace. Hated waiting, but until there was a direction to point him in, the hunt was all digital for now.

He realized after a few hours that Evvek and the

others were silent. Tai'ri glanced up, saw the expression on Evvek's face and stood, abandoning his station.

"What is it?"

Evvek sighed. "We hacked into an encrypted file. Names, locations, dates."

Tai'ri glanced at the screen. He narrowed his eyes as Evvek flicked his fingers and a map sprang up over the desk. Names flew to different points, clustering in coordinates that were already familiar to Tai'ri. Hubs where they'd infiltrated pens, including some they hadn't known about.

"This is where they're extracting the females the *kheter* was feeding them," Evvek said.

"There's too many for her to have been the only one," Ebwenna said.

"Has the broker confirmed a time and location for a showing?" Tai'ri asked.

"No."

"Nudge him. Tell him I'm impatient and if he can't set up something now, then I'm walking. Be careful, we don't want him to disappear."

"You'd think I was an amateur."

"Ebwenna, you and Dayan scout these new hubs. Surveillance only, we need to know who else they have on their payroll."

Tai'ri stood over Evvek's shoulder as the analyst messaged the broker and set up a showing—for that evening. "Good," he said softly once Evvek disconnected from his console. "Now we prepare. I'll update Vykhan."

The conversation with Vykhan was brief, the *Adekhan* a little more curt than usual as he cut the conversation abruptly short, but he gave the go ahead for the op with the broker.

Tai'ri and Evvek left Dayan and Ebwenna at the office—they needed to go shopping. The roles they would play this evening required new outfits.

13

"Yanok, darling," Tai'ri said, stepping out of the transport and looking around with pursed lips. "Are you certain these are the correct coordinates? This district is hardly fashionable."

This was a manufacturing sector stuck in a zoning war, and all production had ground to a halt months ago. At night there was no traffic, either by foot or transport. Just the detritus of half renovated buildings, equipment no one dared steal—not even professional black market scavengers—due to the reputation of the owners.

Couldn't say any more without blowing his new cover. Tonight he would make the first purchase that would begin to build the trust needed to be invited deeper into the enemy web. Tonight he would allow the broker to live, but only as a lure for bigger fish. They'd all die eventually. He soothed his anger with that fact and cloaked himself with the personality of his character.

Wealthy. Frivolous. Completely amoral. Here to buy human female flesh. Tai'ri wanted to punch himself in the jaw.

Evvek, under the guise of Yanok, gave him a look. "Of *course* these are the correct coordinates."

"It has to be the wrong place," Tai'ri complained loudly. "Call the transport back. This is wasting my time." Figures emerged from the darkness. Tai'ri jumped behind Evvek, a scowl on his face. "What is this?"

"Ohmad Lanujahn," a smooth voice called Tai'ri's false name. "We're here to escort you to the ship."

There was only one 'ship' that would be named in that tone. Tai'ri frowned. "It wasn't my understanding that the auction was to take place on Anthhori."

Internally, he cursed. They'd set up for the location they'd been given, though they'd prepared for the eventuality of a last-minute switch—brokers who weren't suspicious didn't evade Ibukay's enforcement force for long. But they hadn't prepared for Anthhori. None of their intel suggested this broker had connections that high—literally.

A shuttle landed on the heels of the escort's statement. He could back out now. But he'd lose the contact.

"I'm sure everything is in order," Evvek/Yanok said

in a conciliatory tone. "No one will break the peace of Anthhori, not even the royal guard."

He'd smack Evvek when he got a chance. The analyst thought he was funny.

"Fine," Tai'ri said. "But I want to formally protest the change in venue. I had dinner reservations and there's no way I'll make them now."

"Duly noted," the smooth voice said.

Tai'ri glanced at their escorts, staring several seconds at each face. Nondescript, dressed in dark uniforms and of varying species. "None of you seem appropriately attired for an interstellar pleasure barge," he said, eyeing them up and down.

"We're working."

Tai'ri grimaced. "Even my help is required to present themselves decently."

"You would *never* allow your retainers to look so unfashionable," Yanok said. "But not everyone can have your impeccable standards."

Tai'ri stared them down some more, distaste crossing his expression. "Oh, fine."

After he was certain the visual implants had captured everyone's likeness and transmitted to the team, he looked away, apparently bored.

They entered the shuttle, Tai'ri fussing absently with the fall of the short cloak around his shoulders. Evvek/Yanok sat at his side, expression a blend of adoring and resigned, adjusting the hem of Tai'ri's cuffs or the drape of his long hair as instructed.

Refreshments were offered during the flight up past the planet's atmosphere. Tai'ri criticized the bites of intricately prepared food, and lectured the escorts on the wines. Yanok stood next to him, anticipating his every request with a general air of tragic long suffering.

By the time they approached the dock of the massive pleasure ship, Tai'ri had escalated from a punch to wanting to strangle himself. He threw himself into his character—if he had to suffer, so did everyone else.

They disembarked into a shimmering black hallway and approached a scarlet entrance. An escort spoke, and the circle swimmed like liquid, retracting to allow them entrance.

Tai'ri stepped into purgatory.

Music pulsed, aliens of every kind meshed together under a sky of glittering diamonds. The only characteristic that united the mob was their wealth and willingness to circumvent the laws and morals that governed the societies each came from. Anthhori obeyed no maxim other than to please oneself, even if pleasing oneself involved debauchment, enslaving others, glorying in death and depraved sexual acts.

And that was just deck one.

"Follow us," the escort said. "We have a private suite arranged for your pleasure."

Tai'ri and Evvek exchanged a look. There had been nothing in this broker's dossier that indicated the display of wealth a suite onboard Anthhori required.

His shoulders tensed, though he maintained a slightly bored, sneering expression, taking care to whisk his silks out of the way of any inferior people lest they become contaminated.

This could go poorly.

But at least he knew for certain the alien female that would be on display wasn't Vivian. Vivian was home, safe since the last time he'd checked on her before deactivating and removing his personal comm for this op. Pity stirred, as well as anger, for the female who had been captured and brought forward for his pleasure. He would do what he could for her, to make up for the fact he had to purchase her to maintain his cover.

They wove through the main crowd and up a flight of wide stairs towards narrow silver hallways leading to private suites. Security was posted every several suites, nodding as they passed.

"I see we are expected," Tai'ri said. "I hope there won't be any more delays."

Their escort remained silent, pausing at a door and indicating Tai'ri should enter. Tai'ri stepped forward and an arm fell between him and the entrance.

"What?" he asked, voice icy.

The escort smiled. "Just a verification process, you understand."

A device appeared in his hand. Tai'ri tapped his foot impatiently as a retinal and fingerprint scan was completed. Not that it would do the enemy any good—

from now on any scans done on him would route to false records and as soon as they were accessed, Evvek's bugs would tag and track. Tai'ri was a ghost again.

"Why wasn't identity confirmation made on planet?" he snapped. "Incompetence. I should turn around and leave."

"It's standard," Evvek/Yanok soothed. "Remember how you've been looking forward to this, sir."

"Fine." He scowled as the identification process was completed, and when the arm withdrew, swept into the suite.

Tai'ri hadn't expected a solo showing, and was unsurprised when his gaze traveled over five clusters of seating strategically arranged to have a full view of the dais but remain private to the other patrons. Servers already attended each buyer, some alone, some with an escort. Tai'ri noted each one, but allowed his gaze to slide away without lingering too long. He was after other fish today, and Evvek's device would also be recording. But they all were pieces that might prove useful in the game.

"See," Yanok said, clapping his hands in delight, "so simple. Perfect. Now we can begin. Magnificent."

Tai'ri glanced around the room, eyeing the empty dais set in the center and a bar manned by a live person along one wall. Richly furnished in reds, purples and blacks—no imagination. These places were all styled by the same kind of decor ever since the discovery of humans. "Adequate, I suppose."

"He's delighted," Yanok murmured to the escort. "Simply thrilled. *Such* amenities."

The escort said nothing.

A vicious twinge of pleasure wove through Tai'ri, and he leaned into his character, spending the next several moments insulting his absent host, criticizing the decor, food and wine and then turning his pithy comments on the stature and dress of the escort.

The room plunged into darkness. A pulse later, light burst from the ceilings, casting patterns along the walls as a sudden deep beat of music filled the air. Doors opened and out streamed dancers, several with instruments, and in various states of nudity. Males, females, Tai'ri counted at least four different species including his own.

A few broke off to attend each patron, but Tai'ri waved his away, annoyance across his face, and stared broodingly into his wineglass.

So the broker wanted to ply them with wine, disorient their senses with mood music likely embedded with subliminals, and rouse their ardor with the old trick of using sex workers. By the time the auction began, the broker was hoping they'd all be slightly more drunk, slightly more disoriented, and all itching for release with something to tease jaded senses.

The entire display piqued his curiosity. Most of

these affairs were quiet, discreet, lights dim and sober. He began to revise what he knew about this particular broker.

He wanted to talk to Evvek, but there would be listening devices everywhere. They couldn't drop character for one moment.

The central dais lit up, and the dancers began to gyrate around it as it opened, the platform revealing their host.

"Welcome," he cried, throwing his arms wide. "Tonight, I am honored to bring before the elite of Naidekai City the highest caliber of alien delicacies for your amusement. After the general viewing you will all be escorted to private rooms for the auction. Let the viewing begin, and unlike other hosts—I encourage you to touch the merchandise."

He smiled beatifically, then stepped off the dais.

"Damn," Evvek muttered as a procession of aliens began to appear on the dais.

Tai'ri studied each, capturing their images to transmit to Vykhan. There was no room for anger, for the sickness in his gut as males and females, at least two humans big with child, stood in front of the audience. Some stood tall, hips cocked. Others grim, and yet others . . .

Some of them might be here of their own accord. The others were not.

The dancers melted away, music softening into a background hum and the lights adjusted. The escort appeared at Tai'ri's elbow and he stood with a loud sigh.

"Finally. Next time I'll be certain to dispense with the preliminaries. I can get far better opera in the Theater district if that's what I wanted."

He and Evvek traded more insults as they walked down another hall, the other patrons leaving in different directions.

They entered a square room with three-way windows and two rows of deep seats. Beyond the windows was another dais under a spotlight, and darkened glass belonging to the other private rooms surrounding it.

Tai'ri sat, and ordered more wine, using his most belittling tone.

Watching the stony faces of their escorts ice over as they stared at a far wall brought him sweet, sweet satisfaction.

Satisfaction turned to ashes when moments later a side door opened, and out walked a slender male of medium height. Their host. "So honored you have graced us with your presence," the broker said in a surprisingly deep, smooth tone.

Tai'ri stared at the Aeddannar. Green skin, wispy white hair and over large, glittering eyes. Purple lacquered nails shimmered, matching the multitude of chains draping his neck and forehead.

"A lack of punctuality is a sign of a deteriorated

mind," Tai'ri said, every emotion in his body solidifying into icy resolve.

The broker approached with a light step, coming a length too close for Tai'ri's liking and lifted his palms toward Tai'ri in a conciliatory gesture. "My apologies. We were finalizing the last touches on our offerings for the evening. I do expect you will be pleased."

Tai'ri sighed heavily. "I hope so. I'll be disappointed if you've wasted my time." He paused. "I would like to know with whom I'd dealing."

"You may call me Zhiannur."

The reply was so smooth Tai'ri knew it was a false name. But still, it was another piece of information.

Tai'ri inclined his head, dismissing the male. Unblinking eyes flickered, then the broker lowered his feathery lashes and spread his arms with a smile and a bow, backing out of the room.

Moments later a seven-foot-tall Hyunthu female emerged onto the dais, green skinned and double jointed, lidless swirling eyes sweeping across the darkened windows as if she could see through each one. Delicately, she picked up a gavel.

A panel slid out of the wall and lit up, preparing for Tai'ri's bids.

"Let us begin," she said in a crisp, cool voice. "Our first offering for the evening, a Drathokian male from the Broma system..."

Tai'ri instructed Yanok to make a few half-hearted

bids, and eventually sprawled in his seat, head tilted back on his head in despair at his boredom.

"Sir," Yanok said eagerly.

"Our next offering, a human female and fetus, from planet Earth of the Solari System."

Tai'ri sat up, not having to fake the exclamation that fell from his lips.

She was medium height, a swath of light brown hair falling over her full chest. They'd draped her in a white cloth across her chest and groin but nothing else except for strategically placed chains of silver and gold, little gems winking in the light. Her hands cupped her protruding uterus and she stared at the windows with a desperate, frozen fear that clenched Tai'ri's heart. This female could have been Vivian, and his baby.

"Bid," Tai'ri snapped. He gathered himself and pointed. Trembling finger, remembering to pitch his voice correctly. "I want that one, Yanok. Get her for me."

He didn't wince when a spate of furious bidding sent the price well over the budget for this operation. Ibukay wouldn't care—in fact, the fact that there was another bidder with deeper pockets than usual meant new players on the scene—and even if she did, Tai'ri wouldn't let this female go to a dark fate. He'd pay for her himself.

"Sold," the auctioneer said.

The panel lit up with instructions on where to transfer funds. It included instructions on the medical care and feeding of his new human as well as the return policy.

Tai'ri fixed it with a glare.

"Sir?" Yanok said anxiously. "You are happy with your purchase?"

That jolted him back into character. "Of course. I wasn't expecting another bidder. We'll have to make economies this week."

"Perhaps forgo this weeks' vacation to Sentari 11," Yanok murmured. "We could do something modest. You were looking at that new line of sky yachts."

"I do want to learn to pilot," Tai'ri said, then rose. "Well, let us go claim our new pet."

14

They were taken to a sitting room, sparsely but elegantly furnished with a single seating arrangement.

Bare walls, one entrance and exit. Furniture bolted down, of course, and not even fabric draping the walls that could be used as a weapon. Refreshments were set out on a low table, and Tai'ri sprawled on the adjacent divan, moodily examining the selection of small bites. Yanok hovered over his shoulder, glanced longingly at the food, but didn't touch it since Tai'ri gave it one disdainful glance then pushed it away. They waited for a short time before the female he'd purchased walked in, arms still curled protectively around her stomach. The green skinned auction clerk entered behind her.

"Everything is in order; the funds have cleared," the Hyunthu said in her precise voice. "Thank you for your purchase. Your package has been sent according to the instructions on file."

Tai'ri inhaled, looking her over. "She comes with a wardrobe? Her medical files?" He waved a hand. "Never mind, I'll dress her myself, though if she catches a chill on the travel to my residence . . ."

He allowed displeasure to show on his face. It curled, true and unfeigned, deep in his gut. Every rotten, corrupt player in the puzzle they killed in battle, tried and executed or imprisoned for life, was one more piece on the path to shattering this filthy industry forever.

The human female's eyes flickered toward him, then back.

"Come," he said, snapping his fingers, and rose.

The door opened, and in walked Zhiannur. "I do so hope you are pleased with your purchase."

"Whether I'll be pleased remains to be seen," Tai'ri said. "This whole affair has been rather shoddy, but I suppose I'll just have to endure."

"No one appreciates your true worth," Yanok murmured, giving the broker a resentful look under his lashes. "We should return. I must have at least three hours for your facials tonight, or we needn't even *bother*."

"Of course," Tai'ri said.

"I can't be expected to work under these time constraints," Yanok wailed, shaping his hands as if he wanted to strangle air. "These things take time. I am already so *stressed.*"

Tai'ri stared at him with alarm. "Please, comport yourself. Wine, victuals, my servant needs refreshment!"

"No, no, we need to return so I can begin the herbal infusions! Does no one *understand?*"

"Bring the alien," Tai'ri snapped, "we depart forthwith."

He strode forward, but the broker stepped in front of him. A bold move, considering the male was a half arm length shorter. "Unfortunately, there has been a problem with the transaction," Zhiannur said.

"What?"

A smile curved his thin lips as he stared at Tai'ri, no humor in his brilliant eyes. "The identity verification was not successful." He lifted a hand.

The door slid open and the weaponed guards who'd been their escorts all evening slipped into the room. The one Tai'ri had spent the evening terrorizing stared at him with particular malice. Whoops.

Tai'ri didn't bother wondering how they'd broken through Evvek's cover. "Haeemah's Mercy." The illusion cloaking him froze, then shattered. "Liked this outfit better anyway."

The Aeddannar moved in a blur. Tai'ri's gloved fingers swiped towards him, clipping Zhiannur on the neck. Zhiannur stumbled briefly, but Tai'ri had to let the scum flee, the job done. The sacrifices he made to delay short term gratification. Then the soldiers—mercs—were on him.

The females dove behind the divan for whatever flimsy cover it provided. Evvek tossed them a circular device. The clerk proved her experience by immediately depressing it and a military grade shield snapped into place around them both.

He put them out of his mind; they'd done what they could to see the females were safe. There was only one exit, so the human couldn't be taken through stealth.

His silk and leather getup shifted, nanotech constructed fabrics responding to the physiological cues of his body and morphing instantly into a thin, impenetrable body armor.

Fit like a glove, hurt his enemies like a bitch.

The mercs fanned out, then engaged.

Neither Tai'ri or Evvek had come aboard with visible weapons. But they were *Adekhan* trained by an acolyte of Haeemah.

Their hands were weapons. Their feet.

Tai'ri disarmed the first merc as he depressed his weapon to fire. Tai'ri was in the line of fire; and then he wasn't.

"You see me," Tai'ri said, moving in a blur, and grabbing the male by his neck, "then you don't."

The fight was short, nasty, and complicated by the presence of the females but in the end, there were few paid soldiers even someone filthy rich could hire to match Ibukay's private guards.

"We need to get out of here," Evvek said, crouching next to the females. "They'll either bring more fighters or try to shoot us down."

"This is Anthhori. If they try to shoot us down, the Station Master will respond with commensurate force."

Evvek grimaced as he helped the females to their feet. The pregnant one watched with wide, angry eyes, clutching her protruding stomach. "I never did like the idea of this place," he muttered.

"You're in the custody of *Bdakhun* Ibukay of Beysikai province," Tai'ri said to the auction clerk.

"You don't have the authority to detain me."

"I can always kill you." He wouldn't, but she didn't know that.

The female stilled, then nodded. "Very well. But I expect due process."

He smiled grimly. She had spine to demand due process when she worked for traffickers. "You'll receive it if you cooperate."

"What about me?" the human woman demanded. "You bought me."

Tai'ri winced. "Yeah, sorry about that. Please come with us, we need to leave before more mercs come. You are free, and I promise I'll see you settled on planet with the appropriate medical care and housing."

"It's not like I have any choices, do I?"

"No, for now, but you will. Let's go."

She nodded, and they left.

Once back on planet, Tai'ri handed the female—Shira—off to a counselor from the same safehouse Vivian had been assigned. He'd explained briefly to Shira that he was a government employee and she was safe.

"I'll stand as your legal sponsor until you decide if you want to return to your home or remain on Yedahn," he said.

She had nodded, tense and silent, expression strained. Tai'ri hesitated. "My mate is like you, human and with child. Spent time in a pen. I'll bring her to meet you soon."

"You rescued her, too?"

"Something like that."

After watching her leave, he'd put her out of his mind, returning to palace base to report to Vykhan in person. Anger was useless, especially the rage that broiled whenever he thought of his mate, or even his sister or mother being taken and brutalized.

These people had to be stopped.

"Tai'ri."

Vykhan didn't look up from the console. Vandria, Evvek's counterpart on Vykhan's team, stared at the screen. "There," she said.

Tai'ri listened to his and the broker's voices mingle before the auction, then paused.

"It's not Aeddannar tech," she said. "His palms are coated with . . . I'll spare you the tech details. Basically, he stole your breath and ran the DNA."

Tai'ri cursed, low and hard. Vykhan gave him a long, level look. "We knew they might have your DNA record as they had you in their custody for so long, and in that case any false records we laid would be useless. You know what this means."

The curses increased in both volume, filth, and frequency. Vykhan waited patiently.

"Until those records are located and purged," his commander continued in an even tone that managed to almost be gentle, "we have to adjust your assignments."

His cover was completely blown. Maybe all of them. He'd expected this. Had already processed each eventuality. "I can still do ops."

"We will assign you where your skills and the situation best merit. For now, it is fortunate you are on leave—" slight emphasis on the last words "—you have much to occupy your time."

He wasn't enough of an asshole to protest being sent home to care for his female and child. Pleased at the thought of spending more time with her. But the need to make her safe, to avenge her . . .

Vykhan smiled a little, as if he understood. But he didn't, not really. Had he ever loved a female? Ever wanted her safety above his own life?

But then his *Adekhan's* expression shifted. Tai'ri instinctively braced himself.

"There is something I need to tell you," Vykhan said.

Tai'ri's chest clenched. Vykhan never prefaced anything. "There was an attack. Banujani will live. Vivian is uninjured."

Tai'ri turned on his heel and ran.

15

Listening to the sounds of the battle was like being in a closet while an action vid played in the living room. Vivian tried to emotionally distance herself, knowing if she let panic grip her then she'd do something unintelligent. Like run out of the cafe screaming and waving her arms. Anything to get it to stop.

But as much as she didn't want anyone else hurt on her behalf, she didn't want her baby harmed either. Hadn't Vykhan said that to her, what seemed like ages ago? Her child was her priority.

So she hunkered in the corner, steeling her will. She wouldn't always be helpless. She wouldn't always have to hide. When the baby was born, and this was all over, she would *do* something. Take action. Become strong and learn to defend herself.

"We've got backup," Banujani said. "Fucking

finally. Down to two enemy combatants, but shield is at 10%. Remember, stay put until you get instructions through your comm. It can't be hacked."

"10%? What does that mean?" But she could deduce.

Her wrist unit blinked green. "Vivian, activate your body shield."

It was Vykhan. Which meant the dampener was disabled and help would be on the way. Had it been ten minutes? Fifteen? It felt like an eternity.

"I don't have a body shield."

"You do. Tai'ri upgraded your unit two days ago. Repeat the sequence after me."

She couldn't rely on the translator, she had to actually speak the Yadeshi words in their language. Her tongue tripped over the guttural syllables, but she'd been studying the language manually for two weeks and it only took her three times to adjust her pronunciation.

A shield sprang up around her body, a shimmer of bright green light.

"Now go to Banujani," Vykhan said.

She pushed to her feet, deactivated the door lock mechanism the way her guard had demonstrated, and walked as fast as she could. She forced herself to breathe evenly, so her fear didn't affect her baby and reminded herself that none of this was her fault, she still owed these people a debt of gratitude for their protection.

Steeling her spine, gathering courage fueled by anger, she stepped outside and ran to the crumpled body several feet away. Finally, she could do something, even if it was so little and so late.

Banujani lay unmoving on her back, one arm flung over her eyes, another flung out with her weapon nearby.

As she approached, Banujani turned her head slightly. "What the—"

"Shush." The shield around her body flared, expanded over Banujani, but even Vivian could tell by the color that it hadn't been made to protect two people. It was thin; weak. Hopefully it would be enough.

Crouching was a problem, equally so with bending. Accomplishing movement, to be specific, was not what it used to be with a five-to-seven pound baby lodged in one's groin.

Somehow Vivian managed to grab the weapon in the dazed woman's fingers and placed herself in front of her injured guard. Banujani's eyes sharpened for a split second before they went fuzzy again. Vivian knew that if the guard hadn't recognized Vivian somehow, she would have roused herself, despite what looked like a serious head injury and rapidly increasing blood loss.

The silence, after the jarring sounds of battle, seduced Vivian into wanting to pretend they were safe. And then she realized silence meant people who were dead or unconscious.

Heads began to emerge from behind tables, from around walls, anywhere people had taken cover. A general din rose, the urgent shouts and conversation of people in an emergency.

"Eh, miss, maybe you should—"

She swung the weapon, the dangerous end hopefully, towards the man who inched closer. He held up his hands and jumped away.

"Stay back," she snarled.

"Got it. Absolutely staying away. Except we don't know quite what it is you're holding, and it looks dangerous. You're pregnant. You sure you want to be holding that thing?"

A crowd was gathering, people emerging from their hiding spaces as the shock of the sudden attack faded. The bodies were gone of course, but the blood and . . . detritus . . . remained.

Banujani whispered.

Without taking her eyes off the crowd, Vivian kind of bent her knees. Anything deeper would force her to the ground, and once she was on the ground, she would need a forklift to get her up again. Which was not an option.

"Can you speak louder?"

"She's losing blood," the bystander said, hands still up. "Look, see my nametag? I work in the cafe. The one that just got the glass blasted out. We have a first aid kit. Authorities should be on the way."

"Banujani?"

The woman nodded. If she thought it was fine, then fine. Vivian nodded. "But just you."

"Sure thing, miss."

In a minute flat, the man ran into the cafe and back out again, and managed to get a basic bandage on Banujani's wound.

"Okay, that should—"

Figures popped out of the air, moving in formation and barking orders.

The bystander cursed and jerked away again, and the crowd dispersed. Vivian relaxed. She recognized the not-cavalry. It seemed like forever since Banujani pushed the distress button.

"Vivian?" one of the black clad warriors said. "May I approach?"

Her fingers clutched Banujani's weapon reflexively, but she recognized the voice and nodded, releasing the weapon. He was there in a moment, snatching it out of the air before it crashed on the ground and the others approached.

In a whirl of time she and Banujani were hustled off. Banujani roused, pain in the brackets of her mouth.

"What's wrong with her?" Vivian asked, then grimaced. Besides a blast from a weapon? Stupid.

"The blast is designed to be disorienting," the guard said. "Remaining still and slowing one's heart rate is the fastest way to recover. The more you move, the worse the effects."

Good to know, in case she was ever blasted.

They approached the house and Vivian blinked as black clad figures swarmed up the side and then winked out of sight, clinging to white walls. She shook her head.

"Amazing."

"The house is secure," her guard said.

They entered and the next several minutes were spent triaging their wounds. Vivian discovered there was a small medical facility in the basement she hadn't known existed.

"We can treat most medical emergencies here," she was told. "Even childbirth."

Another guard walked in, without the head covering and introduced herself. "I'm medically trained. May I assess you?"

Vivian nodded. "How is Banujani?"

"She'll live," was the cheerful response.

Vivian answered questions, suffered the handheld scanner to assess her for internal injuries, listened to the baby's heart rate and answered questions about pain, fetal kicks, and a host of other standard inquiries.

"Tai'ri should be home soon," the medic said kindly.

"Where is he?"

"You can ask him about that when he's home, but he wasn't reachable for some time. As soon as he learned about what happened, he signaled he was en route."

Tension inside her eased. She knew Tai'ri still had duties, and the strong desire to curl up into his side shocked her.

"Whoops," the medic said. "If you speak it, it shall be so."

The door flung open, the threshold filled with six feet of broad shoulders, vibrating with angry male.

"Viv!"

"The baby is fine," she said.

He was at her side in a moment, and it took her a second to realize he was covered in . . . "What are you wearing?"

He blushed. Vivian eyed his face in fascination. It was becoming easier to spot blue skinned blushes. He was dressed in silk and leather, skin tight on bottom, draping and gaping on top. Completely undignified and designed to titillate the senses. Erotic senses.

"You look like you belong in a harem," she said.

"Uh . . ." he stuttered. "What? No, no, it isn't what you think, I was working."

She felt her eyebrows slowly rise. "In a harem?"

Tai'ri glared, his hands brisk as he swept them up her body, assessing her injuries for himself as the medic stood by with a small grin.

"No, not a harem, Vivian."

"Because if you have any other human females . . ." She didn't know what possessed her. She wasn't a teasing type person, and didn't have much of a sense of humor. Maybe it was the giddy relief of being alive and well, and the baby unharmed, and Tai'ri now home, that spurred her.

He sighed and lifted her carefully into his arms with a nod towards his team member. "You're teasing me."

"Yes," she admitted, hesitating, and then wrapped an arm around his neck. "I'm glad you're home."

His breath stilled for a minute, then he brushed his lips against her forehead. "I'm glad I'm home, too."

Tai'ri lifted her into his arms. She wrapped an arm around his neck, trusting in his strength and balance, though she supposed this wasn't the first time he'd carried her.

He remained silent on the lift up to the first level, and into her room where he laid her with exquisite control on the bed. Straightening, he brushed a lock of hair behind her ear.

"I'm going to get you something to drink and eat," he said.

"Nothing heavy, I'm a little queasy."

He nodded, and she settled back onto her pillows, closing her eyes for a moment. When she opened them again, he was sitting at her side, a tray on the nightstand.

"You slept for an hour," he said. "I didn't want to wake you."

She yawned, covering her mouth. "You didn't have to sit here with me."

"I wanted to." He handed her a glass of clear liquid which turned out to be water flavored with something sweet and citrusy, lightly carbonated.

She sipped the chilled beverage, then set it aside and looked at the bowl of slightly steaming grain and vegetables in what smelled like a lightly seasoned sauce.

"There's frozen cream," he said after she'd eaten several bites then set the bowl aside.

"Only if you have some with me." He was taking care of her, but the miasma of the evening he must have had lingered in the dark expression in his eyes, and the subtle tension in his shoulders.

Tai'ri smiled a little then left, returning moments later with two small bowls of the dessert.

"Can you tell me what happened to you?" she asked.

"Just work." Then he grimaced slightly. "I'll have to talk to you about it soon for reasons. But for tonight . . ." he hesitated. "I'd like to hold you."

He'd set his bowl aside and waited, hands on the tops of his thighs. Strong fingers, long and surprisingly graceful. He held himself completely still, as if prepared to accept her no without protest.

It was so little to ask for, just a smidgen of contact. She found she didn't want to tell him no. Of course she didn't want to tell him no. Not the way he was slowly worming under her skin, into her daily existence. Becoming her new normal, her new sense of family.

"Yes," she said. "But I'm going to get comfortable."

Getting comfortable meant moving onto her side, and placing a pillow between her thighs.

Tai'ri settled at her back and his arm slid around her back. His palm rested lightly on her belly. She'd never had someone in the bed with her before, not since she was a small child and her mother slept at her side.

But then his hand moved up her arm, his fingertips lightly caressing her skin. She shivered.

"Stop that," she said.

A silent laugh moved his chest. "Why? I like touching you."

"It's distracting, and I'm trying to sleep."

"Oh, Viv. That's not even close to distracting."

He didn't say anything else, but the promise in his tone was enough, and the brief, searing press of his lips on the side of her neck as he pulled her hair aside.

Eventually she fell asleep, and distantly realized that though she'd told him to stop, she hadn't really wanted him to.

16

A SOFT SCUFF OF FEET BROKE VIVIAN AWAY FROM her tablet. She glanced up at Tai'ri, who stepped onto the deck and then simply stared at her.

He shoved his hands into his pockets. She set her tablet down, poured him a glass of lemonade, and gestured.

"Something's wrong," she said. "What is it?"

He frowned at her, not quite an expression of displeasure. "How do you know something is wrong?"

"Your tell." She nodded at his hands.

Tai'ri sighed. "Figures." He sat though, eyeing the glass of lemonade. "I don't suppose this has something stronger than fruit in it."

"I don't suppose it does."

He sipped, winced a little, but drained the glass. "Before I forget, the art district we went to the other evening has a public warehouse that stocks supplies from several different planets. Do you want to go?"

Poor man. He actually thought he had to ask. "I have plenty of blood I can sell."

"What?"

"It's a joke, a bad one. I would love to go."

He stared at her, baffled. "I don't know why you keep saying you don't have a sense of humor."

"I didn't use too, truly. But maybe something about being here brings out that side of me." Something about not having to work long, relentless days suppressing her unhappiness.

Tai'ri rose, went back into the house, then emerged a minute later with a small glass of clear liquid she just knew wasn't fruity. He sat down. "I bought a human woman."

Vivian considered him, the set of his shoulders that betrayed discomfort. "Why?"

"You aren't upset?"

"I don't feel I'm in full possession of the facts. I can get angry later, if anger is warranted." She spoke slowly, because obviously he was bothered, and expecting some kind of recrimination.

Tai'ri leaned back in his chair, stretching his legs out. He eyed her broodingly from that sprawl, his fingers tapping on the armrest. "I was following a lead of the people trying to sell you. You take out one and another takes it's place."

Her stomach clenched. "It sounds like you're playing whack-a-mole."

"What?"

Vivian paused, mentally side stepping the translator, and used her manual language skills. "Whack-a-mole."

His expression cleared. "Your Yadeshi is getting better. The accent is cute."

"Thank you."

"I get it, though." He glanced up at the sky, appearing thoughtful. "It's a long game."

"So you bought a woman. I surmise you were under cover?"

"Yeah. Thing is, I'm legally her guardian until her citizenship paperwork comes through."

"Interesting. Where is she?"

"At one of the *Bdakhun's* locations. She's pregnant."

Vivian inhaled, wincing internally. "Oh. Poor woman. Is she being sent back to Earth?"

"She hasn't decided. I thought you might like to meet her. You two have something in common."

Vivian knew better than to try and lean across the table with her baby belly in the way, so she settled on a warm smile. "I would love to meet her." And hope that comforting this woman wouldn't destroy the fragile peace she herself was building.

"I'm Shira," the young woman said.

She looked Vivian's age, medium height and lush with the curves of late stage pregnancy, her golden-brown hair in a braid over one shoulder. She'd glanced at Tai'ri when they'd entered, glaring until she seemed to recognize him.

Vivian understood. It had taken her eyes a while to acclimate to a sea of blue faces, to be able to tell them apart from one another. Their species was as homogenous as the human species, which was to say, not at all once one got over the subtle variations of blue skin, dark hair, and blue or green or black eyes.

"I'm Vivian," she said, giving her a smile after Tai'ri introduced them.

Shira's hazel eyes flickered down to Vivian's belly. "They nabbed you too, huh?"

Vivian led her to a couch. They were in a common room, and after a long look at the various women in several seating areas, Tai'ri excused himself. It was a kindness; no one was here because they'd had a nice introduction to planet Yedahn and its people, especially its men.

"Yes, I was taken over a year ago."

"Did he buy you, too?"

Vivian shook her head. "No." She hesitated. "I can't say much because some of the information is sensitive, but Tai'ri is the father of my child."

Shira stared at her with wide eyes. "Oh. The Y.E.T.I program?"

"No, no." Vivian sighed, placing a hand over her eyes. "I'm explaining it badly. Tai'ri and I never . . . I was artificially inseminated by our captors." She'd assumed that had been how all the women were impregnated, but something in the other women's eyes made her shy away from that assumption.

"Oh. *Oh.*" Shira's gaze went to the door Tai'ri had exited. Her shoulders relaxed. "He really is one of the good guys then? They told me he was some kind of government official, and my sponsor."

"Yes, he's one of the good guys. I live with him. We're . . . getting along. He's very nice." Vivian almost blushed, irritated with herself at her banal speaking.

Shira seemed to understand. "He didn't want you living here since you were pregnant with his child, did he?"

Vivian shook her head.

"That's good. I don't know who my sperm donor is. They say the baby is half-Yadeshi, though."

"It's hard, but you're strong, you'll get through this." Vivian wasn't the type to touch people without permission, but she reached out and squeezed Shira's hand briefly. "And if you ever need to talk, I'm here."

They spoke for an hour, the conversation becoming increasingly relaxed. Shira's composure impressed Vivian—and the sparks of ribald humor that peeked out occasionally.

"They told me I can go home if I want to," Shira said. "I don't know. The economy is trashed, we're on our fifth drought in ten years, and I—my family is all gone." She looked down. "But what am I supposed to do here?"

"You can work with me."

As soon as the words were out of her mouth, Vivian knew she should have asked Tai'ri first. But it felt right. If Tai'ri was Shira's sponsor, and the woman had no other friends or family, then in a way that meant Tai'ri and Vivian were the only family Shira had.

"What do you mean?" Shira asked.

"I don't know," she hedged, "but I don't plan on sitting around doing nothing once this baby is born in a few weeks. Whatever I do, you can do with me."

Shira eyed her, then grinned. "Bosom buddies?" She cupped her full chest, hefting it with a mock leer. "Or just bosom?"

Vivian laughed, blushing a little.

Shira's smile faded. "They said they were trying to track down my sperm donor. I'm not sure how I feel about that."

Vivian frowned. "No, I understand. Depending on who he is, if he's notified it could just make the situation worse. I'll talk to Tai'ri. At least with me, they told me I wouldn't have to have anything to do with the baby's father unless I wanted to. That same offer should be extended to you."

When Tai'ri returned some time later, Vivian and Shira cornered him.

"You're my sponsor, right?" Shira demanded.

He halted, shoving his hands in his pockets, and eyed them both. "More like a legal guardian till you decide if you want to stay here and apply for citizenship."

"Ok, well tell the people in charge that I don't want anything to do with the sperm donor."

"Uh..."

"It's the right thing," Vivian said, interpreting his expression. "What if he isn't a good man?"

"He could be dead, for all we know."

"That would be great," Shira muttered.

"But if he's not, and he's a good male, then he should know about his child," Tai'ri countered. "We don't really know how the traffickers are obtaining their ... sperm." He winced. "If it was all from kidnapped people, we'd have more cases of missing adult males." Tai'ri stilled suddenly, then cursed. "Of course. The fucking sperm donors."

He spun on his heel, tapping his wrist unit, and strode to a corner of the room, talking under his breath.

The women exchanged looks. "Looks like we just handed him a clue," Shira said.

"Looks like," Vivian murmured.

Tai'ri returned, leveled a look at them, all hesitance gone now under his mask of professional warrior.

"Shira, nothing will be done without your knowledge and consent. We'll discuss this further later. Viv, we need to go."

Shira grabbed Vivian's hand. "Comm me, okay?"

Vivian squeezed back. "Okay."

17

"This is better than a baby shower," Vivian said gleefully, eyeing her selections as the clerk tallied them up, barely able to refrain from rubbing her hands together.

The craft warehouse obviously believed in old-fashioned service, just as the cafe they'd first met in had. No self-scanning of purchases, but a flesh and blood shopkeeper on the premises.

He'd woken her that morning for the shopping trip back to the artists' sector. Stepping inside the warehouse for the first time, she'd been struck silent by the sheer variety of supplies, and instantly knew she'd need a bigger studio. More storage. More projects to give her more excuses to shop.

Tai'ri turned back towards her, expression baffled. "A shower of babies? That can't have translated right."

She counted herself lucky he'd trailed behind her

for the three hours she'd spent in the store—the size of a warehouse—rather than finding a seat and parking himself. Not that he would—if anyone got even a foot too close to her, he morphed from amused and resigned to bristling and dangerous.

"No, a baby shower. It's an occasion where friends and family gather to give a pregnant mother the stuff she'll need for the baby."

He scowled. "Where is the father? Why isn't he providing his mate and child what they need?"

Vivian laughed, stepping aside as Tai'ri paid for her booty, then arranged for the bags to be delivered. She eyed her purchases as the clerk put them in a labeled bin for pickup. She may have gone a little overboard.

"I'll pay you back," she said.

"I can't hear you." Tai'ri placed a hand on the small of her back. "Are you hungry? I'll take you to lunch and you can tell me more about this showering baby custom."

"It's really just an excuse for a party," she said once they'd chosen a food vendor and found a table in the outdoor courtyard. "It's not just presents, but food, music, games."

"My family has a monthly gathering," he said, stretching his legs out. "If there are any births, we celebrate them. I'll tell my father about this showering baby custom. The males should be the ones to provide for the babies. Trust humans to make females spend their own money."

"Oh, you don't have to—"

"My mother has commanded. Her first few requests to bring you home were very sweet."

"And the last few haven't been?"

He said nothing.

Vivian sighed. She couldn't closet herself away from his family forever, though it brought up the uncomfortable topic of the future, and what her feelings were for Tai'ri. Her plans for herself. All the things parents would want to know. He wasn't pressuring her, but obligation weighed. He was giving her so much, and if all he asked in return was that she come to a family gathering, how could she say no? She could meet him halfway.

"It would be nice to meet your mother," she said. It wasn't exactly a lie.

She was struck when his answering smile strummed a deep chord of warmth in her—because, evidently, she was pleased to make him happy.

"Let's get you home," he said quietly. "You've been on your feet long enough today."

His almost bondmate collapsed into an exhausted heap on the couch when they returned home. She noticed his amusement, struggling into a seated position to begin taking the delivered packages up to her studio.

"I'll do it, Viv," he said. "Sit."

She looked stubborn for a moment, then sighed. "Alright. But just put them somewhere. I'll organize the supplies."

She gave him a brilliant smile, taking the sting out of her territorial words. That territorial streak sparked joy. It meant she was beginning to see his home as hers, beginning to stake a claim.

Even if she didn't really want to meet his mother.

After convincing her that her packages weren't going anywhere and yes, she really did need a nap, he left her curled up on her bed then slipped into his office and accessed his data unit.

"You have intel?" he asked Evvek, responding to the comm request that had been waiting since lunch. It hadn't been marked urgent, so he'd ignored it. Had to remind himself to slow down, enjoy the parts of his present life that brought him happiness, even if that happiness was complicated. He'd never be able to get this time back, and he wanted memories of Viv, big with his child and content. Maybe when everything was resolved, he could look back and pretend like their life had begun in a normalish fashion.

He wanted that for her, too. Her first pregnancy should be filled with nothing more taxing than what colors to dress the baby in. What meals to nourish her body with.

"Yeah, following up on missing males was a stroke of genius." Evvek sounded excited, but looked uneasy. "I began with compiling missing persons reports, male victims, but it occurred to me. The reason they can get away with this is because there *aren't* any missing persons. You start killing males left and right, then you make it harder on yourself. Media attention, males start carrying weapons, etc. Aliens get trafficked, it's just some lurid news story, the *Bdakhun's* pet project. Our own people start turning up dead and missing, there's an outcry. So I focused on males who reported physical assaults accompanied by short term memory loss."

"You think males are being snatched, their sperm extracted, and then tossed back on the street?" His jaw clenched.

"Lure a male to a location where you can grab him. You can even use a female, seduce him. That would almost be easier. Prime the pump, so to speak." They exchanged a pained look. "Then you knock him out, steal the goods, and disappear. You've got material to use to impregnate the females."

Tai'ri rubbed a hand over his face. "Haeemah's Mercy. And I just walked right into their laps. I thought my capture was opportunistic, but if they've been doing this to others . . . what's Zhiannur doing?"

"As soon as his feet hit planetside, we'll be on him."

"But he isn't on Anthhori."

"No, and there's too much signal interference to know what shuttle he's on. There are dozens of interstellar freighters in orbit right now, plus the private small crafts, and—"

"Yeah, I know. Alright, inform Vykhan. The *Bdakhun* will want to alert the public."

Evvek rolled his eyes. "What's she gonna say? Males, party in twos? Don't accept any offers if a hot female tries to take you home? Best thing we can do is keep going after the head of the snake and cut it off."

"I agree, but the decision is hers."

"Sir . . . are we going to tell these males they may have children?"

Tai'ri thought about Shira. "I don't know if the human women will want us to. I'll need to speak to the *Bdakhun* about that soon."

He signed off and stared at his console, considering the situation with him and Viv. Even if these new mothers were unable to mate—what were the odds, after all—they could still be matched with warriors on Yedahn who would care for them . . . if the women didn't want to return home with their half-Yadeshi babies, and the biological fathers were unfit. He made a mental note to discuss a reunification program with the *Bdakhun*. It would have to be handled with extreme care.

And in the meantime, he would talk to his father about showering babies. Because even with traffickers and the weight of his work, every day life still needed to go on.

18

Vivian rubbed her throbbing temple. Daobah, Tai'ri's youngest sister, enjoyed conversation. Incessant conversation, without pauses for breath or contemplation, and Shira encouraged her.

"This is cosmic," Daobah said, holding up a diaphanous swath of . . . what was it? She exuded health and energy, a girlish layer of softness over the muscles of someone who was constantly active. Thick, Vivian's father would say. She wore an ankle length sheer pink skirt with multiple layers of fabric, and a black fitted t-shirt with a picture of an attractive snake shifter man who, Vivian had been informed, was a totally stellar vid star. The man stared out from the shirt with swirling yellow eyes and iridescent skin and every once in a while in a sultry tone said, "Bite me."

Vivian blinked. "That's considered appropriate attire for an infant?"

Shira considered the garment, wandering over from a different rack. She wore a pair of black leggings and an oversized white shirt in a soft material, one shoulder bare. Her hair was pulled back in a haphazard tail and somewhere she'd obtained an electric blue manicure, the tips of her nails long and ruthlessly pointed. Like talons.

When Daobah had showed up at the house to take Vivian shopping, Vivian's only requests had been that they pick up Shira, and that they go somewhere vintage. She wanted to feel and examine the clothing rather than stand in front of digital walls tabbing through endless virtual models to place an order.

"It's cute," Shira said. "Kinda."

Daobah pressed the label. A mini holo advert of a bouncing baby swathed in a rainbow of sheer fabric, her lovely mother twirling her in sunlight, shimmered above the dress.

"I could be incorrect," Vivian said, "but that doesn't seem to reflect an accurate portrayal of the daily realities of motherhood."

"That's called marketing," Shira said. "It's the Great Lie they sell women so we'll have babies." She grimaced, rubbing her stomach. "By choice, preferably."

Despite her words, Vivian knew her new friend was at peace with the idea of being a mother. Angry and exasperated, but welcoming of her upcoming child. They'd talked about it, and Vivian had tried to copy some of Shira's sardonic optimism. Which should be an oxymoron, but Shira somehow made it work.

Daobah put the dress back on the rack. "It's cute, though. But, yeah, the first diaper blowout and this thing will be refuse."

"Diaper what?" Shira exclaimed as Vivian blinked.

Daobah's pale eyes brightened with joyous malice. "Let me tell you about those."

As Daobah ghoulishly described the upcoming pleasantries of motherhood, Vivian glimpsed a petite young woman drift close. A flowery headband held back shoulder length hair, and she wore a fitted pink jumpsuit that managed to look demure. She turned her head and gave Vivian a wink.

"Maybe we should think about lunch," Vivian said.

"I could eat," Shira said. "Again."

"Right," Daobah said. "And after a break, we need to actually buy something, Viv. Shira has four outfits already—"

"I have no standards," Shira said. "Anything works."

Daobah gave the woman a sour look and kept talking. ". . . and there's a small and squally coming any week now."

Vivian suppressed a shudder. The baby kicked, possibly in affront. "Nothing personal," she muttered to it, rubbing her stomach.

Daobah and Shira chose meals from a kiosk specializing in Earth Italian cuisine, and Vivian went for a regional seafood, after filtering for pregnancy and human dietary restrictions.

"So, how's Tai'ri treating you?" Daobah asked when they were seated. She dug into a heaping bowl of pasta, which disappeared at lightspeed. Vivian nibbled on her fish. "I mean, I know other girls think he's cute and all, but . . . ugh. He farts in his sleep." Shira snorted, inhaling her pasta, and began coughing. Daobah slapped her on the back and shoved a drink under her nose.

"Tai'ri is very kind," Vivian said.

"Then what's the problem?"

"I don't understand."

Daobah gave her a gimlet stare, then relented. "Tai'ri's kinda touchy feely, but he keeps his hands in his pocket around you. He just hovers."

"Our relationship will take time to develop," Vivian said. "It's not Tai'ri's fault."

Daobah rolled her eyes. "Help me out here, Shira. You do think Tai'ri is hot, right?"

"Sure. But he's not my man, so I can't comment too hard on that." She grinned at Vivian, who smiled wryly.

Daobah sighed. "Ugh, humans. It's important." Her gaze flicked down to Vivian's lower arms, and only then did she shut her mouth.

Hmm.

Shira leaned forward a little and reached out to grab Vivian's arm. Vivian let her push up her sleeve and stare at the tattoos. "Yeah, about these. Do they have any feeling? I've seen them move on other Yadeshi."

"Some of the time they do," Vivian said, eyeing Shira's mark free arm. Hmm . . .

Shira tilted her head. "You know, I took a tour of a YETI base once. Few years ago, I wanted to see what the deal was. I saw two human girls with marks like these. They'd never tell us what it meant, just that they were for the women who'd married a warrior."

They looked at Tai'ri's sister.

"It's not really that simple," Daobah said, looking uncomfortable, "but I guess if that's the story they give you all, I shouldn't contradict it."

Vivian watched the expressions play across the girl's face speculatively. Tai'ri still hadn't managed to get his console fixed and now Vivian was having suspicions. Why wouldn't he want her to access the datasphere?

She suspected it was something to do with these supposedly medical only markings. Markings which most every Yadeshi person she'd seen possessed.

Markings which lately, the more she allowed herself to relax in Tai'ri's presence . . . stirred. Yesterday, experimenting, Vivian had deliberately meditated and forced herself to think warm, positive thoughts about Tai'ri. Forced being a strong term because as soon as she gently banished her fears, anxieties, and dark memories, her mood turned to the present tense and ... Tai'ri was there. Cooking, helping her learn the house tech, handing her nutritional smoothies and gently haranguing her into drinking water.

Bringing her skeins of colored fibers and boxes of beads and semi-precious stones. Even blue and purple clays and what passed as a kiln.

After a time, she found that she did not have to force herself to think of him warmly. He was kind, thoughtful. He hovered, but that was to be expected in the circumstances. He was a thoughtful, insightful conversationalist who knew the value of silence. Talking to him was easy.

He made her remember that once she had daydreamed about love and old-world marriage and two children rather than the more practical one.

It was time to talk with Tai'ri. About the marks, about the future. About her growing feelings and sense of permanency. And whether his obvious attraction to her was just a product of circumstance or if he wanted something more, long term.

As soon as he came home tonight, they would talk.

"House, where is Tai'ri?" Vivian asked as she entered the house. Banujani set her purchases down on the kitchen island, then stepped out onto the balcony. Vivian briefly wondered if the guard was going to leap over the railing or climb up a wall.

:Tai'ri is in the first guest suite.:

"Viv," Tai'ri called, and she followed the sound of his voice, stopping at the threshold of the room.

His eyes lit up and he stood. "Daobah said you bought things."

She looked around the once simply but elegantly furnished room, which was now a riot of color, patterns and . . . stuff. Three different styles of rocking chairs, one only half assembled. A sensory play corner, and a bed suitable for a small child. Plus swatches of color on the walls, and newly installed floating shelves lined with toys.

"So did you."

When he'd told her goodnight the previous evening, he'd been all in black. Streamlined trousers, long-sleeved shirt, his hair pulled back. Now he was back to his loose pants stuffed into scuffed boots—she cringed at footwear in the house, but perhaps he'd just gotten in—and a short sleeved neutral shirt, his hair a mess around his face and the bracelets tinkling around his wrists.

"It's just some options. I know you're busy, didn't think it was fair to make you do all the shopping." He stepped over a pile of stuff and pressed the wall; a hygiene station slid out. Waist high bathing sink with all the bells and whistles. "Bey said one of these stations is better for a little one than the adult sized bathroom."

"It's very nice."

He looked pleased, the kind of expression she imagined men boasted millennia ago when bringing home a fresh kill for supper. She studied him, trying to look at him through the eyes of a woman interested in . . . romance. Deep soul searching had assured her that despite her time in the pens, her desire for love and sex wasn't gone. Or rather, it was beginning to stir again as time and normalcy created a buffer between her and the past.

"I didn't buy any clothing," he said quietly, studying her return. "Baba said that's female shopping only."

"Daobah gravitates towards clothing more suitable for a photo op than midnight feedings and mess." Her heart fluttered; he held her gaze and she couldn't quite look away. She fought to keep her voice even. "I didn't buy anything—I thought you and I could go."

But she hadn't, not until now. Watching the warm smile cross his face was worth the small lie.

"If you want me," he said with a slow smile. He held out a hand. "We'll do something new and interesting for lunch too."

"Everything is new and interesting, Tai'ri."

He stilled, staring at her, an indecipherable emotion flashing across his face. Tai'ri lifted her hand to his mouth, and pressed a kiss in her palm. Her internal thoughts stuttered just from that small touch.

She cleared her throat, and tugged out of his grasp. "I *did* buy some things, though." To distract herself from the intensity of his regard, she turned and picked up a stuffed animal.

"You know you can buy whatever you want. But why do you look so guilty?"

Vivian set the toy on a shelf, fussing with its placement. She heard the soft scuff of his feet, felt the warmth of him at her back. Close, so close. "I bought craft supplies. I'll update the spreadsheet." The one she'd started to keep track of his shameless spending on her.

Tai'ri laughed, a deep, rich sound, his hands settling on her shoulders, thumbs at the back of her neck. He pressed deep, massaging the stiff muscles. "Of course you bought more craft supplies when we have a baby coming. You don't need to pay me back."

Vivian bit back a moan, but then he pressed deeper and the sound slipped out. He paused for a long moment, then resumed.

"It's not a matter of need," she said, "but of what's right."

He turned her to face him and narrowed his eyes. "I won't negotiate with you on this."

She glared at him, then relented. "Then consider it an investment, not a loan. You'll get a return on your *investment* once I'm financially independent again."

"You're carrying my investment. And if you're going to consider art supplies an investment, and you want to be financially independent, then you should start a business with them." His gaze was warm, but implacable.

Vivian rolled her eyes. He was too silly. A business. "You're going to hang wallpaper? That's so vintage."

"The walls can change color according to your specifications, but I thought something tactile would be nice."

She looked around at the toys and stuffed animals placed cheerfully around the room, then laughed. "There is *plenty* of tactile here, Tai'ri."

He looked pleased. "You like it then? It's a start. Even if you keep the baby in the room with you while she or he is little, their own room is still useful."

She abandoned thoughts of organizing her craft supplies today and began directing the arrangement of all the furniture he'd bought. He moved furniture, a warm presence at her shoulder, obeying her instructions.

When it was time for a break, she snuggled into one of the rocking chairs and he brought her a cupcake, and even let her eat a second before dinner.

It wasn't her home on Earth. But it was becoming home on Yedahn. It wasn't until later that she admitted to herself she'd avoided the talk they needed to have about their feelings, and the future.

19

His family home was nestled into one of the low mountains surrounding the city. As they approached in Tai'ri's double flier, her stomach somersaulted. The house was built into the side of the mountain itself.

It dangled.

"Are you certain of the structural integrity of your home?" she asked. "It appears unstable."

"Six generations," he said. "No one has fallen off a terrace yet—not on accident. I had a great uncle who . . . never mind." He eyed her pale face. "So, there will be lots of chocolate. I asked my mother, who knows someone who knows someone."

She clung to the conversational thread grimly. "But you know the province princess. Your connections trump theirs."

He shrugged.

The flier landed in a circle on the flat roof. They exited, Vivian carefully not looking towards the ledge but beyond, at the view.

The incredible view.

"This kind of view would go for a premium on my homeworld," she breathed.

"My family does well," he acknowledged.

She turned to him. "You do realize I'm beneath you socially?"

Tai'ri stared at her. "What are you talking about?"

"On my homeworld, my class would be considered at least a Tier below yours."

He sneered. "Human vakshit." He slung an arm around her shoulders. "Don't worry about that here. If you want to please my mother, eat her food and let her talk about breathing techniques during labor. Or ancient water birth practices. We've all heard it all, so our eyes glaze over. If you look interested, she'll love you forever."

With that advice they entered an elevator embedded in the mountain which lowered them into the house.

The doors slid open and a shock of riot and sound spilled out.

"Oh, God."

This floor of the home was open, designed in muted earth tones with flashes of jewel bright accents. Low couches, reclining chairs and seating areas with small tables scattered throughout. The ceiling was pulled back and flowed into a windowless wall that let in both air and the city view. As she glanced up, swirling stars floated in the glass, throwing an ethereal light throughout the room.

"Courage," he said.

"Viv!" Daobah pushed through the crowd and came forward, knocking Tai'ri's arm off her shoulders. "Welcome to this madness. Poor soul. Everyone is talking about you."

"Baba," Tai'ri rebuked.

"Whaaa? Go skulk somewhere."

Daobah led her through the crowd, pausing every few feet to name relatives or intercept a child. Proving personal space was a cultural thing, people nodded at Vivian, smiled, and even gave their little one fingered waves, but didn't approach. Tai'ri hovered at her side, his hands rubbing up and down her shoulders, the line of his body tense.

"The marks are riding you hard, aren't they?" Daobah remarked, glancing at him.

"What?" Vivian said. "What do you mean?"

Tai'ri gave his sister, who scowled at him, a look.

"Nevermind," Daobah said. "I talk a lot. If you hadn't noticed." She grabbed Vivian's hand and resumed pulling her along. "Viv, I'll take you to meet the Matrons."

"Who?" Vivian heard the capitalization of the word.

Tai'ri trailed behind. "Mother, The Aunts, Grandmothers, and Great-Aunts."

"I—how many are there of you?" She looked around, feeling as if she was sinking into a giant vat of helplessness. "There are so many."

"We're fertile and horny," Daobah said.

"Is that why the family business is birthing?" Vivian asked, glad for a startling minute that she didn't have younger sisters.

"Yup. People come to us cause they hope the fecundity will rub off. And the only thing that rubs off is dry c—"

"Daobah." Tai'ri's tone was steely now. "We are in company with children. Mind your speech."

She snorted. "As if you can grow up in this family and not know all about everything by the time you're off the tit. The Matrons. The Pit."

Daobah stopped in front of an inset circle of the same warm blonde as the rest of the room. Several women lounged on a wide, circular couch, trays of food and drink scattered at feet and elbows.

If these women were Matrons, it proved human suspicions that the Yadeshi aged very, very slowly. Their hair and skin did not appear to lose pigment, but some of the women bore more pronounced lines around eyes and mouth, and moved slower, spoke quieter.

One woman rose from the couch, her dark hair softened with red and wound around her hair in a multitude of thick braids. Strands of polished stones similar to those on Tai'ri's wrists dangled from her earlobes.

"Son," she said as Tai'ri descended into the . . . pit. He bent his head so she could kiss his forehead, though she wasn't much shorter than he. She wore narrow wine red trousers and a duster that swept to the floor edged in brown and gold. "And this must be Vivian. Come, sit, daughter, we won't stand on ceremony for now."

That sounded ominous.

"Give her the soup, Agata," one of the older women grunted. "Human blood is weak. Bring Abeyya, *yadoana*."

Vivian realized the command was directed to Daobah, who darted back up the dais.

"The male's circle is waiting for you," Agata told Tai'ri. "Go. We know how to care for your bondmate."

He stiffened, glancing obliquely at Vivian, then inclined his head and left as well. Agata patted a cushion and one of the other women helped her sit. Daobah and Abeyya appeared just as a bowl of steaming soup was placed in Vivian's hands. A golden broth swimming with vegetables, some kind of small grain and slivers of meat she recognized as either fish or what passed for chicken.

She picked up the deep bowled spoon and took a careful bite as Abeyya found a spot on the couch and draped herself down, snagging a morsel off someone's platter. The temperature was perfect, not too hot, and the broth flavorful.

Vivian paused. "Oh! I didn't scan to see—"

Agata sniffed. "Really, *yadoana*. Though I'm glad you're conscientious considering the stakes."

Vivian took that to mean the soup was safe, and continued eating. "The stakes?"

"Your child. I spoke with young Ibukay. My mother oversaw her birth decades ago." Vivian paused, startled, then resumed eating when Agata gave the bowl a pointed look. "Have they told you there is a complex battery of treatments human woman have to undergo to prime their reproductive systems to accept Yadeshi genetic material?"

"I believe I underwent those procedures." Her mood darkened and instinctively she looked around for Tai'ri.

Agata touched her shoulder briefly. "I am beyond angry at what was done to you and my son. But we cannot bring ourselves to regret any new life."

"It isn't his fault," Vivian said softly. "He's been very kind."

"So tell me about my son. Is he seeing to your sexual needs properly? Males can be obtuse about these things when we're big with child."

Vivian choked on the tea one of the younger women, perhaps an 'aunt', had handed her.

Agata patted her on the back, Abeyya watching

with amusement. "Don't be shy, we're all mothers here. Many babies, many males."

"Lots of sex," Daobah muttered.

Vivian set her tea down, folding her hands on top of her bump. Sex just hadn't been a topic of discussion growing up. Lineage, genetic matches, etc. . . but not the act that produced offspring. "We just met weeks ago, after a harrowing shared experience."

Agata's head tilted. "True. But he is your bondmate. It is his job to—"

"Mother."

Vivian glanced over, a little intrigued by Tai'ri's timing. He hovered at the top of the circle.

His mother gave him an irritated look. "We didn't call you."

"May I claim Vivian?" Tai'ri tone was scrupulously respectful. "I wanted to spend time with her this evening."

Agata sighed. "Oh, fine. We'll speak again soon, Vivian."

Tai'ri descended the steps and approached to help Vivian rise from the soft couch.

"We have much to discuss as well, Tai'ri," his mother added.

He cringed, though he was smart enough to have turned his face away first. A spark of amusement burst in Vivian's chest, sending tendrils of warmth through her. It was hard not to find a tall, strong man who was afraid of a lecture from his mother adorable.

"They can be overwhelming," he said in her ear as they walked away. "They didn't interrogate you out of respect for the . . . circumstances. That will probably come after the baby is born and well settled."

The vague 'after the baby is here' time in the future that she still had trouble imagining. The babe shifted inside her, punctuating the fact that the future was closer than the past.

Tai'ri rubbed the small of her back, escorting her to a dark corner of the room where there was a plush couch just enough for the two of them, frothy plants and a screen on either side offering some privacy. They settled onto the couch and a lanky young man approached moments later with a small tray loaded with bits of food, and a steaming teapot.

"Introduce your most stellar brother," he said to Tai'ri.

Tai'ri made a show of looking around.

"I'm Yolu," the young man said. He eyed Vivian. "You're way hotter than he deserves."

Vivian laughed. "I don't know about that. It's nice to meet you." She gave Tai'ri a sideways look. "How many siblings do you have?"

"Better save that for another time," Yolu said.

That they were brothers was apparent once Vivian really looked. Yolu's bone structure echoed Tai'ri's, and he carried himself with the same quiet self-assurance. She couldn't imagine Tai'ri with the short, white tipped spiky hair or slashed shirt, though.

"Here." He held the tray out to Tai'ri, who set it on a small side table. "The Matrons said to feed her." With a quick grin, he was gone.

"Your family seems kind," she said. "You're very fortunate."

He studied her face. "Do you think this is a family you would feel comfortable being a part of? Raising our child in?"

The real question he wasn't asking . . . do you think you will stay with me?

Vivian realized she was hungry, for once, and eyed the platter. Tai'ri waited patiently as she used the food as an excuse for more time to respond.

"Whether I'm comfortable or not, the child genetically belongs here as much as it does on Earth," she said. "Eventually I would like to go home, see my parents. If it's safe."

He stilled beside her. "It will be safe."

The thread of darkness in his tone again, the rare glimpse he gave through the window to the other facets of his personality. Not for the first time, she wondered who he was when he was working for Ibukay. The spy, the warrior, the chameleon who could kill coldly, whether in defense or for a mission.

He was still waiting for a reply. "Yes," she said quietly. "I could envision myself as a part of this."

With the admission, something inside her relaxed. One of her barriers crumpled, and she opened up a little more to the possibility of a real future on Yedahn. With this man, as a family.

The baby stirred, pressing in her groin. She rubbed her hand over the roundness that could be a bottom or a head.

"It will be alright, baby," she murmured.

Tai'ri nuzzled the top of her head. "That's the first time I've heard you speak to her."

Tears pricked Vivian eyes with the sting of guilt. The first time she had spoken to her child, who had done nothing wrong and deserved its mother's love.

She took a deep breath, blinked away the tumultuous emotions. She would do better. "Tai'ri, we need to talk."

"Frightening words."

A small laugh escaped her. "No, no. I—" she glanced up at him, met the steady gaze that looked at her as if nothing else could claim his attention as long as she desired it. "I just realized the other day . . . I don't know what the future brings for me. For us. I don't know what you want—"

"Then I haven't made myself very clear." His voice was deep, the words deliberate and shaded with meaning she'd have to be a fool not to hear.

She plucked at his sleeve. "It's just the other day I was thinking that if I had met you under normal circumstances—well, normalish—I would have wanted to get to know you."

His hand slid around the back of her neck. "Are

you trying to tell me that you're falling madly in love with me?"

Vivian wrinkled her nose at him, then laughed. His lips curled, and as warmth unfurled in her chest, her marks moved, sparking and sending tendrils of liquid heat through her body. "And we're going to have to have a talk about these marks."

Hearing the breathlessness of her own voice, Vivian was unsurprised when Tai'ri lowered his head slowly, as if to give her time to pull away, and settled his lips over hers. She opened beneath him, hands sliding up to his shoulders. The room, the din of conversation, fell away and it was just him. His taste, his scent, the weight of his arm sliding around her shoulders and anchoring her to him.

"Go upstairs," someone hooted. "There's children here."

"There's nothing wrong with a display of healthy passion between consenting adults!" someone else yelled.

"That's why we have so many babies in this family!" was the heated reply. "Two this year already! You're not the one who has to plan all the apprenticeships when the younglings come of age."

"Well, three soon. She's about to pop."

Tai'ri pulled away from her, the smile on his face wry. "Welcome to my family."

Vivian leaned her head on his shoulder, and listened to the argument.

20

"You're cooking?" a disembodied voice came from her comm.

"I cook," Vivian said, bringing a deep-bowled spoon to her lips.

"And thank god for that," Shira said. "I mean, the food isn't bad at the safe house, it's just so relentlessly *nutritious.*" She made a face.

Vivian smiled, surveying the meal. Delicate whitefish, noodles, and vegetables simmered in a fragrant broth. It wasn't quite the dish Agata had served her, but it was Vivian's family's version, a recipe passed down for several generations. Well, as close to the recipe as possible since the spices were different, and the available fish and vegetables as well.

"This is nutritious," Vivian pointed out. She'd invited Shira to lunch not just because she needed a buffer, but because she genuinely wanted to get to know her better. Her outgoing personality was a breath of fresh air.

"Yeah? All I see are noodles. A big, heaping bowl of carby noodles."

Vivian laughed and handed her a bowl. "You might as well get started. I made enough for everyone," she added, knowing the guards would hear. "There are two fillings for the dumplings, too. Fruit, and a spiced meat."

She ladled fish and noodle soup into the bottom half of the clay lunch container, then set the dumplings in the top compartment and covered it with a lid.

Repeating that three more times, she said, "Lunch."

A strained silence. "We're on duty."

"Then come one at a time." She poured tea into thermoses. "Besides, there's nothing more threatening going on right now than the occasional fly by dropping from a bird."

Moments later a black clad warrior morphed into existence, a flash of movement and light coming over the balcony before it solidified.

"I will *never* get used to that," Shira muttered, slurping up a noodle as she balanced her bowl on her stomach. Banujani gave Shira an amused look.

Banujani's first shift on duty after her injuries, Vivian had attempted an apology. "It comes with the job. Besides, you're Tai'ri's, which makes you one of us.

We protect our own. No guilt." Banujani had grinned. "And I hear you were about to skewer a civilian, too."

"You know," her guard said now, perhaps reading Vivian's expression, "if you feel guilty about me getting hurt, you can cook more often."

"Setting the bar, Banu?" another voice said through the comm. "Damn. All a warrior wants is a dumpling."

Vivian handed Banujani a container and thermos. "Take this and come back for the others, unless you can carry two sets at a time."

It wasn't until she'd begun cooking this meal that she truly understood how disconnected from herself she'd become. It was time to contact her parents. But first she had to get through lunch.

"They're here," Banujani said.

Shira sighed, setting her bowl down. "I guess it's time to pretend I'm civilized." She shifted, looking a little uncomfortable. "It's not like they're *my* in-laws, I don't know why I'm nervous."

"Tai'ri is your sponsor, that's why—like temporary adopted family. Just be yourself," Vivian said.

House announced Agata and Abeyya a moment later, and Vivian waddled towards the entrance to welcome them inside.

Agata swept down the hall, Abeyya at her back. "No need to come open the door, dear, it's coded," she said, and kissed Vivian's cheek. "Hmm . . . Kholorian paprika. And garlic from Isthmus 2." She turned to

Shira. "And you must be my son's ward. How lovely you are."

Shira's cheeks pinkened, but she smiled. "Yup, he's my hero. I got the better end of the deal, though."

"Hardly," Abeyya said. "He was annoying growing up, and he's just barely improved." But her amused expression took the sting out of the words. "But tell me about your baby."

They ushered Vivian and Shira to the table on the balcony and dished up a carafe of soup as they all chatted, bringing in the platter of dumplings and teapot as well.

"Well seasoned," Agata said. "Your own recipe? I've never tasted quite this combination before."

"Adapted from a family recipe," Vivian murmured.

"My only family recipes came in dehydrated packets," Shira said. "I almost want to learn how to cook now."

"You should," Abeyya said. "It can be very rewarding, and you'll have your own child soon."

Shira's expression darkened a little, then she shrugged. "Yeah, I guess I don't want my kid growing up eating the cardboard they passed off as food."

"We'll have to order some of your home world spices so you can prepare us something," Agata said. "And spend some time looking through recipes to see what you like. Family dishes are so important."

They chatted, Abeyya interjecting questions here and there about Vivian and Shira's health, the babies.

She recognized a subtle but thorough medical assessment taking place.

Shira reached out, grabbing Vivian's hand. Their gazes met for a moment in understanding. Vivian saw the same echoes of pain, fear, grief and anger in her new friend's eyes. Shira just seemed to hide her feelings better.

"Our parents won't be here when we birth," she said.

Agata's look was compassionate. "Have either of you asked the *Bdakhun* what possibilities there might be to bring them to Yedahn?"

"Somewhat. I haven't contacted her in some time," Vivian said.

"She may want to give you space to settle in and regain your strength. But if she gave you an opening to contact her, don't hesitate to use it. I'm sure a temporary visitation allowance could be made, perhaps even a travel stipend. You should have your parents with you as soon as it can be arranged."

Vivian sighed. "They would be mortified if they knew they were receiving special treatment."

"I feel that the sight of a new grandbaby would make them promptly forget such mortification."

"I think so too."

Her parents would dote on a new grandchild, even if they would be embarrassed by the undignified method of conception. But maybe she was being unfair. In a moment of clarity Vivian understood that she blamed them, partially, for her kidnapping. She'd wanted to rebel, to be part of a movement that worked against the controlling status quo, fought back against a government so restrictive of every day movement that it was a wonder the total number of breaths of each citizen wasn't measured and allotted. Part of her desire to rebel had been her parents constant support of the status quo.

Being recruited to take part in an underground movement had excited her, knocked her out of her restless ennui. The fact that the meetings were late Friday night after curfew had only added to the mystique.

It turned out that it was easier for traffickers to nab women who were out, alone, after curfew.

She should have stuck to crafting.

Vivian laughed out loud, then shook her head as the other women looked at her inquiringly. "I was just telling myself I should have stuck to crafting. I'm very good at it."

"Ha," Shira said. "The only thing I do well with my hands is eat."

Abeyya laughed. "I'm positive you're selling yourself short. You should open a studio, Vivian. Small, with enough room for perhaps ten students per session. You could teach Earth crafts, sell your own work, invite local guest artists in for evening lectures and socializing."

"It's a wonderful idea," Vivian said.

"But?" Abeyya prompted.

"I don't have the finances to open a business."

Abeyya snorted a quick laugh. "My brother, and our family as a whole—and I do mean *our*, Vivian—is quite well off enough to front a reasonable start up loan for a small business."

"Especially with all the alien culture hysteria," Agata murmured. "Earth crafting could be very lucrative. I don't think any humans have a shop that caters to that market, at least not in this city."

Shira's eyes widened. "Hell, if the locals want aliens, give them aliens, Vivian. I need to find something to do soon, too. I'm positive after the new mom glow wears off I'd go batshit sitting around all day."

Vivian agreed, though she wouldn't have used those exact words. She was already beginning to feel restless despite Tai'ri's thoughtful attempts to keep her occupied.

Vivian struggled with her pride and wondered if she was being foolish. She'd done nothing to earn this family other than get captured and impregnated. It was highly serendipitous that the sperm used to knock her up was from a man of wealth, status and good lineage on this planet. She realized any other woman wouldn't hesitate to take advantage . . .and was it not her right, after all, even if Tai'ri was an inadvertent father as well?

Vivian looked up, mentally shaking off her indecision. It was time to take another step forward.

"I would like some time to research and put

together a proper business plan and proposal for financing," she said. "But I think I'll take you up on the offer." She glanced at Shira and hesitated, lips curving in a smile. "Everyone is craftsy, you know, it's just a matter of finding the medium that speaks to you. I could use a partner. Two humans are better than one."

Shira blinked rapidly and looked down at the table. "I wasn't fishing."

"You don't have to. Tai'ri is your guardian, that practically makes us sisters."

"Okay . . . okay, what the hell. I'm in if you want me."

"Excellent," Agata said. "Planning will give you both something to do outside of the babies those first few weeks after they're here."

"If Tai'ri gets his console working," Vivian said. "Though I can't quite figure out if it's the console or the connection to the datasphere he's having trouble with."

Agata lifted a brow. "He's having trouble with neither."

"That's what I thought. These marks aren't just medtech, are they? Tai'ri has been reluctant to discuss them."

Agata sighed. "I didn't agree with Tai'ri's request not to discuss the marks with you. It's paternalistic, though we understand his desire is to spare you further distress."

"His desire is to avoid the fallout of acting impulsively," Abeyya muttered.

"Yes," Agata said. "He should have controlled his instincts better. Intentions mean nothing when they infringe on another person's autonomy. But, and I hope you don't take this the wrong way, we can't bring ourselves to regret the fact that the child exists."

Shira looked between them, eyes wide. Flickers of alarm traveled up Vivian's spine. The baby kicked.

"Please tell me," Vivian said.

Agata sighed. "The nanoink used to comprise the tattoos do impart significant healing benefits to the individual. But the tattoos are one of our oldest traditions, though they've evolved with time and advancing technology. Originally, they were simply a marriage ritual, and the process of receiving them quite painful."

"Are you telling me that Tai'ri and I are married?" Of all the things she was expecting to hear, this wasn't it.

Shira's eyes widened. "Oh *shiiiiit*."

"No," Abeyya said. "Nothing so dissolvable. And not yet. Until you accept the marks and consummate the bond, your link with Tai'ri will remain tenuous."

"Though it would be difficult to remove the marks at this point," Agata said quietly.

"We call those who exchange marks matebonded," Abeyya said. "It happens when the properties in the tattoos recognize another person as being especially compatible, and not just on a genetic level though that is a good portion of it." Her nose wrinkled. "Our Inkmasters are forbidden from disclosing the process used to produce the ink or what goes into laying the tattoos after birth."

That caught Vivian's attention. "Will I be required to tattoo my baby when she's born?"

"No, nor you, Shira, though it's rare that parents these days choose to forgo it. The marks themselves, when exchanged between a pair, confer a certain amount of mental and emotional awareness. Not quite telepathy or empathy, but similar enough."

"And this is all tech?"

The Yadeshi women exchanged a glance. "The Inkmasters are sworn to secrecy."

Vivian was nonplussed. "And you all just trust that they'll . . . do the right thing?"

"It's a sacred trust," Abeyya said, a little stiffly. "There has never been an Inkmaster who subverted a bonding mark."

"They weren't originally intended for humans, though," Shira said. "They couldn't have been."

"No. The fact that they work on humans is a delightful surprise, and one of the reasons our planetary council pursued the treaty with Earth so aggressively," Agata said.

"So when I was in the hospital, Tai'ri tried to . . . bond with me."

Abeyya looked as if she was trying to choose her words carefully. "We think because of the child, and Tai'ri's distress when seeing you unwell, the marks responded. Because they can heal, they must have—"

Vivian held up a hand. "The marks are sentient? Or is that another thing your Inkmasters can't disclose?"

Silence. Then Agata said, "There are entire forums dedicated to nothing but discussion over the exact nature of the Ink."

"Except I don't have access to the datasphere. Did Tai'ri think I would be angry when I found out what he did?" Especially since it appeared they were married—no matter what Agata and Abeyya said, that was the bottom line—and without her consent. "Never mind. I'll deal with Tai'ri."

Abeyya winced. Agata smiled a little. "Be gentle. I don't believe he intended to do what he did. He simply acted in the moment."

"I understand." Vivian throttled her rare temper. She would discuss it with Tai'ri, but it wouldn't be appropriate to vent her anger to his mother and sister, who had been nothing but kind and certainly weren't at fault, for anything.

How much of her anger, and what she was angry over, she would take some time to work through before he came home for the evening. This whole time she thought they'd been working toward an understanding of perhaps forming a more long-term relationship—and the whole time he'd known they were married, the point moot. He'd let her make a fool of herself.

"When I speak to him, I'll keep his intentions in mind," she added.

21

He might have to stay away from Vivian for a few days.

Something had shifted after their last kiss. Until now, he'd been able to control his hunger, keep the fire banked. But he'd *sensed* her internal submission, even if she didn't fully realize herself that she was in love with him.

He was trained to see these things, monitor the tells. And with the aid of the fledging bond—not yet fully formed or consummated, but still present—he could filter out the truth of her feelings.

The entire day his temper had snapped, until Evvek had finally kicked him out of his own office. Tai'ri didn't blame the analyst. A male in the new throes of a bond was often difficult.

He entered the house, pausing just inside the

entrance as his attention zeroed in on the living area. She was awake.

Damn.

Tai'ri took several moments to recite a chant for peace and Silence, desperately banking the raging tides that roared back to life as soon as he realized his female was waiting for him in the dark, alone, restlessness and yearning spicing her blood.

He wasn't *Adekhan* trained for nothing. He would sit down, have a pleasant evening conversation, and retire to bed without ravishing her. Without giving in to the increasing demand that he sate himself, make her come so hard there was no doubt in her mind what his *intentions* were.

Tai'ri snorted, moving forward. She actually thought he was going to let her leave him.

Silly *yadoana*.

Vivian ordered the lights dimmed and waited for him in the living area. Normally she would be asleep this time of night, but they had things to discuss.

Access to the datasphere—though, to be fair, if she had pushed it he likely would have caved. She had to admit to cocooning herself in her own little bubble in this house, only willing to dip her toe into the greater world outside. She hadn't been ready to fully face her new reality, especially after the series of attacks. She was . . . readier now. Which meant forcing herself to pin down this relationship.

His attempts to keep the full nature of the marks away from her.

The consequences of impulsive actions. Mostly hers.

True anger was impossible, knowing he'd acted to save her and the baby's lives.

He entered the home like a ghost, footsteps silent. It was only her increasing awareness of his presence that alerted Vivian. She sat up straighter, shifting to relieve some of the pressure on her ribs—it turned out that breathing was neither simple, nor optional, while pregnant—and trained her gaze on the hallway leading from the entrance.

Tai'ri's shadow stopped. She hadn't bothered to raise the lights, and her human eyes made out his outline. Dressed all in black, a dense shadow softened only by light from the twin moons streaming through the balcony windows.

"You're still up," he said finally, moving into the room.

"I couldn't sleep." That was a neutral enough conversation starter. "It's hard to get comfortable."

Something is his posture softened, perhaps the stiffness in his broad shoulders. He moved towards the kitchen. "Bey says these last few days are the most difficult. She says some of her mothers offer bribes to help them go into labor early."

Vivian smiled ruefully. "I might have offered a bribe too, if it had occurred to me."

"Be over soon. At least this part. Something to drink?"

"Thank you."

She waited in silence as he washed his hands, then selected bottles of fruit juice and poured it into glasses. He crossed to the couch and handed her one, and settled in the couch opposite her, stretching his legs out.

Vivian sipped, frowning. Despite his even tone, his energy crackled. It occurred to her that he must have been . . . working . . . and hadn't quite transitioned back from whatever mental state that required.

"I'm sorry," she said. "I'm interrupting your decompression time." She set the glass down and began to push herself up. This was clearly not the time to start a discussion that may well become heated.

"Sit, Vivian. Finish your juice."

She stilled, startled by the unfamiliar edge in his voice, then settled back into the couch to finish her juice.

When she finished, he spoke again. "Now tell me what you wanted to talk to me about."

Well, he wasn't stupid. Not that she had ever thought he was.

"Your mother and Abeyya came for lunch today—though I suspect that was actually an informal prenatal checkup."

"How did it go?"

"They told me what the marks mean."

The air around him charged, and then settled, in a single breath. For a split second she had felt a surge of unimaginable anger, fear and then nothing. Acceptance.

"I didn't want to tell you," he said. "At least not until after the baby was born."

"You didn't have the right to make that decision for me." But her voice lacked heat, even to her own ears.

"No. But I made it. And your response?"

"To your attitude, or to the revelation?"

Tai'ri laughed. "My attitude?" He sank further into the couch, leaning his head back. Moonlight filtered over his face as he shifted his position. His eyes were closed, a small smile playing over his lips. "You've been a big, walking attitude since this all started. But now I'm going to endure whatever else you decide I deserve to handle." He sighed. "Go ahead, *yada'ami*. I can take it."

She opened her mouth, closed it. For the first time, understanding a little more what the marks meant, she reached into the rope of awareness between them and . . . felt.

Resignation, low burning anger, frustration. All emotions she was intimate with, but none of them hers at the present. Grief. Old grief, juxtaposed on new. And—

She jerked out of the bond, cheeks burning. How

could anyone walk around feeling like *that* all day and remain sane?

Tai'ri sat up, eyes snapping open. "So, they really did tell you what the marks mean."

"The discussion wasn't as detailed as I would have liked, but I imagine it's something that needs to be explored over time." Her voice remained even enough, even under the weight of his narrow-eyed gaze. "We aren't married, not the way humans understand marriage. And we aren't fully bonded the way you people understand it. I haven't—we haven't . . ." she looked away, a little annoyed at her own skittishness. "We haven't had sex. I haven't consented to the bond, whatever that entails."

"No. They tell you the marks can't be removed?"

"Yes."

Tai'ri shrugged. "We can stay in this limbo. It'd be miserable for the both of us. The marks may be shielding you from the worst of the effects because you're pregnant."

Vivian looked down, unable to meet his gaze anymore. "I just—how do we go forward from here? You're just as trapped as I am."

"Viv—I'm not trapped. Nothing has happened since I was released that I didn't want. I want you. I want this child. You saw my family? Family is what I know. Even if I wasn't prepared for it to happen the way it did."

A thought, a memory, an emotion swam under the

surface of his words and was yanked back, shut into a black box. She thought of the old grief flavoring his emotions and knew they would have to discuss it. Soon.

"I'd intended to rip you a new one," she murmured. "Somehow it's easier to be angry with you when you aren't present. You're always so . . . kind and rational. Anger is hard."

"Be angry." He settled back into the couch, locking his hands behind his head and gave her a crooked smile. "Yell and curse and hit if that's what you need."

"I doubt that would be either comfortable or healthy, especially for this baby. They don't need to hear all of that."

He tilted his head. "It *is* just a single baby?"

"Oh! No. I just can't call them 'it'." And they were digressing. She narrowed her eyes. "I'm realizing you're an expert on steering a conversation where you want it to go."

His eyes glinted, and he leaned forward, resting his elbows on his knees and clasping his hands. "I am a super-secret master spy, Viv."

She tried to smile. "I know. What happened to me could have been so much worse, I tell myself that."

"Vivian."

"Some of the other women, I know they didn't fare as well." She stopped, picked up her glass to wet her lips with the last drop of liquid. "My child's father is wealthy, well connected, kind and intelligent. They'll have a big, supportive family. I'm lucky."

"You were kidnapped, raped, and impregnated." His voice was steely. "You are not lucky. You don't have to accept what happened to you, or brush it aside."

Her hands curled around the glass. "I agree with you. I've asked myself, how do I go on? How can I have a normal life? Those months in the pens—" she inhaled, forced her hitched breathing to smooth out. The yawning cavern of panic in her mind threatened. The familiar warmth came to her rescue as usual, an insulating blanket.

Only now she had a name for that blanket. Tai'ri. Had he been manipulating her emotions all along? Softening the stress and trauma of her memories?

Yes. He had. But intent counted for something, and she wouldn't throw that away in a fit of anxiety.

"I'm a coward," she said softly. "My whole life I wanted to make a difference, to buck the system. And the one time I did—or thought I did—I wound up kidnapped. And it wasn't even real work for change. We'd meet in an attic on Fridays and discuss our grievances against the government. We talked, but we didn't do."

Tai'ri shook his head. "That kind of change takes decades, centuries. Overthrowing a government is only a flash of blood and brilliance in vids."

She shrugged. "Which makes me sound even more stupid."

"You aren't stupid." He frowned at her. "What you

strike me as is a female who was raised to be productive and obedient and work within the system. You have a streak of creativity, of independence that clashes with your upbringing and you had begun to explore how to reconcile both sides of your nature. The timing was . . . poor. But getting kidnapped wasn't your fault. What happened to you wasn't your fault. Not being thrilled with the results, even if you know our baby isn't to blame, isn't your fault."

"No, the past isn't my fault. But choosing to become bitter and dwell in it is my fault."

He was silent for a long moment. "There's a healing process. And grief never goes away completely, it only mutes."

Seeing the haunted look in his eyes, she was tempted to ask what shape his old grief took, but wasn't quite brave enough to open what she suspected was an old wound. Not that she feared he would harm her—but she didn't want to lose the steady rock of his presence.

A rock she had come to depend on. Once again, she admitted to herself that she hadn't been treating him very well. If she couldn't quite accept him as a lover, yet, she could at least stop treating him like a potential enemy.

"I'm sorry, Tai'ri," she said softly.

"What for?"

She shook her head. "I need to be a stronger

person. Not just for myself, but for this baby. For the family you've offered me."

He stood, then came to crouch at her feet. "You have a family. We aren't replacing yours. And you'll see them again, I promise. And, Viv? You're probably the strongest person I know."

Tai'ri took her hands in his, his fingers caressing the insides of her wrists. She looked into intent blue eyes, and blue was such a paltry word to describe their color and did nothing to frame the expression they held. Had a man ever looked at her like this? Never.

A blush warmed her cheeks and Tai'ri smiled, the curve of his lip drifting upward. His hand slid around the back of her neck, applying gentle pressure.

"You're distracting me," she said.

His smile widened. "There are other distractions I can offer, Viv."

22

Throat suddenly dry, heart thumping, she licked her bottom lip. His eyes flickered downward, watching the inadvertent movement, and the smile hardened into something like a snarl. He closed his eyes, smoothing his expression.

Another ripple in their . . . bond. A feeling of iron clamps wrapping around the growing heat. Was that him, suppressing his sexuality?

"Are you okay?" she asked, feeling foolish as soon as she spoke.

Tai'ri opened his eyes again and her breath caught. His blue irises *burned*. She wasn't frightened, he would never hurt her—but as soon as she gave a single word of encouragement, the smallest physical tell, he would sweep her down a path from which there was no return. And if she wasn't one thousand percent certain, she couldn't allow them to take that road.

But . . . her lips ached. Just a touch, a caress. Surely she could taste the fruit without being dragged to the underworld?

"Vivian, if you don't want me to touch you, you'd better stop looking at me like that."

The growled words didn't deter her growing certainty. "Like what?"

"Like blue is your new favorite color."

Vivian laughed softly. How corny. But it was deliberately corny, he was trying to lighten the sudden surge of heat between them. Tai'ri began to ease away.

"No," she said without thinking, reaching for his fingers as they slipped away from her wrist.

He froze.

"I'm not ready for *everything* yet, but I want—" was she being unfair to him? Selfish?

Tai'ri tucked a strand of her hair behind her ear with his free hand. It struck her, that this man, this warrior, allowed her to imprison him when he could so easily break free from her hold. Her fingers around his wrist were welcome manacles.

"You have to say it, Viv. Tell me what you want, no matter how much or how little."

"But what about you?"

He arched an eyebrow. "What about me?"

"It isn't fair."

He narrowed his eyes. "If you were any other person saying that vakshit, I'd be upset. That's not how this works. What's fair is that we take this relationship at your pace." His expression gentled. "I keep telling you I can do slow, Viv. Trust in me."

"I do." Speaking the words out loud, the truth of them rang in the air. Internally, a sense of rightness tightened between them, and again she *felt* his satisfaction. His yearning and hunger.

Leaning forward, she rested her hands on his shoulders and brushed her lips against his, uncertainty vanquished by his permission to explore as much as she wanted—and then back away when she had gone as far as she could.

He exhaled, his breath warm on her skin, and his hands rose to settle on her waist. Such as it was.

"This will kill me," he muttered. "But it's the best way to die."

Tai'ri took her mouth in a kiss, straightening from his crouch. He drew her up with him, slowly, until they were standing. She shifted to accommodate their child and wound up with her back to his chest, partially cradled in his hold.

Her cells fired, her already tender breasts protesting. Her body tensed inadvertently, a fine tremble running through her limbs. There was a faint taste of mint on his tongue, and his hands ran up and down her arms, restless but soothing.

"Bedroom," he murmured.

She nodded. It would be more comfortable, though she wasn't sure what they could *do* with her unwieldy body. Though it wasn't like pregnant women didn't have sex or make out, so she supposed they'd figure it out.

"You're thinking really loudly," he said as they walked down the hallway.

"I do that," she whispered, struck again by nerves as they entered her bedroom. His choice surprised her, she'd have thought he'd take her to his room. But then it made sense—he would want her to feel in control, comfortable.

Tai'ri gently urged her towards the bed, pausing to kick off his boots. She almost grimaced, because outdoor clothes on her clean sheets, but she'd discuss bed etiquette some other time.

"Take your shirt off," he said. "Lie down on your side." He began to prowl the room restlessly.

Vivian stilled, heart rate jackknifing. After a moment she slipped out of her blouse, revealing her rounded belly with the faint lines of stretch marks, and her swollen breasts cupped in a plain white bra.

He stopped in front of her and settled a hand on the top of her uterus, feather light. The baby chose that moment to shift, and he made a noise.

The emotion in that noise struck her. She glanced up at his expression. His eyes were shut tight, a look of almost pain crossing his face.

"Tai'ri?"

He opened his eyes. "I never thought I'd feel this."

Something was there, a feeling she was able to

sense. An old anguish in his voice. "Tai'ri?" This time his name was partial question, partial demand.

"When I was young, I was in a relationship," he murmured. "It wasn't happy, but I tried. She became pregnant."

Vivian inhaled, surprised. She knew he didn't have any children, so what . . . ?

"She miscarried. I held the baby for a few moments. She fit in the palm of my hand."

"Oh, Tai'ri, I'm so sorry."

He met her gaze. "You don't know how much this child means to me, Viv."

"This baby isn't your lost little one." She spoke as gently as possible. He couldn't use this child as a way to heal old grief.

"I know, *yada'ami*." He kissed the top of her head. "But it *is* my child. A new chance."

Tai'ri nudged her toward the bed and she climbed awkwardly on top, settling on her side. "Now what?"

"Now I give you a massage," he said, lips on her shoulder. "I know you're tired."

"But—"

"Quiet, female. Let me take care of you."

He already did, in so many ways. Vivian bit back a moan when strong fingers dug into her back and spine with expert pressure. He worked the worst of the tension from her muscles, neck and shoulders as well. Her entire body relaxed and her eyes drifted shut as she wallowed in the feel of his hands on her skin.

"This has got to be better than sex," she said.

He snorted. "You don't set the bar high. That makes my job easier."

Another kiss on her shoulder, and she felt her bra give way, the strap pulled down as his weight settled on the bed behind her.

"Yes?" His hand inching towards her breast. She nodded, and he cupped her flesh gently, massaging that as well. Her pleasant glow evaporated, her entire body tensing as he plucked at her nipple, teeth nipping her earlobe.

She shivered, tingling all over. "Tai'ri."

"I know, *yada'ami*. How about this?"

Vivian's breath came faster as his hand left her breast, sweeping down her body, under her uterus. She wore loose bottoms with a simple waistband, and his fingers slipped beneath, finding the curls between her thighs.

"Here," he said, and moved slightly, grabbing a pillow and placing it between her knees.

Then his fingers found her clit, delving between her folds and fondling the bud as her hips involuntarily bucked. Yadeshi women must have similar anatomy, because he touched her as if he knew what he was doing.

Vivian moaned as he played her body, stoking a fire deep inside that her body clamored to have quenched.

"Let go, *yada'ami*," he said, voice a deep growl. "You don't know how sexy you sound."

She must, since his hardness pressed against her backside. But there was none of the grinding she might have expected; tension ran through his body, his control exquisite. She grabbed his wrist as her orgasm rose, crested, wanting him inside her body. Her already strained muscles clenched, but she didn't care.

"More?" he asked. "You have to tell me. Tell me what you want me to do to you."

Heat bloomed in her cheeks, complimenting the heat in her core. "*Tai'ri.*"

He chuckled. "That's my name. I want to hear you say it. Torment me."

If the strain in his voice was any indication, he was already being tormented. She felt bad, but he was an adult and knew how to handle his sexuality. If he said he could wait, then he could wait.

Were Yadeshi men the same as human men? Recalling some of the explicit vids that had come out when the YETI bases were first built—which she had watched as a very guilty pleasure—Vivian's blush deepened. She knew her skin hid most of the color, but still.

"What if the baby hears?" As soon as she said it, she knew it was ridiculous, and sighed, closing her eyes tightly. "Never mind, that wasn't rational."

But he stopped for a moment, then cleared his throat. "They actually can hear, you know. Uhh. . .oh, fuck. Forget the dirty talk. We'll save that for later. So I'll be able to look my own baby in the eye."

Vivian couldn't help herself; she laughed. "Now

that is definitely not rational." But so adorable. If there was any part of her that wasn't already enamored with this man, those parts were rapidly disappearing. "But maybe I can show you."

Her hand still on his wrist, she directed him down. "Here." She didn't recognize the husky, subtle demand in her voice. "If you please."

"I *do* please." Amusement, need, and some indefinable emotion tangled in his voice.

As his fingers slipped inside her body, Vivian stopped trying to figure him out and just felt.

"Do you want to know how you feel?" he asked. "Tight. Wet." She clenched around him, his words an aphrodisiac. "That's right. I feel you. Your body wants to come. I'm going to get you there. Again. And again."

So evidently he'd figured out child friendly dirty talk—which could be a useful skill down the road. Vivian's chest moved in silent laughter, but laughing and orgasming around his fingers as he plunged in and out of her body was too much.

She cried out, her nails digging into his wrist. He murmured into her ear words she barely heard, but his dark, heated tone said everything.

Languor suffused her limbs, and it was some time later she realized she'd drifted in a half daze. At some point he'd dimmed the lights even further, the rise and fall of his chest at her back soothing.

His groin still pressed against her backside, though. Vivian licked her lips. "I—thank you. That was very nice." Her cheeks renewed their burn. What was the proper after foreplay etiquette? She sounded like she was thanking him for dropping off a casserole.

Lips brushed her cheek, and she felt the warmth of his silent amusement. "What about you? You—I can—"

"Go to sleep, Vivian."

"But—"

"*Yada'ami*, you can barely keep your eyes open." He sounded, strangely enough, satisfied.

"So, what, that was a hot toddy or something?"

"I love when you snap at me. Now go to sleep."

She wasn't going to keep arguing with him, especially when he was right. The exhaustion she'd been pushing aside rushed forward to claim her, and she gave in, letting her mind drift away as his hand settled lightly on her belly, his warmth a cocoon of safety. Of acceptance. Of . . . love.

But she had one question before she slept. "These marks . . . they do way more than what you're telling me, don't they?"

"We'll talk about it soon."

23

"I really don't like surprises," Vivian fretted, walking laboriously at his side.

He reminded himself to check his natural stride; he'd teased her that she moved slower than an earth turtle. The half amused, half disgruntled look she'd given him was delightful; she hadn't said he was wrong, though. Tai'ri made a mental note to tell Vykhan he'd been right—he'd needed this time off work to spend with Viv.

"You'll like this surprise," he assured her. "You're female. Why wouldn't you?"

They crossed a gleaming multi-colored stone tile plaza into a triangular building that appeared made of translucent sheets of glass, the interior a steamy jungle forest.

Vivian balked as they came closer. A large, purple, furry animal reared up on two hind legs and opened its mouth in a yowl behind glass. "I am absolutely not going in there."

Tai'ri tucked his tongue in his cheek. "You think I'd let anything eat you? Though I'm sure you taste amazing."

"You are not amusing."

"You trust me?" He took her hand, satisfaction that she didn't pull away warm in his gut. In the transport she had fallen asleep on his shoulder, rousing only when he nudged her awake. Her trust was an honor, and a weight. She'd slept, heavy with child, confident he would guard her. Which he would, with his life.

The shimmering doors parted as they entered, revealing a bustling shopping center. She sighed, rubbing the side of her belly. "I should have known."

Tai'ri solemnly refrained from laughing at her.

"I can't believe how advanced your holo tech is on Yedahn," she said. "I thought the jungle was real."

"It would be a feat to maintain a miniature habitat complete with large predators in the middle of a bustling city."

"Is that a convoluted way of calling me gullible?"

"Course not." He squeezed her hand in retaliation. "I enjoy teasing you, but I would never insult you."

"So where are we going? Baby shopping?"

Her voice lacked resistance for once, and he almost changed his plans then and there to take advantage. "We can, but I've booked us into a spa for couples.

They specialize in late stage prenatal massages. They have human chocolates on the menu."

"You fight dirty."

Tai'ri allowed his smug silence to speak for him.

Vivian looked around as they were escorted into a circular private room done in shades of grey, blue, and white stones. A skylight allowed the midday brilliance to set shimmering crystals embedded in the stones afire. Living plants circled the room in tiers. Refreshments were arranged on a ledge; sparkling waters and juices, sliced fruits and different flavored ices, some creamy.

Tai'ri helped her sit on a low divan. They'd changed into plush white robes before entering, hers with an extra swath of fabric to accommodate her belly. The fabric felt like clouds against her skin.

"I've never done a couple's spa day before," Vivian murmured.

"Never?" He gave her a sidelong look, eyes glinting. "You could have one every day, all you have to do is beckon, Viv."

As if she would. "We aren't really—"

"Are you going to say that after last night? I'm your child's father, and soon to be your lover. Caring for you is my right and my duty."

He caressed her cheek, the tips of his fingers featherlight as always, eliciting a shiver of feeling down her aching spine. Exhaustion trumped most other emotions or sensations these days, and a constant low thrum of discomfort, but his touches always reminded her that there was more.

Once the baby was born, how would things be different?

"I don't want to be a duty," she said. "But I take your meaning."

Tai'ri slid an arm around her and she leaned against his shoulder. Their arms touched and his marks uncoiled. Hers began to glimmer in turn, splitting and moving restlessly on her skin.

"Why do they do that?" she asked.

Tai'ri lifted her braid, toying with the end. She'd taken to confining her long dark hair into a tail for simplicity's sake.

"Part of the preliminary bonding," he said. "They're syncing."

"I need to learn more about your culture and these marks."

He glanced at the refreshments. "Are you thirsty? Hungry?"

She lifted her head and gave him an even stare. "Why yes, for knowledge."

"Females armed with knowledge are dangerous," he muttered.

"Why are you stalling? You know I'm going to have to learn about everything they entail eventually."

Tai'ri smiled. "Maybe I just don't want you to know yet exactly how deep I am in your thrall."

But she felt there was something else he was keeping from her, something about—ah. "Tai'ri—are we fully, officially bonded? I thought we had to . . . consummate the bond before it was complete."

His voice deepened. "We do."

"Out of curiosity, what happens if we don't? Will the marks go away?"

He narrowed his eyes, straightening slowly from his relaxed slouch, and began to answer when a male entered, dressed in a sleek jumpsuit that managed to look stylish even thought it was a uniform.

"I'm Kaidell," he said, gaze stuck on Vivian as his eyes widened. "I'm ecstatic to serve you today."

Vivian shifted, a little uncomfortable by his regard. Other than Tai'ri and Vykhan, she hadn't interacted with any men since her time in the pens. Her breathing quickened, but she forced herself to remain calm, trying to mitigate the unexpected stress response.

"I requested a female," Tai'ri said softly.

The masseuse bowed. "Our apologies. There was a scheduling conflict this morning and because of our cancellation policy . . . ."

"I should have been informed. Vivian?" His arm rose to her shoulders, fingers tightening around her upper arm almost possessively.

Vivian didn't speak at first, waiting until she was certain her voice would sound normal. "I'm sorry,

Tai'ri. I don't think—would a cancellation be too much trouble?"

"I completed a tutorial in human physiology this morning," the masseuse said earnestly. "There are few structural differences between Yadeshi females and Earth females. I assure you—"

Tai'ri cut him off. "I'm certain you're well qualified. But I requested a female, or if none is available, we'll use the room until our time is up."

The male's eyes widened. Vivian's panic receded a bit as she watched a violet stain on his cheeks. "Well, our facility isn't licensed for services beyond those listed on our menu."

"We'll simply relax and enjoy the refreshments," Tai'ri said, voice dry.

Vivian blinked. "Oh. He thinks—" she shut her mouth, amused as well as embarrassed. "I see."

"We happen to have a whirlpool available right now," the masseuse said. "Might I offer that as an alternative?"

"A whirlpool?" She glanced at Tai'ri. "We did have an impromptu massage last night—" she stopped, blushed, then gathered her composure. "I wouldn't mind floating around in a pool."

Tai'ri gave her a vulpine smile; slight, charming, and utterly male. "Whatever *yada'ami* wants."

"Then it's settled," the masseuse said brightly. "This way. No bathing suits are required."

"I was, in fact, counting on that," Tai'ri said.

The pool was set into the floor, the tiles a warm, textured stone. The skylight continued into this room as well, sun rays bouncing off more strategically placed crystals. Birds chirped, and a gentle breeze scented with sand and sea wafted through the air. The masseuse excused himself after giving them a tour of the discreet wall panel with options to program temperature, scents, sound and water pressure.

She fled to one of the discreet stalls for a quick solar shower, then changed out of the fluffy robe into a silky summer one. Walking to the edge of the pool, she dipped her big toe in, then looked around. Tai'ri wasn't back yet, and the clear water offered little in way of coverage. She couldn't enter the pool in the robe; that would only betray the depth of her nervousness and make her look silly.

Taking a deep breath, she allowed the fabric to drop down to the ground and stepped forward.

"Let me help you."

She jumped, startled, but Tai'ri's hands on her shoulders kept her steady. "You don't make *any* noise."

"Bare feet." His voice was warm with amusement, and something else. "Stone floors."

His hands moved down her arms, a deceptively innocent caress. Except that she was naked, and he was naked . . . and doing absolutely nothing to hide the hardness of his body pressing against her.

Then he moved, stepping in front of her so she had a view of sleek muscles, smooth skin, taut buttocks.

"Oh . . . dear," she said.

Tai'ri faced her, and Vivian hastily looked up, keeping her gaze firmly on his face. He smirked, eyes glinting as he stepped backwards down the pool stairs, then held out his hands.

"I'd ask if you like what you see, but you're only looking at my face."

"With good reason." She slid her hands into his, and he assisted her down the stairs. Water of a perfect ambient temperature lapped over her thighs, then her belly and up to her chest as she descended.

"You don't have to be so shy with me, Vivian. My body is yours. Look your fill."

She shivered, the crooning dark rumble of his voice pebbling her nipples, sending sparks of lightning shooting off in her core. Her inner muscles clenched, and she worked to loosen the tight muscles of her jaw. She was *supposed* to be *relaxing*.

"It's a little hard for me," she said. "I've never been extroverted, despite being a teacher. And I haven't . . ."

"Have you had a lover, Vivian?" he asked gently.

She waded towards a bench, one hand still clasped in his, and sat, using the time to regather her maturity. She was an adult, damnit.

"No, though I'm not a virgin, either."

He stepped close to her, his hands settling on her waist. It wasn't the most modest position, considering his height. She tilted her head back on the ledge, closing her eyes.

"Coward," he murmured.

Vivian sniffed.

"But you were telling me why you're so shy with me. You're not a virgin, but . . . ?"

"I've only had two short term dating relationships, and I wouldn't give either of them the label of lover."

He winced. "That bad?"

"They weren't entirely satisfactory." She frowned, eyes still closed.

"Of course not. *I* am your mate. I will satisfy you." His hands drifted up, up, cupped her breasts and squeezed gently.

Her breath caught, and he played with her nipples, tugging and stroking until her hips began to squirm on the bench. She licked her lips, and heard his low grunt.

Vivian opened her eyes and made herself look. Do more than look. Reaching out, she wrapped a hand around the thick, heavy erection waiting so patiently for her notice.

Breath whistled through Tai'ri's teeth, and he said an indelicate word.

"Do you want me to stop?" she asked, fingers exploring. He felt like life, the warm, satiny steel of his erection pulsing under her touch. Nothing inhuman, so to speak, about his penis. Despite the blessed size, it was humanoid enough. But then, Earth women had been assured of that years ago.

"Only if you want to," he said through gritted teeth.

"I'm beginning to want more than I thought I would," she murmured. "You make it difficult to resist you."

"Good. Goddess damnit." He blew out a heavy breath, then squeezed his eyes tight. The tendons of his neck stood out in harsh relief as she worked her hand up and down his shaft, faster and faster. "No, don't stop."

"Good. Because I owe you for last night."

Tai'ri stilled, then suddenly his hand was around her wrist, not painful, but tight enough she couldn't move. His eyes flashed, an edge of danger she'd never seen in his gaze when he looked at her.

"You owe me?" he asked, and some instinct warned her to choose her words carefully.

"I don't mean like *that*. But there's no such thing as any long-term healthy relationship where there's no reciprocity. And I may be shy, but I can admit I like touching you."

He was silent for a long moment, eyes narrowed on her face. She waited patiently, then slowly, he released her wrist.

"You know I would never—" he stopped, as if he couldn't even say the words. "I would never—"

"I know, Tai'ri," she said, voice very gentle, reminding herself that they *both* had wounds.

She increased the speed and pressure of her

caresses, a deep feminine satisfaction settling into her at the sight of his tense shoulders and utter abandon when he finally came. Almost helpless under her touch as he slumped forward, bracing his hands on either side of the ledge.

"Vivian," he said, then lowered his head and took her mouth. Dominant, nearly savage, his tongue shoving between her lips. A hand wrapped around her neck, holding her still as her lips opened under his.

Vivian gave herself up to the kiss, gave herself up to the pleasure when his fingers found her clit, rubbing and flicking with incredible speed. Her hips bucked, and she grabbed his biceps, tearing her mouth away so she could gulp in lungfuls of air.

Fingers slipped into her sheath as he worked her bud, one hand pumping in and out, fingers hooked inside her as he adjusted the angle and pressure according to her cries.

"That's right, *yada'ami*," he growled. "Come for me."

The tremor began in her core and spread to her toes, overtaking her in a rush of pleasure. Her spine arched, the sides of her uterus sore from the sudden spasms. She screamed, and he kept rubbing and fucking her until she slumped, pushing his hands away.

"Stop, stop, that's enough," she cried. "You're going to kill me." But she laughed, a deep, throaty release of energy. "Oh my god. I didn't know a man could do that with just his fingers."

He pressed a kiss on the corner of her mouth. "I am not a man. I am a Yadeshi warrior. And I am yours." His voice lowered to a whisper. "And just so there is no mistake—there is more than one method of *consummation*. *Enja*. You are mine."

24

"Clever bastards," Evvek muttered, then sat back in his seat. "So look, this is what happened."

"Give me the short version," Tai'ri said.

After a blissful day and then evening spent with Vivian, he'd come into base this morning only to learn that the tracker he'd planted on Zhiannur had gone dark after the Aeddannur finally landed planetside and disappeared into the city.

He happened to be in the area, so why not check in?

"The short version is that the *V'dahn* needs to upgrade the city's infrastructure. Our quarry disappeared into a black hole between signals. I looked up telecom records and residents have been complaining for years, until they just started moving out. It's a dead zone."

"He went into Sector 7."

Evvek grimaced, then kicked the leg of his desk. "Yeah. I've been saying for years that ignoring that sector would bite us in the ass. Lack of resources, blah blah, not a priority, blah fucking blah, slated for future rehabilitation, my ass. But they have to have some kind of signal to get data in and out. Probably hardwire. I just have to find it, track it to the hotspots and then we've got our guy."

"But as soon as he comes out, you'll have him again anyway."

"If he doesn't find the tracker, yeah."

"How long will it take you to find that hard wire?"

Evvek gave him a baleful look. "You aren't supposed to be involved."

"How long did you all expect that to last?" he demanded.

Eveek stabbed a finger at him. "You clear it with Vykhan."

"Fine, just get the op set up." It took ten minutes of fast talking and ignoring Vykhan's icy stare before the *Adekhan* relented.

"Just gather intelligence," Vykhan said finally. "The *Bdakhun* wants you to remain alive for the birth of your child."

Ah ha. The *real* reason he'd been pulled off duty. A female's tender heart.

Evvek had been listening to the conversation. "Take your team out on standby, and try not to trip over my people. It won't be that long."

Tai'ri made eye contact with Ebwenna and Dayan and jerked his head. The next phase of the hunt would yield prey.

Slum wasn't quite an accurate description of Sector 7; more like a ghost town. Evvek was right. Ignoring this sector had been a mistake, even though the reasons for doing so were sound. The traffickers' playbook for years had been to bury their pods near transportation hubs close to medical facilities, the datasphere and physical traffic disguising their movements. Tai'ri had explored Sector 7 years ago and after the third fruitless search, decided to monitor but otherwise turn Ibukay's strapped resources elsewhere.

That was on Tai'ri. Should have kept a better eye on it; intelligence gathering was his job. Vykhan was their heavy artillery and their strategist, but infiltration and data were on Tai'ri. He'd have to do better.

"Diabolical," Evvek muttered, after reporting that his people found the hardwires and tapped in manually, rigging a signal. "They're using short ranged frequencies older than my great-grandmother. They'll have security, sir, but the perimeter will be limited."

"Sentries."

"As usual, look up. And listen for unusual birdsong."

"Funny."

Tai'ri, Ebwenna, and Dayan blended into the foot traffic, scarce as it was. People lived here, those who rejected the various programs set up to assist struggling persons with employment. Many who no longer qualified for any program or chose to support themselves outside the accepted social norms.

Petty criminals, addicts, unregistered aliens. The occasional hard eyed youngling—though they tended to stay away when Tai'ri and his team came through. Despite his chameleon like abilities, the children quite often saw through whatever disguise he wore to the government official beneath. Their mothers fled to these black holes in the city in order to keep their children when otherwise agencies would have taken over.

Evvek murmured directions in their earpieces. They wore loose, dark, utilitarian clothing and light jackets with hoods to shadow their faces. The hoods were lined with tech to disrupt remote audio/visual surveillance so neither their images or conversation could be recorded. When they closed in on their quarry, they'd activate cloaks to make them 'invisible.' Eb and Day had their nano suits on under their clothing, but Tai'ri's was still regenerating from the last use. He'd been requisitioning a backup for years, but the budget didn't stretch and he was good enough at his job that Accounting justified the denials by saying a backup had never been needed. One of these days Ibukay wouldn't have to run her teams on a pauper's budget.

"Alright, you're nearing the hot spot," Evvek said finally. "Zoning maps of this block are twenty years old. Don't expect anything to be up to date. We haven't even had an aerial scan in thirty years."

"Who appointed the city chancellor?" Ebwenna muttered. "She has one purpose. I hate when bureaucrats don't do their damn jobs."

Yeah, he'd be having words with the Chancellor, but his own chagrin prevented him from replying. He'd made a classic mistake, allowing the enemy to lull him with their apparent pedantic routines. How many of the pens they'd raided over the years had been feints?

Damnit.

They slipped into an alley a block from a two-story walk-up, a residential building made of actual gray bricks, a flight of wooden stairs leading up to a manual double door.

Ebwenna stared. "Haeemah's Mercy. Are those things even functional?"

"You can go first," Dayan said with a grin. "I'll carry you to a medcenter if it collapses under you."

"This building is ancient. Weren't all the graystones supposed to have been torn down a hundred years ago?"

"Get this," Evvek said. "This whole sector was originally earmarked by the city historical society. They wanted it preserved for posterity. But then shit happened."

"Not much posterity," Dayan said, looking around with a doubtful expression.

"Entrances?" Tai'ri asked.

"Front and back, fire escapes on both floors. Metal ladders if they haven't rusted off. I've got these vintage photographs, nothing—"

"Up to date. Right," Tai'ri said. "Activate cloaking. We'll go around back. This is a scouting mission only. Do not engage."

Their camouflage snapped into place. They'd appear to be nothing more than another bit of old building, crumbling concrete sidewalk or whatever piece of the landscape the tech latched onto.

They walked briskly toward the building, skirting the front. The space between the graystones was narrow, and they entered a small courtyard with a decoratively dilapidated fence.

Tai'ri kept his eyes peeled because of that fence; attacks always came from above. And despite the apparent wear, the beams stood straight, the wood solid with no gaps between slats. On either side the neighboring graystones sat dark, windows busted out. Perfect for a sniper.

"You're almost within range," Evvek said. "Body count coming up in three, two . . ." He counted down then went silent as the trio entered the perimeter of the rigged security field. "I've got a satellite in place. Scanning the building now."

They moved toward the back entrance. An old-fashioned padlock guarded a rusted latch. "Oh, nice," Ebwenna whispered. "I can practice my lockpicking."

"You took Medieval Covert Ops too, huh?" Dayan said.

"You know *Adekhyun* Numair insists on a classical education."

"Is the chatter necessary?" Tai'ri asked. They spoke in voices pitched low enough not to carry, but still. "Ebwenna."

She nodded and moved forward ahead of them, crouching in front of the padlock. "It's rusty enough I could probably just sneeze on it."

Tai'ri kept his gaze trained on the nearby buildings. The lock broke open with a clang and they all froze. Ebwenna's hand rested lightly on the latch and she eased it open, pushing the door open a millimeter, then waiting for instruction.

No one jumped out of the neighboring buildings, though, and the sound of scattered foot traffic continued as usual in front.

"Oh, fuck," Evvek said. "The basement is hot, sir. I'm counting twenty warm bodies packed in two rooms. Three moving around in hallways, two sitting."

Tai'ri's shoulders tensed. "It's a pen."

"Sir, you need backup." Evvek's voice was shorn of its usual banter. "You're not made, there's time to—"

An alarm blared. "Too late."

"Sir—"

"They know we're here." If they retreated now, the people in the basement would disappear. "Let's go."

They were trained, and experienced. Ebwenna stood, stealth a fond wish, and kicked the door open as they all drew weapons. "That's always satisfying."

Tai'ri entered first.

"I can't wait till I can have a real drink again," Shira said, staring mournfully into the glass of protein smoothie.

"A glass of wine would be nice," Vivian acknowledged. They sat on the deck in chairs that cradled their backs and allowed them to put their feet up. "Though I'm not sure about—"

Sudden, searing pain. The glass slipped from Vivian's fingers as she half doubled over, gasping, the pink liquid spilling onto the deck.

"Viv!" Shira exclaimed. "Is it the baby?"

She couldn't breathe, it was as if a giant weight pressed down on her chest. Every muscle in her body seized, and when she inhaled her lungs burned. It felt like she was trapped in a burning building. It felt like—

"Tai'ri!" she gasped.

Vaguely she was aware of a sharp voice, then a mask slammed over her mouth and nostrils. Fresh, cool air infiltrated her lungs and moments later the pain and fire receded. But not the certainty. She pushed the mask aside, swinging her feet cumbersomely to the ground and struggling to get up.

Banujani pressed her back down. "I called Abeyya, Vivian. Stay still."

"It's not me, it's Tai'ri!" She realized the skin on her arms was crawling, fire ants marching in whorls. She glanced down, and the marks writhed, edged in angry light.

Banujani stood and strode to the edge of the deck, speaking in a low voice. Vivian took the chance and stood, knees unsteady, but clung to the chair until she felt solid on her feet.

"Is he hurt?" Shira asked softly. "I've been reading up on the marks. They can help you sense when your mate is in trouble."

Vivian swallowed and took a deep breath. "I know."

Banujani turned, the expression on her face carefully neutral. But her eyes were angry. "We know his last location. They're sending help."

"It won't be enough." With every fiber of her being she knew that. "I . . . what I felt. As good as your medtech is, it won't be enough."

Banujani was silent, weighing Vivian's words. "Right. All we can do is wait."

The guard continued to pace the deck, occasionally speaking in a low murmur, face hard and expressionless. Shira and Vivian watched her, Shira's brow furrowed as she glanced occasionally at Vivian.

But as they waited, the wrongness increased. Vivian's marks crawled, then suddenly slowed, settling back into stillness. A pit formed in the bottom of her stomach.

"Banujani, something is really really wrong," Vivian said. She ached with the need to do something, but she wasn't quite sure *what*. It snapped into place. "I need to go to him."

Her guard shook her head. "Out of the question."

"Tell me he's fine, then. Ask your people."

"I'm getting updates." Banujani came and crouched in front of Vivian. "I know waiting is hard. But they sent a backup team with a medic and as soon as we know—"

"It will be too late!" She grabbed Banujani's hands. "I don't know how this works, but I'm telling you that if I don't get to Tai'ri, he's—" she faltered.

The woman sighed, stood, and walked away, the cadence of her voice harsher, faster as she spoke. Vivian watched her closely, spotting the moment Banujani stilled. Went utterly quiet, then turned and pinned Vivian with a look.

"I'm going to ask you something," Banujani said. "And it will probably piss everyone else off, but you deserve to make the choice."

Vivian's fingers clenched the chair. "Banujani."

"Tai'ri is injured, bad. They're stabilizing him, but the op went sideways. There's tech built into the marks that can help speed healing. But it'll leach energy from you, and no one knows how it would affect your pregnancy. No one else will tell you this, but I will. You can help him, but there might be a cost."

She didn't even think. It wasn't a matter of choosing Tai'ri over their baby, it was a matter of faith. "Let's go."

"You fly like a madwoman!" Vivian yelled, and she never raised her voice. "Take this thing off manual!"

"I can fly better than a machine any day," Banujani snapped. "Do you want to get there in time or not?"

Vivian ground her teeth and checked her safety harness for the fifth time, then gave up and closed her eyes. When they landed on a rooftop skyscraper, she released the harness with shaking fingers and exited the flier.

"I called ahead for a scooter for you," Banujani said. "You can't walk fast."

The scooter was a flat round disk with a tall stick for her to hold on to. Banujani gave her a thirty second crash course on the voice commands and then they were off, Banujani at a dead run with Vivian flying through the air beside her.

"Why don't I have one of these?" Vivian muttered, thankful for the momentary mental distraction.

"Abeyya wants you to walk," Banujani said, not even out of breath.

People dived out of their way, though the hallway was wide enough once they left the rooftop and entered the skywalk leading into the facility. Inside the facility they slowed enough to get through security, Banujani impatient at every retinal checkpoint as they were scanned into secure levels.

The scent hit Vivian, and the bright, clean light. The sense of controlled urgency and low tones of staff who went from room to room.

"So . . . this part is going to be tricky," Banujani said.

They entered a small room and two people immediately looked up. One of them was the petite woman Vivian had seen shadowing her. But now the cheerful prettiness of her face had hardened into something cold, focused.

"Banujani." Her voice was flat. "She shouldn't be here."

"You don't even know why we're here, Eb," Banujani countered.

The man next to Eb shook his head. "We can guess, lovey. There's only one reason why you'd bring her here against explicit orders to keep her on lockdown."

"Tai'ri is dying," Vivian said, certainly settling into her chest as she spoke. "I can help him."

"Tell us the truth," Banujani said. "How is he?"

The pair exchanged grim looks. "We took fire, but we cleared the building," Eb said. "He went in for a final sweep while we were getting everyone to safety. The explosives must have been on a delayed timer, or someone from a remote location set them off, but there was an explosion, and half the building fell on him. They also flooded the place."

Banujani grimaced. "So broken bones, burns, poison gas, the works. A tube can't handle all of that at once. The nanos in his marks would have burned out already keeping him alive."

"I know what you're suggesting," Eb said. "But we don't know how a human attempting to split the marks would affect her. And she's pregnant."

"I have to try," Vivian said. Throat dry, heart racing, she stepped forward. "Please help me. If he dies —he's all I have here. All *we* have." And she couldn't, *couldn't* imagine the coming months and years without him. "He saved me. Let me save him. Please."

The man sighed. "We'll have to find a *kheter* ruthless enough to open the tube and let a pregnant human bondmate attempt to split the marks."

"Then let's find one," Banujani said. "That should be easy enough around here."

25

"I remember you," the *kheter* said, eyeing Vivian. "Interesting."

She wasn't anything like the first woman who had treated Vivian; medium height, round, her expression skeptical rather than cold and her hair in a messy bun on top of her head as if she didn't have time to be bothered with it. She glanced at Banujani.

"*Bdakhun* Ibukay would have my head, then my career, and I just qualified for a panel at the regional conference. No. You're not supposed to be back here anyway."

Banujani sized the woman up. "*Bdakhun* Ibukay has a gala scheduled next quarter."

"I know." The woman sat back in her chair, unfazed. "Her trafficking platform. Fundraising."

"If you do this, you'll be the only *kheter* to have supervised a gravid human bondmate splitting her marks to aid a trauma patient. I'll guarantee you a forty-minute presentation at the gala. In front of all those rich donors."

The *kheter* pursed her lips. "Yes, but if it goes sideways—"

"But if it doesn't?"

"Look, does she even know what she's doing?"

"Do any of us? The marks don't come with instruction manuals. We *all* wing it."

"True." The woman chewed at her lip, then stood. "Alright. But if it goes sideways, I'm telling the Board that I was under duress."

Eb pulled out a slim weapon and pointed. "Take us to Tai'ri or we kill you."

The *kheter* clapped her hands. "Perfect."

Tai'ri was assigned a simple white room, the stark walls inset with different displays. He rested inside a long tube with a transparent top and when she saw him, her stomach churned. Her mind stuttered, because even with the hours he'd spent in the healing device already he looked . . . like meat. She barely recognized him. Vivian froze, staring.

"Once I disconnect this," the *kheter* had said, "you'll have minutes. His nanos haven't even started regenerating. If you can jumpstart them, once he goes back in they'll take over." She paused, fixed Vivian with a steely look. "Just jumpstart him, don't try to go any deeper."

Whatever that meant, but she wasn't going to argue.

Vivian stepped to his side, waited until the lid of the tube decompressed, rising slowly.

"Physical contact will be needed," the *kheter* said. "Don't worry about introducing infection."

Vivian reached in and took his hand carefully, closing her eyes to the sight of him because if she continued to look, she might lose faith. "I don't know what to do."

"I've seen your marks react to him," Banujani said. "When that happened, what was going on?"

The tattoos responded when he was close, when his low voice and subtle, sly caresses filled her senses and tried to push away her doubts, her past. So she called forth her memories of him, of his smile, the taste of his lips, his growls when he was making her come. Warmth bloomed in her body, and the memories came faster and faster. She didn't resist the emotion they dredged up, not this time. She opened herself fully, and the marks awakened, jarred into life as if by command.

How did one tell nanos to get to work?

"Whatever you're doing," the *kheter* said, "keep doing it, and do it faster."

The nanos responded to stimuli, obviously. Thoughts, emotions, memory, touch. Probably scent, too, some kind of pheromone. If visualization sparked them to wakefulness, perhaps visualization could be used to command them.

She opened her eyes, took in Tai'ri's still, battered form, then imagined him whole, healthy. Imagined her marks flowing into him, repairing damaged tissue. Imagined her strength as a glowing rivulet between them, and pushed it into him.

Vivian grit her teeth. It was . . . hard. Spikes behind her eyes warned her of the very real physical consequences of doing whatever she was doing. Spikes that became pics. Her heart rate increased her breath coming faster as if she'd been running a hundred-yard sprint. While pregnant. Her throat burned, dry.

"It's working," she heard from a distance.

She threw herself into the healing, pushing, pushing as if she were trying to push the baby from her womb. And as she directed all her force of will at those thoughts, her womb rippled. A sudden, sharp tightening. She gasped. The tightening released, then grabbed her again. Startled, she cried out, thrown from her concentration.

"That's enough," the *kheter* said. "Get her away from him!"

Hands tore her fingers, clenched hard enough around Tai'ri's she was shocked she hadn't broken his bones, away, almost dragging her backwards. Vivian gasped again as her womb tightened, and continued in a low, painful undulation. She grunted, almost bending over.

"Fuck," Banujani swore. "*Kheter . . .*"

Vivian looked at Tai'ri through the haze of pain. The raw, deep fuchsia purple of his face was fading back into dusky blue. If he was healed then everything was worth it. The baby was full term; if she went into labor now, the baby would be fine.

"He's healing," the *kheter* said, then turned, eyes both triumphant and grim.

Another ripple and she couldn't help the low moan that tore from her lips. Perhaps if she hadn't been so suddenly tired, she might have been able to handle the pain. But she couldn't focus, her thoughts and feelings scattered in a dozen different directions.

The lid of the tube was about to close when Tai'ri's eyes snapped open. His hand smacked against the lid, and it paused, then began to open.

The *kheter* whirled. "No, you can't move! I need you to lie back down and let the tube do its job."

He ignored her, gaze fixed on Vivian as his lip curled back in a snarl. He barely waited until the lid was open before throwing his legs to the side of the bed and lurching to his feet.

Completely nude, he stumbled forward. "Vivian," he said hoarsely. "What?"

She wasn't afraid of the snarl; she sensed he was acting on instinct. Disoriented, angry, in pain, and trying to decide if she was being threatened.

"You were dying," she said.

Her knees crumpled a moment later; only Banujani kept her upright, and the woman lifted Vivian into her arms.

"She used the marks," Tai'ri said, the expression in his eyes terrible. "Damn you all."

"You can dress us down later," Banujani said. "Any chance I can talk you back into the tube?"

"No," Tai'ri said.

Vivian moaned as another wave hit. "Right, we need to get to Maternity," the *kheter* said. "Now."

Vivian woke, a deep ache under her ribs, remembering the *kheter* snapping instructions, Tai'ri stumbling at her side. She didn't think he'd even bothered to grab a sheet or hospital gown to make the trek to the maternity level. The fact that he hadn't tried to take her from Banujani told Vivian that Tai'ri was still very, very hurt. But he hadn't left her side, not as the medics worked to pause her labor, the room quiet and grim as everyone worked.

"If we can't stop the labor," she'd been told, "then the baby is old enough now that it can be born safely. But hybrids are tricky, and we'd prefer the child stay in utero another few days at least, even two weeks. So don't worry, just focus on calming your nanos. And your blood pressure. The baby is reacting to your stress."

Tai'ri had said nothing, standing at her side as he

held her hand. Someone, eventually, found him a gown to slip over his shoulders.

Movement drew her attention, and she turned her head. Tai'ri approached with a glass of water in his hand, and settled on her bedside.

She studied his face. Lines bracketed his mouth, and his skin looked delicate. But his color was normal, and his hand steady as he lifted the glass to her lips so she could sip. The tension in her body drained; even through their fledgling bond she felt his strength and health. He was fine now.

"How long have I been asleep?" she asked.

"The day you healed me, plus another two full days. Your body needed to rest."

The baby stirred as she drank more of the iced water. Stretching, a little kick, and then settling back down.

"I'm trying to decide whether to be impressed, or very, very angry," he said.

She settled back into her pillow. "I think I managed these marks pretty well for being an alien and a beginner."

He took a deep breath, exhaled, and waited a moment before speaking. "Vivian, they barely kept you from going into labor."

"It would have been fine. It was a risk, I know. But the alternative wasn't acceptable."

Tai'ri closed his eyes, mouth tight, but when he opened them again a wry expression settled onto his face. "At least I know for certain that you like me now."

Her lips curved. "See? Positive thinking. Do you think we're both well enough to go home now?"

The answer was yes. After a flurry of last-minute exams and instructions, they were released from medical care with a warning not to get too comfortable—they expected her labor to begin again at any time.

They stepped outside under the bright sunshine, fliers whizzing by, and began walking towards one of the transportation hubs. There was a shimmer in the air and Vykhan appeared at her side, dressed in his flowing gray, his braid draped over one shoulder.

She glanced at Tai'ri, who looked at his commander but said nothing.

"Your bond is true," Vykhan said, staring straight ahead as they walked. "And, you, Vivian—you're stronger than I thought you would be."

"Thank you," she said politely. It was meant as a compliment, after all, even if it was slightly backhanded. She didn't think that was his intent, however.

He fixed Tai'ri with a look. "I am informed Vivian's time is nearing."

Tai'ri tensed at her side. "You're going to take me off active duty again."

"You need to focus on your mate and child, Tai'ri."

Vykhan's tone was gentle, for him. "Trust us to finish the hunt. She deserves a mate who is fully present. You will never get these days back."

"My sister must have given you talking points." He stopped, looked down at her. Vivian let him take her hands and waited patiently as the thoughts rolled through his eyes.

"I want to spend time with you," he said finally. "Rubbing your feet and your belly and watching the child move and grow. Cook, shop, complete the nursery."

"But?"

"I want to hunt down the people who hurt you. I want them dead."

"You almost died, Tai'ri." She loosened her hand from his grip, lifted it to cup his cheek. "Can't your team take over the hunt for you for now? A few days?"

"You've done enough," Vykhan added. "We can take it from here."

Giving in, Tai'ri nodded. "Alright. But I want in on the final takedown."

Vykhan smiled. "Agreed. Now go home. And stay there this time."

26

A week later the pains began as fluttering cramps, almost as if her period was due. Vivian noted the discomfort and continued on with her day.

By late morning, considering the pains were steadily increasing in strength and frequency, she started to suspect that she might be in the early stages of labor.

Vivian set down her paintbrush as another cramp seized her lower groin. She exhaled through it, a little pleased at her forbearance.

She picked up her brush and resumed the delicate blue flowers she was painting over a white porcelain bowl. When it was done she would carefully smash it into pieces and then meld them back together again, highlighting the cracks with gold.

Setting the bowl aside, she stood, rubbing the small of her back, and thought about the small bag she'd packed for her stay at the birthing center. Everything was ready to go, especially since the center provided toiletries and any small comfort items typically requested.

Taking the lift down to the bedroom level, she walked slowly towards her room. Walking today had become more difficult as it felt like every muscle was involved in the pressure around her uterus.

She took her essentials bag from the inset wardrobe and put it on the bed, staring at it. She'd been sleeping in Tai'ri's bed the last week, but she'd kept all her things in here, all her energy directed towards fussing with the nursery.

"Viv?"

Glancing over her shoulder, she watched Tai'ri walk in. "I was about to check the bag again."

He stopped behind her, placing his hands on her shoulders. His fingers dug into specific pressure points and her eyes fluttered closed.

"I feel your pain," he said softly as he massaged her strained muscles.

"That's going to be inconvenient."

He kissed her temple. "I wouldn't permit you to go through the pain alone. Do you think it's time?"

"I'm sick of being pregnant, so whether it's time or not, it's time."

"That . . . makes sense. Finish checking the bag, I'll go alert your guard and Abeyya that we're coming in."

They didn't leave right away, Vivian electing to

walk around until the pressure was strong enough she no longer felt comfortable at home. Tai'ri helped her walk to the flier between contractions, and she breathed her way through them during the short trip.

Abeyya greeted them at the front doors, whisking them inside and to the suite Vivian had already chosen.

"First births can take time," Abeyya said. "I wouldn't advise lying down unless you want to, and make sure you eat and drink when your body prompts you."

The lights in the suite were dim, the windows to the outside darkened to control the stream of sun. A breeze came through from hidden vents, and Tai'ri started a playlist of soothing instrumental music she'd already compiled days before, having thrown herself into preparations since the scare in the medical center.

But as fast as the contractions came, they stopped just as suddenly.

Vivian sat on the edge of the bed, frustrated and tired. "Was this just a false alarm?" she asked Abeyya, who'd come back in at Tai'ri's summons.

"Well, it's not uncommon for labor to slow or even stall, especially with first babies. We have a few options." She pursed her lips.

"Yes?" Vivian prompted.

"We can send you home or you can stay here, and you may be in labor for several hours, even a day or two."

"No!" Vivian's fingers curled into the bed. "I want this baby *out*."

A smile lurked in Abeyya's eyes, the corners crinkling. "You and every other mother at this stage. We can give you chemical or manual inducement, but I prefer not to intervene with hybrid births. Or at all, really. The third option is much more fun, but sometimes uncomfortable for the mother."

"Yes?"

Abeyya glanced at her brother and seemed to be struggling to suppress a grin. She coughed. "Well, sperm has powerful chemicals that promote labor."

Vivian stared at her, perplexed. "Sperm? How would I . . . do you mean ingestion, or a topical application?"

Abeyya coughed harder, then apparently gave up. She started laughing. "You'd think at my age and after so many years as a midwife, I'd be more mature."

"You'd think," Tai'ri muttered. "She means sex, *yada'ami*."

"What?" She couldn't have heard that right.

He placed a kiss on her head. "Sex can stimulate contractions."

"Surges." Abeyya sniffed.

"Whatever. The point is, fun for me—maybe even fun for you, Viv."

Vivian shifted on the bed to face him. He sat cross-legged behind her, having never stopped the massage, and gave her an innocent look.

"So both topical and ingested," she said.

He grinned, and it wasn't sweet. At all.

"I'm willing to try anything at this point."

"Are you certain?" He hesitated. "I'll admit I thought you'd want to wait until you weren't pregnant anymore for our. . ."

Vivian took his hand. "I'm certain."

Tai'ri stared at her, then his expression shifted. Warmth, desire, a quick, visible battle with the edge she sometimes saw in him as he looked at her, quickly suppressed. One day, when the time was right, she'd explore that edge. Tease it to the surface. But the time wasn't right for that side of him, not yet.

Or that answering side of her.

"Well," Abeyya said. "I'll check on you in an hour?"

"Really?" Tai'ri scowled at Abeyya. "Give me a little credit, Bey." His elder sister patted his head on her way out, laughing softly.

And then they were alone.

Tai'ri looked at Vivian, then slipped a hand around the back of her neck and leaned forward, nipping her bottom lip. "I guess we'll have to abridge the birth story until the baby is at least sixteen."

She huffed, smiling, then hesitated. The room was beautiful and comforting, but she was beginning to feel cloistered.

"Do we have to stay inside?" Part of the reason

she'd chosen this suite was for its access to a small private garden.

Tai'ri moved off the bed and came around in front of her. He took her hand, helping her stand. "No."

They crossed the room together and entered the garden. The stone privacy wall stood at least nine feet, blanketed in an array of plants, both flowering and not. A thick carpet of not quite manicured grass cushioned her soles. Large, plump pillows sat on a low couch.

Vivian looked up, closing her eyes briefly as sunlight bathed her face in warm rays. The climate here reminded her of parts of the south in Mid North America. Tai'ri went back inside a moment, then she heard the music begin to drift out into their garden, adding to the background hum of birds and fliers.

Which made her think . . . "Do people ever look down?" she called out, opening her eyes.

He didn't respond right away, but moments later a shimmer of air arched in a bubble from the side of the wall to the top of the stone surround, then dissipated.

"We can see through," Tai'ri said, emerging again, "but from above it will be opaque."

He approached with deliberate, graceful steps, gaze fixed on her face. The sunlight bounced off his hair, bringing out the subtle highlights and adding a sheen to his skin. His eyes glittered like gems and she was struck again how beautiful he was. By her own ordinariness next to him.

Vivian admitted to herself, though, that *he* didn't

seem to think she was ordinary. She was coming to accept that whatever he saw in her was real to him and not just a product of their mating marks was a process.

His hands cupped her face, and he lowered his head to kiss her again, then trail his lips to her earlobe. "May I undress you?"

She wet her bottom lip and nodded. She'd already changed into a simple halter sundress, inexpensive and disposable, but pretty. Her feet were bare, and she'd forgone both bra and underwear as well.

So as his fingers slipped under the halter neck and tugged, pushing the fabric down over her body, she was completely naked underneath.

Her nipples pebbled as he stared down at her. "Beautiful," he said. He reached behind and undid her braid, lifting the strands of her dark hair and draping it over her shoulders. "There's never a moment I don't want to touch you, to taste you."

"I wasn't ready for a long time," she said, voice not quite steady. Her skin felt hypersensitive, her body reacting even to the faint breeze.

He lifted his gaze to hers. "I know. And now?"

"What could be more perfect than here, and now?" The fragrance of real flowers, the clarity of the sun, and the father of her child looking at her like she was his world. And could there be any reason more meaningful to make love for the first time than to aid in the birth of their child?

"Nothing more perfect," he said.

She tugged at the hem of his fitted cotton shirt. "You're too tall."

He pulled it up and over his head, tossing it aside to reveal broad shoulders, strong arms, and a chiseled chest. The flat, hard abs she'd enjoyed looking at every night this week in the shower. Now he only wore his loose, lounge style pants, already tented from his erection.

Tai'ri backed her slowly towards the divan. She bumped against the cushioned edge. He kneeled, his eyes on hers, and settled his hands on the inside of her thighs, pushing her legs apart, exposing her inner body to the air. Lowering his head, he brushed a kiss on her plump flesh.

Vivian blinked at him. "But we're supposed to have sex. Not that I'm protesting." Not at all. Her heart lurched into a gallop, her body already clenching, a low throb beginning in her clit.

"This *is* sex," he said. "And this isn't just for the baby." He grabbed a pillow and stuffed it behind her back so she could lean back. "Can't touch you for several weeks after you birth. This memory will sustain me."

His deep, husky voice was muffled slightly because he buried his face in her body. Vivian closed her eyes, tensing as he licked between her folds, spreading her open to reveal her swollen bud. She shifted her hips again, getting just the right angle, and gave herself up to the pleasure.

The sides of her uterus clenched as she came the first time. The ripple morphed into a low thrumming pressure, but the pressure fizzled out again. She grimaced slightly, torn between frustration her labor was still stalled and desire for more of Tai'ri's touch.

"That's not the look a male wants to see on his mate's face when she's coming in his mouth," Tai'ri said.

Vivian blew out a breath, opening her eyes. "It's not you, I just want this baby to come."

"We haven't even started." The corner of his mouth curled as his eyes glimmered with blue heat. "That was just to get you wet, *yada'ami*."

He slipped a finger inside her sheath, then a second. Her hips bucked restlessly, her body demanding a harder, deeper penetration. "See?" He withdrew his fingers, glistening from her natural juice. "But this isn't what you need."

Her gaze lowered to his waist and the waiting erection. She pushed herself up and reached for him, her palm grazing his hardness. His teeth clenched together as she slid under the waistband of his loose pants, cupped him, her hand unable to circle his width.

Tai'ri stood, shed the pants, and reached on either side of her for more pillows, which he tossed to the ground.

She eyed him. "I am so not getting on my back."

He gave her a look. "Your back wasn't what I had in mind, Vivian. I want you on your knees."

She wet her bottom lip, then with his help maneuvered herself to rest her knees and forearms onto two soft pillows. They gave, accepting her weight, and she lowered her upper body to the ground with a sigh of relief as pressure eased off her spine.

Tai'ri caressed her buttocks, then slipped between her thighs and played with her clit. "There's nothing prettier than the sight of your ass and pussy waiting to play with me."

She blushed, though he couldn't see it, still not quite used to his explicit talk. Her body loved it, especially when his erection nestled between her cheeks, then rested against her entrance as his hands came around her body, cupped her breasts.

"Tai'ri," she said, a warning in her voice. "Now."

"So demanding." Amusement and a darker emotion in his voice as he slid inside her.

Vivian bit her lip. His width stretched her body, filling her in a way she'd never experienced before. Her inner walls clenched around him, greedily wanting more. She gasped as he fully sheathed himself.

"You feel so good," he said roughly, hands tight on her breasts. He massaged her nipples, his touch exciting a tingling and feeling of increasing fullness.

"Tai'ri" she moaned.

He slid out, slowly, then sheathed himself again. And again, his strokes almost too careful. "Is this good, *yada'ami*? Tell me what you want."

Her fingernails dug into the ground. "I won't shatter if you fuck me, Tai'ri."

He paused. She wanted to look over her shoulder at his face, but she felt the ripple of surprise through their bond. "I don't want to hurt—"

"Tai'ri!" Her buttocks bucked against him, grinding. "I need this." She hadn't realized until he was inside her how much she had needed it, how much she had been suppressing her own body.

"Very well." He increased the speed of his strokes and gradually, the strength behind them. Which each stroke bursts of pleasure bloomed inside her, a slow building arc of tension as her body clamored for a final release.

He switched rhythm, changed his angle. Vivian knew she wasn't quiet and didn't care. All that mattered was she was finally experiencing what it was like to be completely mastered, and completely cherished, by a man who cared not just about her pleasure, but her heart.

He spoke to her, murmuring some things she heard and tried to respond to, and other things she didn't understand and didn't bother to try.

Part of her knew he was holding back, holding something *important* back, keeping fine control over the depth of his strength. She felt it, the slightest distance, hesitation. Not emotional; his heart was hers. She knew it as surely as she knew they would soon have a child in the world.

What's more . . . her heart was his. How could it not be? This man who'd given her all of him, who was here with her during a day in her life she would never forget, probably the most important day of her life.

The orgasm grabbed her, shattering her thoughts until she was nothing more than a mass of emotion, her consciousness floating on bright waves. Dimly, she heard Tai'ri cry out, his hands caressing her back with slightly unsteady fingers.

As she came down from the high, she pushed up. He helped her straighten, then settle back onto his thighs, her body still trembling.

She tried to speak, stopped and cleared her throat, then tried a second time. "Do you think that worked?"

She felt his chest move with his silent laughter. He pressed a kiss on her shoulder. "We should probably keep doing it until it does."

27

They'd made love again several times over the course of hours. Though she'd been doubtful, her contractions began again, coming strong enough to break the water sac and after that, Abeyya told her brother to keep his pants on. Not that Vivian was thinking about sex at that point. She stood under a hot water shower to alleviate the pain, and finally entered a pool staff set up in the room.

The pain felt like hovering on the edge of death. Even with the weightlessness of the pool surrounding her, and Tai'ri a supportive, thankfully silent, presence at her back, the contractions gripped her uterus with the ruthlessness of a rabid dog and dug in.

They'd dimmed the lights and Vivian's mind drifted, Abeyya's occasional murmur filtering through her semi-trance. She knew Daobah was present now as well, fetching fruit juice and honey sticks for Vivian to suck on. Her appetite was nonexistent, but the sugar and juice kept her energy levels up.

"Vivian?"

She opened her eyes. Abeyya crouched on the edge of the pool, speaking softly. "We're monitoring the strength of your surges. Do you feel any urge to bear down?"

It took her a moment to respond. "I don't feel like it."

"That's fine. You're doing very well. Relax into the surge, and if you don't want to push, then don't. Your body knows what to do."

Vivian wasn't so certain of that, but it was barely an hour later when the need to escape—and the panic that escape was literally impossible—morphed into a sudden, lighting urge to bear down.

Abeyya was there, and Daobah.

"Get me up," Vivian gasped after the third bearing down. "On my knees."

There was no reason to her demands, only an instinct as old as the universe. Tai'ri helped her onto her knees and Vivian reached between her legs.

"Is the baby crowning?" Abeyya asked.

Later, Vivian would remember her calm, encouraging tone with gratitude—it helped ease her panic. She nodded. Her palm rested gently on something small, round, fingers running through what must be locks of thick silky hair.

"I feel the head," Vivian gasped. Then she laughed, the sound closer to tears.

Another surge. She leaned into it, and the baby's head emerged. "The head! Can the baby breathe?" What had Abeyya told her about water birthing? She couldn't remember.

"It's fine, Vivian," Abeyya said. "Your baby won't breathe until they first touch air."

The point was moot for with the next surge the baby's tiny body slid out of the birthing canal. Vivian caught the child, lifting them out of the water and clasping them to her chest.

A single, poignant moment later and a clear, piercing wail filled the room.

Tai'ri kissed her cheek, and Vivian felt wetness on her cheeks, not all of it from her. "Well done, *yada'ami*."

She was up and walking two hours later.

After allowing the cord to stop pulsing, and her body to release the placenta, Vivian and Baby emerged from the pool. Once the birth was over, she'd wanted nothing more than to dry herself off and dress and then find some place warm and snug to relax with her new child.

"Do you want to see what gender the baby is?" Tai'ri asked. "I didn't look." They'd made the choice to wait, drawing out the anticipation as if it were a gift to unwrap. Vivian had wanted to save the moment for when she was dry and clothed and free of pain.

Vivian gazed at the tiny face almost obscured by her swollen breast. Abeyya swore the baby would be able to breathe, even though it looked like the poor child was being suffocated.

She couldn't stop staring. The baby's head was topped with a thick swath of blue-black hair, not surprising considering Vivian and Tai'ri were black haired. But under the sun subtle highlights of blue gleamed, echoing Tai'ri. The infant's skin wasn't the deep blue of Tai'ri's, but closer to lavender. A baby blue with blushes of rose underneath.

"Yes, let's do the reveal," she said, mouth curving in a smile.

She gently delatched the baby from her nipple, then slid them out of the sling. Vivian settled the baby on her thighs, then undid the cloth diaper. After a few seconds, she refastened the diaper, then nestled the baby back into the sling, their bare skins touching.

Tai'ri's fingertips touched Vivian's cheek, gently urging her to turn her head. When she did, he lowered his head, his lips brushing hers.

"We have a daughter," he said, then smiled.

She stared into his eyes, utterly captivated by the joy she saw therein. And realized his joy was only a reflection of her own.

Vivian tabbed through the documents on the thin tablet that had arrived by messenger an hour ago.

It was fortunate she was sitting, because shock momentarily stole all the sinew from her muscles. She rubbed Baby's back as she read, then tapped her comm unit.

"Viv?" Tai'ri's voice came immediately through the unit.

"Can you come down here, please? Ibukay sent me some documents."

"She—I'm coming."

Moments later Tai'ri emerged onto the balcony. He came immediately to Vivian and placed his hand over Baby's head, bending down to kiss Vivian's cheek.

"Let me see," he said.

She waited as he skimmed the files. "I see," he said finally, voice neutral.

"Are these what I think they are? An application to the court to approve my citizenship status based on Baby's birth?"

"Pending the official registration of her birth. We have to choose a name."

Two days after the birth, and she still hadn't pulled the trigger. They'd spent the last several evenings compiling lists, debating meanings, respective cultural traditions, and were at an impasse.

Tai'ri wanted a traditional family name, of course,

and so did she. They would have to compromise. Which wasn't the problem, but Vivian was simply . . . waiting. Wasn't she supposed to feel a click? Just *know* what her child's name was?

"You know you can literally pick any name on our list, Viv," Tai'ri said, once again proving the strength of their burgeoning bond. It was stronger after the birth, even without consummation.

"A name is forever, it has to be the right one."

He shrugged. "Whatever we pick, she'll wind up choosing some trendy, anti-establishment use name when she's in her rebellion phase, anyway."

Vivian stiffened. "There's no need to assume Baby will not be a responsible, productive member of society."

He gave her a strange look. "I didn't say she wouldn't be. Don't human children rebel against authority figures as a rite of passage into adulthood?"

She stared at him, expression stony. That had landed her in the pens. "That would be extremely foolish. A one-way ticket to a state run program and never seeing your family again. Especially if you are a Low or Mid Tier teenager with no connections or family wealth."

He shoved his hands in his pockets. "Well, it's different here. Our young adults are encouraged to explore their developing identities, and that frequently involves changing names and . . . " he ran his tongue around his teeth " . . . some benign time spent in a repentance facility. Not much time," he added hastily. "Minor disruptions are best handled with counseling and work sentences. But quiet and reflection sometimes is the best course for a child who has not learned to protest within the acceptable confines of law and order."

"That's anarchy. And you sound like you're reciting a text."

"I read. And it's not anarchy. They have to get it out of their system young, so they can settle down."

She rubbed her hand on her forehead. "We're digressing. What are we naming the baby?"

He finally took a chair, stretching out his legs, eyeing the pitcher of iced tea. "I need something stronger for this conversation."

She snorted. "Once the birth is registered, I can file for citizenship. And then I can apply for the permits to open my studio and hire local staff."

He looked pleased. "Went over your business plan while you were sleeping. Solid."

"That's all you have to say? Even without Ibukay's recommendation, my plan to start an apprenticeship program and hire local staff right away is designed to weigh in my favor. It will be seen as contributing to the economy rather than simply taking from it."

"Like I said. Solid. But first we have to name Baby."

"I have a surprise for you," Tai'ri said, stepping onto the balcony.

When they'd arrived home, Vivian settled onto the living room couch, the nearby table laid out with everything she would need. Diapering supplies, drinks for herself, an entertainment pad for reading and vids. Tai'ri would be home for several more weeks as well, working from his home office and spending time with them.

She glanced up from her breast where the baby was nursing. He held a large data pad in his hands, and a black box. She watched him connect the pad to the box, spend several minutes inputting some kind of code and speaking to Evvek when she finally priced together the technical jargon.

"Tai'ri? Are you setting up an interstellar comm link?"

He glanced at her and smiled. "Surprise. Going to take an hour or so on our end. The relay is—well, never mind. But your parents are on the other end on a YETI ship, standing by."

She waited, nerves dancing during the time it took for the relay to connect. The signal dropped several times before fixing. She didn't mind—normally no one but government officials and people with very deep pockets were able to use the interstellar relays. She'd take even a shoddy connection over now. Ibukay must have come through.

Her parents' faces appeared on the wide monitor.

Vivian blinked rapidly, maintaining her composure. She knew that her apparent calm, more than anything, would work to reassure her parents that she was well.

"Mother, Father," she said. "I'm happy to see you."

Her mother said nothing as they studied each other. Nadine Huang considered hair dye vulgar and allowed her hair's few silver strands free rein. A few lines at the corners of her eyes were new, stress or age Vivian couldn't tell. Her golden-brown skin was still smooth, taut over fine bones. Behind her, her father stood with his hands on his wife's shoulders, his expression more open. Tightly curled dark hair was cropped close to his scalp, and deeper grooves bracketed his eyes and mouth, his dark brown skin still smooth and youthful. Joy shone from his dark eyes.

"Daughter," he said. "We're overjoyed you are alive and well." He hesitated. "We don't fully understand what happened. Why are you on Yedahn?"

Vivian's eyes closed for a moment. She had hoped Ibukay would have explained everything so she wouldn't have to fumble her way through awkward explanations, but she should have known better. Ibukay would have said only what was necessary to get her parents on the call, and nothing more.

Taking a deep breath, she began a halting explanation beginning with her kidnapping, and ending with . . . Mayleen.

Her mother stared at Tai'ri as she spoke, then

shifted her gaze to Vivian. "He is very blue," she said in Mandarin.

"He is Yadeshi, mother."

"Blue is a good color. It is for healing."

"He can understand Mandarin," Vivian said apologetically, but her heart lightened. It was her mother's tacit blessing. "Tech."

Nadine's gaze scanned the room behind Vivian. "This is your home?"

"Yes." She had deliberately chosen the living area with a view of the sleek kitchen and balcony. The elegant furniture and crystal embedded countertops screamed prosperity.

"He is not poor." A glint of satisfaction in her mother's dark eyes.

"No, mother."

"We hope he's kind as well," her father interjected in Standard. He understood Mandarin better than he spoke it.

"Very kind." Vivian smiled. "He and his family have welcomed me and Mayleen into their family."

Her mother's stare was keen. She switched back to Standard. "You aren't coming home. I can hear it in your voice."

Vivian froze, then swallowed. "No. I . . . don't think it's best, considering the baby."

"Good."

"I—what?"

Nadine's expression softened. "We know you

chafed for something more than what we could provide you. What this world could provide you. Perhaps on Yedahn you can be who you were meant to be."

"Let us see our granddaughter," her father said.

Vivian unwound the cloth sling and shifted the infant in her arms so Mayleen was facing forward. Her tiny head turned, eyes closed as she rooted for a nipple.

"Oh," her father breathed. "She's perfect."

"Well done, Vivian," her mother said. "A strong looking child. We have both requested a leave of absence. We will be there with you in a few months."

Vivian blinked. "I would love to have you here, but . . . ." She didn't know how to ask the question about their finances—her parents had never thought it appropriate to discuss money with their *child*—especially with Tai'ri hovering at her back.

Her mother waved a hand. "Your princess will incur the expense on behalf of her government, as it was one of her citizens who illegally took you from your home."

Vivian stared at them, a little shocked. They had accepted help? She'd been so certain they would turn down an offer of aid.

Her father grinned at her. "The look on your face, girl," he said. "That is what happens when a daughter thinks she knows better than her parents."

"You'll stay with us, of course," Tai'ri said. "It would comfort Vivian to have her parents in her home."

Well, yes and no. Father would take over the kitchen and mother would attempt to take over Vivian's new business. Neither of them would let her hold her own baby, if the looks in their eyes was any indication.

Her chest warmed. "I can't wait until you are both here."

28

Vivian stood naked in front of the full-length mirror, twisting and turning as she eyed herself critically. Experimentally, she bent down, touching her fingertips to the floor. Then her boobs started leaking, so she straightened and started to dress.

The first fifteen pounds had melted off, mostly blood and water weight. These last fifteen would need a little more attention. She should probably swap her morning fruit filled buns for more vegetable soup.

"House, locate Tai'ri," she said as she finished slipping into undergarments, a belly wrap, simple leggings and an oversized t-shirt.

:*Tai'ri is in the gym.*:

She left the bathroom, padded to Mayleen's bassinet and looked down. The tiny baby slept, arms and legs sprawled, plump belly rising and falling with her breath. Carefully she lifted the child, then left the bedroom and made her way to the lift, and to the basement gym.

The room was across from the med suite, and when she stepped inside she stopped, staring with unabashed interest at the tall, leanly muscled man going through a series of exercises.

"Is it lunchtime?" he asked, stopping after several moments.

"No. Abeyya said I could begin some light exercise this week. I want to learn self-defense too."

He approached, touched the tip of the baby's nose gently, then lowered his head and gave Vivian a kiss. It held all the pent-up hunger and frustration she'd also begun to feel over the last weeks as her body healed and her libido seemed determined to get her pregnant again.

But learning to care for a new baby, and exist in her new body, had belayed opportunities to pick up where they'd left off the day of Mayleen's birth.

"We can start with some stretching and go from there," he said.

Vivian walked to the corner of the room where there was already a bassinet for the baby, and set her inside, then turned once she was certain Mayleen would remain asleep.

"Stretches. Let's begin."

It felt so good to use her muscles. To walk and jump and stretch without the cumbersome weight of a pregnancy. She still marveled at how light she felt, and how fast she could move.

Which was why she pushed for more than stretches. "I can do more," she insisted. "Try me."

Tai'ri, who'd been standing to the side watching her with a professional eye, shook his head. "You'll injure yourself. You just gave birth."

"Six *weeks* ago, Tai'ri. You said you would train me." She pinched her upper arm. "I'm flabby."

He gave her a reproachful look. "You aren't flabby. You're motherly. You aren't a warrior."

And that was the problem, wasn't it? "Maybe if I'd been a warrior, I'd never have been kidnapped."

They stared at each other. "And then we would never have met. Had Mayleen."

"I want to be able to defend myself. I want to be strong."

He came closer, cupped her face in his hands. "I agree. I just want you to give yourself time. I know you think six weeks is enough time, but your body is recovering from more than a regular human birth. I talked to my mother, and *she* said twelve weeks, minimum. A fourth trimester."

Yes, Agata had warned Vivian as well about a fourth trimester and not to be so eager to follow standard human guidelines of six weeks to recovery. "In fact," his mother had said, "on Yedahn we really give the mother a year before we expect her body to return anywhere even close to pre pregnancy."

"What if there's no time?" Vivian asked. "What if someone comes after us again?"

His expression hardened. "Then they'll die."

"Or?"

Tai'ri grimaced. "Alright. Alright. I wanted you to have time to relax and enjoy the baby. Once I start training you, I'm going to train you the way I would one of my people. I'll demand your full attention."

"Good. Let's start now."

Vivian giggled, curling in on herself in self-defense as Tai'ri tickled her mercilessly.

"That's what you get for not defending that block," he purred, fingers torturing her sides.

"Tai'ri!" she howled. "That's enough."

"There are consequences for sloppiness. Though I could punish you in other ways."

Both of them stilled at the tone in his voice. Vivian uncurled from her ball and rose to her knees to face him. He crouched, eyes hot and roving over her body. She really didn't understand what he saw; she was sweaty, plump, hair frazzled from sweat and her belly was . . . not what it once was. Her boobs were leaking through her thin tank top again; she'd forgotten the cloth pads.

But she narrowed her eyes at him. He wasn't going to dangle the bait of his body in front of her as a distraction. "I'll fight you for it. If I score two hits in five bouts, you make lunch. If I don't . . ."

His gaze brightened, smile turning feral. "You realized you just gave me the best excuse to kick your ass."

She rolled her eyes. "With what? A feather boa?"

"I don't know what you're trying to say."

"She's trying to say your training sucks," Banujani's flat voice said.

Vivian started, though Tai'ri rose, seemingly unsurprised by her presence. His second in command fixed him with a look. "All this giggling makes me ill. I thought you were supposed to be training her."

His shoulders hunched. "I am."

"You're flirting. I've been watching you. You're not taking it seriously, you'll get her killed."

His expression hardened, a cold expression snapping into place. "Careful, Banu."

Banujani advanced into the room, stabbing a finger at him. "You can't train her. You wince every time she gasps or flinches, and all you can think about is sex."

He opened his mouth, closed it.

"I'll take over from here," Banujani continued, then fixed Vivian with a stare. "And *I* don't think you're cute."

Vivian pursed her lips, struggling not to laugh. Tai'ri's face struggled between sheepishness and indignation.

"She may have a point," Vivian said. "If you're worried about hurting me . . ."

He sighed, rubbed a hand over his face. "Fine. I'll still work with you on your conditioning, though."

"If there's anything left of her once I'm through."

Vivian's smile faded as she looked at Banujani. Okay, so . . . now she was starting to worry. "Banujani? You don't really mean that, do you?"

"First position, First Form," the woman barked. "Sir, get out."

Banujani didn't wait until Tai'ri cleared the mat. She rushed. Vivian dropped clumsily into place, and proceeded to learn the difference between training and flirting.

Two weeks later, Vivian stared up at the ceiling and considered staying on her back.

Banujani's face came into view. "You could have blocked that."

"Your disappointment pains me."

"Not as much as getting knocked on your ass."

"That is true." But her breasts were tingling, and it had distracted her for the split second it took for Banujani to become offended she did not have *all* of Vivian's attention, and express that discontent. "I'm getting better, aren't I?"

Vivian didn't know how to interpret the ominous

silence, and after a moment scissored to her feet. It was amazing what one could learn during training sessions that lasted a minimum of five hours, six days a week.

Banujani was standing several feet away, arms crossed. "Your progression is satisfactory considering you're human, a civilian, were in absolutely no physical shape—"

"I was in excellent health. Am."

"For a civilian." Banujani strode forward and pinched Vivian's upper arm. "Well, you've got a bit of definition now, but you were all flab a few weeks ago."

"Mid Tier teachers don't really need muscle tone. Tai'ri hasn't complained about my curves."

There was something about training with Banujani that brought out the bolder side of her tongue. Perhaps it was only that getting hit and kicked several times a day put things like manners and discretion into perspective.

Being the target of kidnapping maniacs also lent one perspective.

"Again," Vivian said.

They drilled for another thirty minutes, Vivian grabbing her focus and wrangling it until all thoughts of the baby receded. Her worries and dreams about the studio, Tai'ri and whatever danger he embroiled himself in on a daily basis. She banished it all, and focused.

She would get this. She would get stronger and she

would learn how to protect herself and not be a sitting duck or a burden to her new family.

Banujani signaled for a stop. "Your endurance is getting better, but you get sloppy when you start to get tired. It's the little one's lunch time, anyway, I'm guessing. You were grabbing your boobs." Curiosity crossed her face. "Are they like, psychically attuned to the baby?"

"Well, no. Boobs aren't sentient. It's just that the baby is on a schedule and everything just seems to . . ." she waved a hand in a vague gesture " . . .flow. Literally."

"Huh. Ok, well, we might as well go eat, too. Tai'ri left little sandwiches and flower shaped fruit in lunch containers." She shook her head. "Never thought I'd see the day."

She saw little of Tai'ri over that week. He left early in the morning and didn't return home until late at night. She knew he kept tabs on her because at night, if she was awake when he came home, he questioned her about her training and mentioned little things that had happened with the baby. She began to suspect he had cameras in the home and shrugged. Of course he did.

She missed him. It was difficult to find time just for them between their work schedules, the baby, and her own exhaustion between on demand nursing and

Banujani's ruthless determination to turn her into a deadly killing machine.

Under Abeyya's gimlet eye and Banujani's tutelage, she made progress.

But she wasn't happy with the small daily progress. Tai'ri's frequent long silences as he stared at her and held Mayleen drove Vivian to push herself to her limit. Instinct, the bond growing between them, or just experience told her fear drove him the way it did her. Too much fear for them would make him sloppy—Banujani told Vivian all the time to center herself, release her anxiety over being injured, and flow into the fight.

"A little fear keeps you smart, and on your toes," Banujani lectured, "too much freezes your instincts. Silence the fear. Silence every emotion except for the fact that you must live, defeat your enemy, and protect your child."

Vivian evaded a strike, grabbing Banujani's wrist and using the woman's body weight against her.

Banujani slid out of the hold, the meat of her palm flying towards Vivian's face in what she knew would be a punishing blow.

Vivian deflected, evaded, moved back in for a strike. Her breaths came fast, her gaze locked on Banujani's sinuous movements as they circled each other.

Center. Focus. The only must is that she defeat the enemy.

Silence.

Flow.

Vivian moved faster, feet light, muted slips of sound on the mats. Kick, spin, evade, block. Strike, jump back. Accept a hit to the ribs to create an opening to move under Banujani's defense. The pain sparked, and she pushed it aside.

The pain was nothing to childbirth, and the building tingles on her arms, the heat. As the pain from the tattoos increased, her arms seemed to strengthen. It was as if the moves became second nature, or perhaps some of the medtech that allowed Tai'ri to imprint the marks on her had also transferred some small part of his own memories, guiding her. Her feet and hands shifted seamlessly into position the better she tapped into her center. When she faltered, that connection faltered. When she pushed aside doubt . . .

Banujani flew back several feet as Vivian's hand connected with the woman's chest.

"Halt!" Banujani shouted. "What in Haeemah's name—"

Vivian halted, but the strange oneness with herself remained. She stood, still and ready, gaze trained on her mentor.

"The first step to Silence," another voice said from behind, "often takes pupils years. You have achieved this in weeks. Interesting."

Vivian turned. Vykhan stood in the threshold of the gym. House must have let him in.

"I have incentive," she said, hearing her voice distantly. "I won't be taken again." Her voice sharpened, anger seeping through. "My daughter won't be taken. Tai'ri won't be—" she couldn't say it. Killed.

She couldn't imagine a life or her new, small family without him. How quickly he'd become so integral to her, and they hadn't even . . . she yanked her mind away from that path, attempting to dampen her body's automatic blush.

Looking into Vykhan's eyes, her blush dissipated. He stared at her with hawk like intensity, bright and avid, a penetrating judgement that seemed to pierce through to her soul, rake it over the coals and then retreat . . . without finding her wanting.

He smiled. "I believe you. I believe you will survive this." He nodded at Banujani, who'd come to stand by Vivian, then turned and left.

"That was high praise," her mentor said. "But let's see if you can do that shit again."

29

Vivian curled around Mayleen, inching her arm ever so slowly away from the sleeping baby, then tucked her boob back where it belonged. After she'd crept off the bed she stood for a few moments to make sure the baby was really asleep this time.

"House, monitor Mayleen," she murmured. A light flashed on the ceiling, House didn't respond verbally, programmed to remain silent when Mayleen slept unless in emergency.

Vivian tip-toed out of the bedroom and down the hall. It was late and Tai'ri should be home soon. She'd taken to waiting up for him rather than falling off to sleep with Mayleen. The darkness that shrouded him lately disturbed her, and the fact that he seemed to gather it inward. To her, to Mayleen, he was the same caring, gentle father and partner as he'd always been.

But in his eyes she saw a maelstrom waiting to be unleashed.

He couldn't live like that, it wasn't healthy.

She had a pretty good idea of one of the underlying causes.

Rather than curl onto the white couch with a tablet to wait for him, she stepped out onto the deck. A word to the house and the hard surface under her feet morphed into the same firm spring of the training gym down below. She pushed the table and chairs out of the way and then stood in the center. An evening breeze brushed her bare skin; she wore a thin-strapped tank and loose pajama bottoms and nothing else. She'd pulled her hair back into a tail to stay out of her face, baring her neck as well.

She was exhausted. Her mind was exhausted, but the internal drive to *do* something spurred her. While she waited for Tai'ri she practiced, slipping into each beginner Form, making minute adjustments based on the instinct shivering into her limbs from the tattoos. Testing her realization from earlier.

Breathe.

Focus.

Silence.

She whirled, and her kick connected with strong hands. Tai'ri, clothed in black and silent as a shadow, threw her onto her back.

She scissored to her feet, engaged.

He wasn't nearly as harsh as Banujani. He pulled

his attacks at the last moment, fingers skimming her body where Banujani would have let the blow connect. Where it was a fight with the female guard, with Tai'ri it was a . . . dance.

But it had been a long day and no matter how her blood fired her limbs, those same limbs were on the brink of collapse. Banujani was right; her endurance *was* poor—and she had other plans for tonight. Though it occurred to her she could have gone about this in a less disheveled way.

"Enough," Tai'ri said, voice deep and quiet in the night.

Vivian halted, panting, drawing in great gulps of air into her lungs. "You're home."

His mouth quirked in a smile. "I'm home." He took her hand and drew her inside. "You're tired, should be resting." His fingers brushed her face, leaving heat where he touched her, and he turned to the inset fridge.

Tai'ri poured them one of his post workout smoothies he prepared in batches. "I wanted to wait up for you. I wanted to ask you about the marks."

He leaned back against the counter, sipping his drink, and stared at her. "Ask."

"Today while I was training, it was as if I slipped into a trance. I'm a raw beginner, but . . . it didn't feel like it. The moves felt familiar, as if I'd done them many times before."

"Good."

She watched him, narrowing her eyes. "I don't know much about your people's medtech with these tattoos, and your Inkmaster's seem to be priests or something, but can the marks transfer data? Memory?"

He considered her. "We aren't fully bonded. Threads are there."

That didn't really answer the question. She waited.

"Yes," he said finally, "that's one of the possible benefits. Doesn't always happen like that, but it can. Interesting."

"I'm getting stronger. Faster." She tilted her head, looked up at him through her lashes. "I landed a blow on Banujani today."

He lifted a brow, eyes glinting.

"Come on, you know that means something. Banujani is *ruthless*."

"If she underestimated you enough that you were allowed to hit her, she won't make that mistake again."

Vivian grimaced. "Well, I guess my bruises would be lonely without company."

He set his drink down and then lifted her up into his arms, striding to the couch. He sat, cradling her in his lap.

"Let me see," he demanded. "She shouldn't be so hard on you. You're a beginner."

She nuzzled his neck with her nose, inhaling his unique scent, then pressed a kiss against his skin.

Tai'ri stilled. "What did Vykhan want? Why was he here?" His voice was slightly hoarse.

"Hmm. He just said I was on the first step to Silence. Then he left."

She'd been exhausted, but resting in his arms renewed her energy. Energy, and the desire that simmered in her blood, growing stronger as *she* grew stronger.

Strong enough to hold her own against that darkness he kept hidden. Strong enough to be his bonded mate. completely.

She shifted, turning to straddle his lap and looked into his half wary, half slumberous gaze. Her hands rose, tangling in the hair at his nape.

"You sure you want to start something, Viv?" he asked in his soft drawl.

"Mayleen will sleep for at least another hour." She didn't recognize the seductive croon of her own voice.

He blinked. "Ah . . ."

"Are you *blushing?*"

"I don't blush, female." He narrowed his eyes, an edge to the smile he now gave her.

She lowered her head, her lips hovering over his. Then she slipped off his lap and began to walk away, an extra sway to her hips when she glanced over her shoulder. "Well, I guess it's been a long day for you. I'll just—"

He was on her as she stepped into the hallway, arms swiping her feet off the floor again. Tai'ri pressed her back against the wall, her legs wrapping instinctively around his waist.

"It hasn't been that long a day," he said, heat in his eyes, a faint growl in his voice.

Slowly, carefully, his eyes never leaving hers, his hand slipped up her body, under the tank and palmed one of her breasts. Vivian inhaled sharply. He pushed aside the sleep bra she wore, the warmth of his bare hand on her skin. Her breasts tingled, the nipples sensitive and almost raw.

"I can't decide if it makes me perverse, or simply hungry that every time I watch my daughter eat I'm jealous," he said quietly.

Her muscles clenched. He gently massaged her breast and despite the light initial discomfort, fire sparked and her hips ground against him instinctively. Under her open legs his body was already hard, making clear his intentions for the night.

That was fine. Those were her intentions as well.

He took her lips, kissing her with a barely restrained savagery. Still holding back, not wanting to hurt her. She returned the kiss, fingers clenched in his hair. Well, she would just have to prove she wasn't afraid of him, of their passion.

Tai'ri shifted suddenly, flipping her over so her back was pressed into the couch, his body braced over her. The strands of his hair tickled her face, his eyes glimmering as he stared down at her.

"You know I can't hold back any longer," he said, jaw tight.

She wrapped her legs around his waist. "Don't."

He hauled them up, Vivian in his arms, and strode out of the living area and down the hallway. Instead of their bedroom, he took them to Vivian's old room. House would alert them when Mayleen woke, or if the baby was in any distress.

"I've been watching you train," he said, then tossed her onto the bed. Not at all gentle.

Vivian stretched, arching her back. "Oh?"

He wrapped his fingers around her ankles and yanked. Hard. Vivian laughed as her hips all but dangled off the edge of the bed; he kept control of her body, though, slowly spreading her legs wide open.

"You *are* getting stronger. Faster. I'd wondered. But if the marks are feeding you my cellular memories, it makes sense." A slow, wicked smile curved his lips. "Do you know what else many couples can feel once bonded?"

It was hard to breathe, even to think when he looked at her like she was a cream puff. "No, what?"

"They can feel each other. During sex. Imagine."

She did. Oh, she did. "Well, we aren't going to feel much of anything with our clothes on."

He braced her feet on his shoulders, and she took a second to be glad she'd fixed up her toes yesterday. Hands sliding up her legs, his fingers curled around the stretchy band of her leggings and stiffened, as if he were fighting an impulse to rip them off her. Then, with exquisite gentleness, he began peeling the fabric from her body, tossing the clothing to the floor when he was done.

With her feet on either shoulder, her mound lay open to him, bare to gaze and touch. Slowly, as his fingertips grazed the insides of her thighs, his eyes roved over her naked flesh, the plump dusky lips covering her opening, the dark curls she'd neatly trimmed the same evening she'd worked on her toes.

"One last chance to change your mind," he crooned. "I won't stop tonight until you're mine, but I'll give you this one last chance to tell me no."

30

"Take your chivalry and toss it out the door. I don't want it. I want you."

His eyes burned. "Bold. House, seal the bedroom door. Don't open except at my command."

:*Sealed, Master*:

Vivian's mouth dropped open. House . . . sounded like *her*. A husky, naughty, very well satisfied her. "When did you change House's voice? Wait—*master?*"

He only smiled and asked, "Do you know what I want, what I've been tormenting myself with for weeks now?"

The conversational tone of his voice was a lie. She shivered. The chokehold he kept on his emotions loosened, began filtering through their connection.

If this muted inferno was what it felt like now, how would it feel when they were fully bonded?

"It will be more," he said. "No, I can't read your mind. Your face tells me everything."

"I should work on that."

His thumb caressed her bottom lip. "After tonight, we'll only be able to hide from each other with effort. It doesn't work like that for all bonded," he added. "The bonding never works exactly the same way."

"That's why no one could ever tell me what to expect, what it meant. I thought everyone was being evasive."

He shook his head. "No, they just didn't want to lie to you."

She opened her mouth, drew his thumb inward and suckled, their gazes locked. His eyes flared; he withdrew the thumb and replaced it with his fore and middle fingers, and after his skin was completely moistened, he pulled away again, only to lower his hand to her entrance. And with one quick movement, slip inside.

Vivian inhaled, trembling. He hooked his fingers inside as his thumb pressed against her clit, and he returned his weeks of torment, fucking her with his fingers as his thumb rubbed her clit faster and faster. Bringing her to the brink of orgasm and then drawing away.

She blinked, staring at him, mind scrambled, but he just raised his fingers to his mouth and licked them clean. "That," he said, "is what I've been imagining for weeks. How you taste. Well—that's one of many things I've thought about."

"Tai'ri..."

He smiled, a little cruel, a little smug. "Did you think I was going to let you come so easily? No, *yada'ami,* I'm going to draw this out."

"Mayleen will wake up."

"Then we'll pause, and when she goes back to sleep, resume. I will take my time, no matter how you beg me."

She sat up, her streak of usually well-hidden rebellion sparking. "Maybe you'll be the one begging me." She cupped his erection, full and heavy through his pants, and began to unfasten his clothes when he put a hand on her chest and shoved her back down.

He clicked his teeth at her. "I don't think so." Tai'ri dropped to his knees. Took her ankles again and spread her legs impossibly wide. "Scream if you want. I insist."

A cruel, talented, greedy tongue invaded her body. Her hips bucked as she ground against his mouth, instinctively tugging her ankles. He didn't let her go, licking up and down her folds with relish, latching onto her clit and suckling. When he delved into her core she grabbed his head, fingers burying in his hair and holding him to her.

"All this syrup for me," he murmured, returning to her clit, his mouth glistening.

He really was determined to drive her insane. He knew just the right pressure, just the right timing to bring her body to the precipice . . . and then back away, leaving her wanting. She writhed, willing to beg, willing to do anything.

" . . .anything, Tai'ri!" She'd said that out loud?

He laughed softly. "Anything? Hmm. That's an offer." He kissed his way up her body. Her clit throbbed, her inner walls trembled and burned with a need for release.

"Anything."

He grabbed the edge of her tank top and peeled it over her head. As she tried to pull her arms out, in a quick twist of movement he wrapped her wrists in the stretchy cloth, turning the tank into a binding, her arms over her head.

Leaning back, he admired his work. "There. So pretty, *yada'ami*. Even with you glaring daggers at me." He pursed his lips. "Fine. You've been patient. What would you like?"

"To return the damn favor," she growled.

Tai'ri laughed. "Why not? It's not like I can't end this whenever I want."

"Undo this." She lifted her arms.

"No. You'll just have to make do."

With a scowl, Vivian rose on her knees. "Now lie down and put your hands over your head."

Tai'ri smirked, but complied, stretching out next to her on the bed and putting his hands under his head. His biceps flexed, and he fluttered his eyelashes at her. "Now what?"

She straddled his waist. "I'm going to tie up your wrists."

"Really? How do you think that's going to work for you?"

Vivian glared at him, but he held out his hands, wrists together. She found her panties and used them like a scrunchie, twisting to secure him properly. "There."

"You know we only have about an hour before the baby wakes up?"

She slapped his face lightly with the back of her bound hands. "Be quiet. It's my turn."

He narrowed his eyes. "So that's how you plan to play? Careful. I'll take you up on it."

"I am not planning. I'm winging it."

And winging it felt good. Powerful. Her body still throbbed, need prickling her temper. But this was more than her temper, this was a side of her that had slowly been emerging during the training, weeks of learning her own strength and—she surmised—some of Tai'ri's natural aggression also rubbing off on her.

"Well, you just have fun, dear," he said in Standard, accent flawless. "Because when you're done, it'll be my turn again."

Vivian quailed a bit, but then remembered who she was playing with and snorted. This was Tai'ri. The man who would cut off his own head before he made her feel unsafe. But . . .

"Do you have any limits? Any boundaries I

shouldn't cross?" Evidently her kittenish little slap only spurred his lust. His eyes glittered, his lip curled up over his incisor.

He gave her a considering look. "I don't think you're capable of crossing boundaries. Play all you want, *yada'ami*."

Though her wrists were bound, there was enough give for her hands to move above the joint. Vivian stroked his erection and considered the problem of his shirt. His hands were bound, and it seemed counterproductive to release him to take off the shirt. But it had to go.

"There's a blade strapped to my ankle," he said. "Don't cut yourself."

That little goad ensured she found the blade, clumsily unsheathed it then carefully, remembering her mandatory emergency first aid class in secondary school, she cut open his shirt down the middle.

"Much better," she murmured, tearing the strips of cloth away from his torso. He flexed his pectoral muscles, showing off the tone and definition. "Barbarian show off."

"You love my body," he purred.

She leaned forward, her hair falling over his chest, and licked his nipple, wondering if it was as sensitive as her own.

"I do. And it's all mine. *Enja*."

"Say that again."

"Mine?" She kissed her way across his chest. "*Enja.*"

But he was right. As much as she wanted to play, her body and the fact that the baby would wake soon prompted her to abandon the leisurely exploration. They had time.

It was simple enough to unfasten his pants and peel them off, releasing his body. "Hello," she purred.

She wanted nothing more than to climb on his lap, impale herself, and ride her way to a shattering release. But as much as he had imagined tasting her, she had imagined tasting him.

And payback was a . . . well, payback.

Her lips closed over his erection, though closed was highly inaccurate. Her jaws ached, struggling to accept his width. Tai'ri growled as her tongue played on the tip of his head, his hips surging deeper into her throat.

She choked, used a bit of her own saliva for lubricant, and began to learn her way around her man's cock. Licking, moving her head up and down as her hand grabbed his base. As she got the hang of it, she moved faster, tasting the salty sweet liquid that rewarded her efforts.

"*Vivian,*" he said, her name a curse.

She registered movement and snapped her head up. "Put your arms back over your head. I didn't release you."

He snarled at her.

"Bad temper won't help you." She stared at him until he complied, his hot eyes promising revenge.

Vivian returned to his cock, gratified at how he swelled and hardened to an impossible width in her mouth. At a certain point, there was no earthly way she could take him any deeper, not when his size increased. It must be a Yadeshi thing. Did Yadeshi cocks ever stop growing? How big could it get while inside her?

"If you're going to do this to me, at least turn around," he said in a rough voice.

Vivian looked up, tilting her head. "Turn around?"

"Turn your back to me and put your pussy on my face, Vivian."

Her eyes widened as she considered the position he described. A moment later she complied, rising to her feet and turning, lowering herself over his face, legs spread wide.

She leaned forward, gripping the base of his cock, and at the same time felt the touch of his tongue on her clit.

They feasted.

But at a certain point her body rebelled. Vivian cried out as an orgasm rippled through her limbs.

A sharp sting on her buttocks, then a second, jolting her out of her reverie. She lifted her head and looked over her shoulder.

"I want to come in you," he growled.

She scrambled off him. Play time was over. There was no further give in his voice, and his eyes burned.

Turning, she straddled his lap just as he tore his wrists free of her binding.

"Cheating!" she exclaimed.

His hands seized her hips, lifting. Vivian licked her bottom lip, reached between her legs and spread her folds. He lowered her down, the tip of his cock slowly pushing in.

In, in. Deeper, spreading her walls wide until he was sheathed to the hilt.

"Fuck me," he demanded.

Vivian rode him with blind urgency, his punishing grip on her hips urging her faster and faster. He flipped her onto her back, throwing her legs over his shoulders, and plunged deep inside.

Vivian screamed, but he didn't stop, just continued plundering her body with his relentless strength.

As her desire rose, her mind opened. The marks on her arms flared, in sync with his. Waves of pleasure coursed through her, and she didn't understand what she was feeling. Him inside her, or her inside him. His hard cock grinding against her spot, or his body clenched by her soft, greedy walls.

It wasn't only pleasure she felt.

"Vivian," he said, voice hoarse. "*Enja*. Everything I have is yours. Take me."

He kissed her, wild and desperate. All the passion, all the love, all the angry fear mingled with her own emotions. Where he began and she ended ceased to matter.

"Mate," she whispered against his lips, and cried out, the second orgasm stealing away everything but breath.

Seconds later his hot seed flooded her body, his teeth grazing her neck and then biting down, worrying at her flesh as the waves erased any semblance of the kind, civilized man.

He half collapsed against her, his chest smashing her breasts, her hands trapped between them. He lifted himself off enough to tear the bonds from her wrists and flip onto his back, pulling her across his chest. Somehow without leaving her body. His cock lodged between her thighs, pulsing in time with the residual sparks of pleasure.

Vivian braced her forehead on his chest as he caressed her back, hands slipping down to knead her buttocks.

"Mine," he whispered again.

31

"We're going to focus on something different today," Banujani said. "I want to see how deep your bond goes."

Vivian rose from her stretch, giving Banujani a thoughtful look. "What do you mean?"

The guard eyed her intently. "It occurred to me we aren't using your best weapon."

She reached out, taking Vivian's wrist in a firm grip and pulled her arm out. Vivian didn't resist as Banujani pushed up her thin sleeve, revealing the bonding marks.

"You scored a hit on me. That's not easy to do. We know the marks can transfer experiences between partners. It's not common, but it's not rare."

It was easy enough to follow the train of thinking. "You want me to see how much is there and if I can access it at will."

Banujani's lips curved in a pleased smile. "It's a shortcut, but there's no reason not to utilize every tool we have while you're learning. Doing things the long way is for fools. We just want to keep you alive."

"I have no argument with your logic."

Banujani released her. "So, we're going to meditate." She moved to the center of the room and lowered herself gracefully to the ground, giving Vivian an expectant look.

"Come on, we don't have all week."

Vivian settled onto the mat facing Banujani. "Are we doing the find your Silence sequence?" They'd started out training with a day of learning meditation, and breathing, and controlling fear and adrenaline during a fight.

"Yes, but this time instead of Silence, we need to find your memories."

Banujani's soothing voice droned in a low hum in the back of Vivian's mind. She sent her mind into her own past, drawing up memories of her youth and stepping into the sounds, scents, the bright light of a midday sun while on a learning excursion. The umami aroma of her father's curry jambalaya and her mother's intent expression as she turned the pages of a real book.

But these weren't the memories she needed. She recalled the cool wetness of clay in her hands as she spun the wheel, her fingers shaping the lump in front of her into a bowl.

Her fingers flexed, the movements second nature.

She relaxed into the knowledge, remembered her fingers. Then asked them what else they remembered. The shape of clay, the precise strokes of a paintbrush.

The familiar strain of muscles as she fended off an opponent. A skilled opponent several decades of experience ahead of her.

An enemy intent on taking her life.

Her hands flexed, her arms and thighs bunching with decades of muscle memory as she opened her eyes. She saw Banujani as they rose, and she didn't see her.

"Wear the memory, don't let it wear you," she heard the woman say. "If you can't stay in the present, you'll get yourself killed. Now defend yourself."

Banujani attacked.

Vivian snapped into action, meeting the strikes as if the knowledge to do so was embedded in her DNA. There was no hesitance . . . until a part of her mind panicked, realizing this wasn't normal.

She tumbled out of the trance and wound up on her ass for her efforts.

"Sloppy," Banujani said, but there was a thread of approval in her voice. "But not bad. Get up. We do this again. Until you can use the knowledge to save your life and someone else's."

Vivian collapsed another container and stood, twisting to relieve some of the ache in her back.

"Yeah, that's about how I feel," Shira said from the corner where she was nursing her son. "All this tech, and they can't fix weak back muscles. Exercise they say, meditate and use a good pillow, they say. Whatever. I've done all that."

Vivian laughed. Mayleen's weight on her chest was a gentle warmth. If it wasn't for her training regimen, her back would have been a mess.

Ten weeks after Mayleen's birth and her head was whirling from the breakneck speed at which things got done in Beysikai province. She had expected the paperwork approving her business permits to take months. She was no one special, after all.

It had taken two weeks, including the tax filing required to permit her to hire Shira as an assistant, with no special consideration because of Tai'ri's connections. At least none that she had indicated on her forms.

"I didn't realize I ordered so many supplies," she said, looking around. "We might not have enough space."

Contractors had already come and gone, outfitting the studio with custom display shelves, storage units and tables and chairs for classes. She'd chosen light, cheerful colors that managed to retain a sense of elegance without descending into childish. The front was a pane of glass letting in natural light, and the artificial lighting embedded in the ceiling and walls added to the glow. Right now they worked with the artificial lights off, since Mayleen was asleep.

"There's enough space," Shira said, and stood, slipping Ori back into his sling and straightening her clothing. "He's had his lunch, now it's time for mine. What do you want? I feel like walking."

"Whatever you decide is fine."

Shira nodded. "I'll bring back something for Yolu, too." She left the studio, walking at a leisurely stroll.

They'd fallen into a routine this first week in the studio. Paint, install fixtures in the morning. Work on the website and program offerings. Start to unpack shipments around lunchtime and then break to eat. After lunch they'd work for a few more hours then Yolu would accompany the women for a walk in the park before Vivian headed home and Shira was escorted to the small apartment she'd chosen in a nearby neighborhood.

"Shira said she's getting lunch," Yolu said, entering the studio. He'd been outside dealing with a damaged delivery. "I told her to order triples. Stupidity makes me hungry. I can't believe the way people handle packages marked as fucking delicate these days. Excuse my language."

As they unpacked, he collapsed the biodegradable shipping containers and stacked them along a far wall. Each container's items were put away properly before opening another. It prevented what could have been a giant mess.

She suspected he was tidy as a security precaution, however. It was hard to fight when tripping over piles of random stuff scattered over the floor.

He left to deal with another delivery. Tai'ri had been adamant—until they caught the broker who'd gotten away that horrible day Tai'ri had almost died, the women had to maintain their security. Which meant Yolu handled couriers, and Banujani and the team were still guarding Vivian.

A buzzer sounded. Vivian turned as Yolu walked through with a delivery person in tow. Most of the supplies they were unpacking were delivered by pod drones, but the occasional real person came by with more expensive items requiring additional delivery verification.

"This one almost went to the neighbors," Yolu said. "Sloppy."

The delivery person ignored Yolu, approaching Vivian with a datapad to press her thumbprint against.

"It happens," Vivian told him, then said thank you to the delivery person. "I'm glad the neighboring businesses are honest."

Yolu gave her a side eye, but shrugged and began to open the new box.

A comm came through from Shira. "Hey, Vivian, I'm at the new Italian place three blocks down that makes the pasta from scratch. The wait is forty-five minutes. You want me to wait, or should we ditch them for the fried fish joint?"

"Pasta," Yolu said. "I'm growing."

"You heard him," Vivian said, signing off. "Maybe we should just go with delivery from now on. I hate that she has to wait with the baby for that long."

"One of the team is shadowing her, she'll be fine," Yolu said.

She and Tai'ri had spent a week scouting locations for her studio, settling on this small but trendy district that was a mix of business and residential zoning, household incomes in the target range of Vivian's ideal customer. She wasn't aiming for high end, not yet.

"I probably should have leased the studio with the kitchenette," she said. "Tai'ri leaned hard on this one, though." And considering he was financing the entire venture, she hadn't felt quite bold enough to completely discard his preference. In the end, she liked this space well enough that going with his choice pleased her well enough.

"It was the dojo," Yolu said. "It's close, and he cares more about security than lunch."

Vivian agreed and resumed sorting through her packages.

She'd met the owner of the dojo when canvassing the district, asking questions about the foot traffic, crime, and other details that helped her and Tai'ri settle on this location. She'd also be lying to herself if she didn't admit being three doors down from a business that trained citizens in hand-to-hand combat made her feel safe. "Do we have any more inventory coming today?" Yolu asked. "I thought this delivery was it."

She glanced automatically at the front door. "It was supposed to be. Maybe something came early." Vivian began to head to the front when Yolu held out an arm.

"No," he said sharply. "Stay back, I'll see who it is."

Vivian eyed him, but stopped. On her chest, Mayleen stirred and Vivian cradled an arm around the sleeping infant. She would wake to eat soon.

Yolu stalked to the front door, his demeanor shifting from laid-back young man to deadly-in-training protector. One of the reasons Tai'ri had allowed her to work without him present—and until the threat assessment was lowered to zero—was because his younger brother was already in training in combat and protective services.

"Delivery for Vivian Huang," a feminine voice chirped.

"What vendor?" Yolu demanded. "I want to see the tracking number."

Vivian tensed, reacting to Yolu's active hostility towards the female. She started to chide him but stopped. The woman's pale eyes latched onto Vivian when she involuntarily shifted, the gaze too focused to be casual observation. The deliveries had been coming and going all week. Some people smiled and chatted, other people glanced around the shop with casual curiosity, some just shoved a signature pad at her and then took off, not even making eye contact.

But no one just stood there, staring.

Vivian moved towards the back of the shop as the female burst into action, shoving Yolu out of the way and running towards Vivian.

"Run," he yelled, and launched towards the woman. Vivian pressed the distress signal on her comm.

She had her instructions.

"Sir, come see this," Evvek said.

Tai'ri rose from his own console, approaching. A message lay stark on Evvek's console. He read it once, insides icing over.

"It was business before," Evvek said, turning to give Tai'ri a grim look. "It's personal now. I already alerted Vykhan."

"I am here," their *Adekhan* said, stepping into the room. "My team received a similar threat on the *Bdakhun*."

Tension thrummed through Tai'ri. He used the energy, channeled it into cold resolve. No one would threaten his family and live.

"I expected something like this," Vykhan added, expression thoughtful. "We nip at their heels, and this requires a response."

It hit Tai'ri—this was more than Vykhan's usual calm, this was an utter lack of surprise at the sudden escalation of threat after so many weeks of quiet.

"You expected the attack on Vivian at her studio," Tai'ri said.

Evvek inhaled. "Oh, fuck."

Cool eyes met his own. "Her presence out in the open is a temptation to our enemies. By appearing to relax our guard, we invite them to show their hand. So we may cut it off."

"Using Vivian and Mayleen as bait?" Tai'ri snarled.

Vykhan did not move. Tall, cold, proud, so certain of his rightness. "I would not allow your mate or child to be placed in true danger. Even now—"

Tai'ri's comm blared. It was Vivian's panic tone. "It's too late. Let me go, Evvek."

Evvek released him and Tai'ri ran, his anger at Vykhan gone. Nothing mattered now but to get to Vivian and Mayleen.

32

"If he tells you to run," Tai'ri said, "you go for the nearest exit. You run straight to the dojo and request sanctuary. They'll know what to do."

She stared at him in suspicion. How could he promise something like that? Recalling how Tai'ri had clasped the dojo owner's arm, it clicked. "You're friends with him, aren't you? No—former colleagues I would bet."

Tai'ri smiled and shrugged. "He's retired from the Province Heir's detail. Most of his students are prospective or family of other warriors who serve. We take care of our own, in more than one way."

Shelves shattered behind her as the thud of a body flying crashed into them. She whirled, for a split second ignoring Tai'ri's instructions. She couldn't leave Yolu to fight alone. But one of the first things Banujani had taught her in their beginning sessions was that her best defense was her feet.

"Look, yadoana, I get you want to fight and defend yourself. Right now we're going to learn about running and hiding. Then we'll graduate to what you can do to keep from dying if someone gets their hands on you. Your job is to hold out long enough for help to arrive."

"What about ass kicking," Vivian insisted. *"When do we get to ass kicking?"*

Implacable eyes stared at her. "When you can run fast enough and hide long enough that I can't find you."

"But—"

"Don't be in such a hurry to fight. Trust me, you'll get your chance one day, and then you'll wish you hadn't had to defend yourself."

So they'd drilled running and hiding.

Mayleen woke up, wailing, and Vivian knew she would sacrifice anyone, even her own brother-in-law, to keep her baby safe.

She ran, arms securing Mayleen against her chest, counting the seconds, activating her comm. "Banujani!"

Sixty seconds gone, the guard should respond in less than thirty. Please let Yolu live for thirty more seconds. It only took one to kill.

"Get to the dojo, Vivian," Banujani's voice said. "I'm on my way." There was a grunt and a thud and the comm cut off.

The sounds chilled her, so reminiscent of the first

attack. The enemy must have engaged Banujani to distract her while the second came to the studio.

Vivian burst through the back entrance of the dojo and ran through the short hall to the open training area in front. The owner, Kuifi, turned smoothly, no alarm on his face. His gaze sharpened as she stopped.

"Attack," Vivian gasped. "One assailant in the studio with Yolu." She rubbed the crying baby's back, trying to soothe her.

Kuifi called three names, gestured, and they were out the front door at a dead run. A woman jogged crossed towards Vivian. "I'm Kuifi's assistant, Morien," she said calmly, large navy eyes kind. "Are you or the infant injured?"

Her hair was braided tightly to her scalp in looping designs, and for once someone didn't top Vivian by a foot in height. Form fitting workout gear revealed a figure that balanced musculature and feminine curves.

"No," Vivian said. She blinked rapidly. "I wanted to help. I just left him there."

"You did the correct thing," was the firm reply. "*Aja'eki!* What is the first method of defense?"

"Run!" the class roared.

"Would you like to feed your infant?" Morien asked. "We have a meditation room. With reinforced privacy doors. No one will get in there past us."

The message was clear enough. Vivian nodded. "Oh, wait! Shira. Shira is out with her baby getting lunch for us." Panic began to set in. If they came for

Vivian, was Shira a target as well? Why *wouldn't* she be?

"Where is she?" Morien asked.

Vivian gave her the name of the restaurant even as she jabbed at her comm. "Shira?"

Her friend's voice came through immediately. "Yeah, I'm on my way, girl. I've got three bags. Next time Yolu's coming with."

"Shira, we were attacked at the studio."

"What? Oh, *fuck*. Is everyone okay?"

"May I?" Morien asked. "Shira, this is Morien at the dojo. I need you to get off the street. Enter the first crowded business you see and take a seat away from any windows. If you can find a storage closet and barricade yourself, even better. We're sending someone to get you. Keep your comm on."

"Got it," Shira said, and there was only her fast, soft breathing and then the din of patrons in a business.

"I'm going to go get her," Morien said. "This room is secure. Remain here until one of us comes to get you in person."

The baby nursed for an hour at least before the door slid open, revealing her bondmate's enraged face.

He lunged inside the room, aborting the movement only when she instinctively hunched over the baby, shielding her from her father.

Tai'ri's hands curled into fists at his side, and he took a deep breath. "Viv, you're well?"

She stood now that he was calm and wouldn't accidentally hit the baby grabbing for them both, and slid an arm around his waist. His arms enveloped them, his head burying in her hair.

"Banujani and Morien briefed me on the way here," he said in a hoarse tone.

"Tai'ri, is Yolu okay?"

His hands ran up and down her back, though she suspected it was more to soothe him than her. "He's injured, but he'll be fine. He conducted himself well. Shira is safe as well."

Her knees almost buckled in relief. She had to keep her calm for the sake of the baby, but it was so difficult. "Can we go home? I want to check the shop first, but . . . I need some time."

"Of course, *yada'ami*."

"We might need to shut the business down for a time," Tai'ri said when they were home. He stood at her shoulder, watching as Vivian bathed the baby in the nursery sanitation unit.

Vivian didn't respond immediately, wanting to choose her words. Mayleen kicked her feet, beaming a toothless smile up at her parents as Vivian gently wiped her body down with a damp cloth, pausing to tickle her bulging belly.

"The threat assessment has changed?" she asked. It was a silly question, because of course now it had, but she was stalling. He wasn't going to like her response.

"We received messages today from Zhiannur. Threats against your life and the *Bdakhun's*. It's usually difficult to provoke an emotional response from an Aeddannar, but he seemed angry. That makes him dangerous."

He handed her a towel and she draped it over her shoulder, then lifted the baby. Mayleen peered at her father, shoving a tiny fist in her mouth.

Vivian settled into the reclining chair and dressed the baby. Tai'ri pivoted to face them, but didn't approach.

"What do you expect him to do?"

"Today was just a warning shot. He's toying with us." Tai'ri stared at her, grim and angry. "He's as slippery as water, and this has gone from salvaging a lost investment to assuaging a personal insult."

"*He* feels insulted that we're not amenable to his kidnapping Mayleen and I?"

His lips twitched, but settled back into a thin line. "Yes."

"What will it take to finally capture him?"

"It's not just him." Finally, he crossed the room and crouched at Vivian's feet, staring at the now nursing baby. "It's whoever is financing his cell as well. We managed to eliminate operations when they set up in Naidekai, but our resources are being stretched thin.

This isn't the only city in the province where aliens are being funneled."

"Why aren't they just being stopped before they come on planet?"

He touched her cheek. "That's one of our duties, but we aren't a government agency, we're a task force with funding up for renewal annually."

Tai'ri stood, left the room, and returned with a water bottle infused with chopped up fruit. She sipped obediently, recognizing that his particular form of self-soothing was to fuss, even if it was just bringing her water.

Vivian watched him pace. "I don't want to stop working, Tai'ri. I don't want to be shut up in the house, as lovely as it is."

He pinned her with a look. "Are a few weeks of lounging around the house worth more than your life? Mayleen's?"

"That's why I'm training so hard, so I can't be taken easily. If you're having trouble finding this person, locking me in the house will just prolong the inevitable. I need to stay out." She smiled as winsomely as possible. "I make good bait."

He growled.

Mayleen jerked and began to cry.

"You startled the baby."

He approached, sinking down to his knees. "No, don't cry, *yadoana*. I'm sorry."

Watching him coo at the baby was one of her

purest joys in life. Vivian grinned. "Big bad warrior, worried he hurt a little baby's feelings. It's so adorable."

He arched a brow, kissing Mayleen's head, and then straightening. His expression hardened. "You stay home, Vivian."

She looked at him, smiled. "No. I'll go to the shop, and I'll be prepared. We'll draw him out, Tai'ri, and end this."

33

In the end, she wound up compromising. Because much of the work could be done on her home console, Vivian wound up staying home with the baby until later in the afternoon each day. Shira dropped Ori off, and the women traveled together to the shop to spend a half day there. Behind the scenes Vivian knew Tai'ri was watching, waiting. Sending Zhiannur messages designed to coax him out into the open instead of sending his goons.

"Shira's late," Yolu said. He lounged on the futon style couch she'd had brought up from the basement media room to her home studio.

"Like you're ever punctual," Daobah replied with a delicate sneer. The young woman had finally gotten a break in her studies and Vivian had pounced, roping her into becoming a part-time mother's helper for Shira and Vivian as they worked.

Vivian looked up from her datapad, then glanced back down at the time and frowned. "Hmm. Maybe a rough morning."

Her muscles ached from *her* morning. Each day Banujani pressed her a little more, a little more. Each day Vivian was able to slip into muscle memory a little longer while staying aware of her present. She hadn't been able to hold it as long as that first day, two minutes max, but she was improving. Painfully.

They would be opening in a week or two and were currently marketing as well as finalizing the setup of the studio and supply shop. To make their income goals, they needed a certain quota of new students enrolled by the end of the first month they were open. The classes were currently forty percent occupied, and each day brought a trickle of new interest. The marketing could easily be done from the home office.

Shira usually arrived at Vivian's house the same time every morning, give or take fifteen minutes. Shira didn't have a bondmate, or a House, or a Banujani who could pop in and change the baby while Vivian showered if Tai'ri had already left that morning.

Thirty minutes late was tardier than usual, but not unreasonable. "I'll comm her." She rubbed Mayleen's little back in circles as she attempted to contact Shira.

Yolu waited, meeting Vivian's worried gaze when Shira didn't answer. He tapped his comm. "Banujani? Shira's late. Did her guard check in?"

Thirty seconds passed. "No response," Banujani's

voice said.

Vivian stood, datapad and marketing forgotten.

"Absolutely not," Banujani said, arms crossed. She leveled a flat, unpleasant stare at Vivian, who'd demanded to come with them to Shira's flat.

"What are you expecting to find?" Vivian asked.

"Her guard's comm is offline. The longer I argue with you, the longer it takes to get to him and Shira."

Vivian, a few weeks ago, would have winced and backed off. She met Banujani's gaze steadily. "I'm Shira's only friend here. Our babies are going to grow up together. I'm going with you. You'll have to physically restrain me to keep me here, and I know that's against Haeemah's Precepts."

"How would you know?"

"I've been reading."

Banujani grimaced.

Vivian kissed the top of Mayleen's head and slipped her out of the wrap, handing her to Daobah. She hated the thought of being away from her baby for even a few hours, but if Shira and baby Ori were in danger, Vivian would do everything possible to help them. Fear surged for a brief moment, but she allowed it to wash through her, and replaced it with the Silence of resolve.

Breathe.

Focus.

"Let's go," Vivian said.

"No signs of a struggle," Banujani said, voice grim. "Whoever took her was professional. They would have wanted to make the extraction seamless."

Vivian stared down at the empty crib. She'd already been in the kitchenette where a half-prepared meal sat as if abruptly abandoned. Ori's diaper bag rested on the couch, half unzipped and stuffed to the brim with supplies. Shira wouldn't have left it behind.

Silence was hard. She wanted to yell, to burst out in tears, to find a dark corner and curl up and hope the enemy didn't come for her as well. But she'd survived so far, and she was stronger, and devolving into a gibbering wreck would not help Shira and Ori.

Steeling herself, she left Ori's room and entered Shira's. A co-sleeping bassinet sat on the full-sized bed. They'd picked them out together a week before giving birth. Shira had gone into labor only three days after Vivian.

She swallowed, looking around, and noticed a slip of real paper in the bassinet. Vivian frowned. They had several sheaves of real paper in inventory, but Shira wouldn't use it for personal purposes. Vivian approached, then froze when she recognized the Yadeshi characters on the paper.

Someone had spelled the Yadeshi phonetic translation of her name.

"Vivian?" Banujani called. "We need to track. I'm taking you home."

Vivian opened the paper, skimmed the short handwritten note, and slipped it inside the pocket of her slim pants.

She turned, leaving the room, and met Banujani's gaze. "That's fine. You'll keep me updated?"

Banujani stared hard, but there wasn't much she could protest about Vivian's calm acceptance.

"We'll keep you updated," the guard said after a minute.

Vivian warred with herself.

She lifted Mayleen out of her crib and sat in the rocking chair. The baby stirred, and Vivian let her latch onto a nipple. "Love you so much," she murmured. She would do anything for this child. Tear the world apart to keep her safe and happy.

But there was another mother and baby out there who weren't safe and happy, and the thought of what could be happening to them right now was as agonizing as the thought of what could happen to Mayleen. Mayleen was safe behind this fortress. Ori and Shira weren't.

After the baby was sound asleep in her crib again,

Vivian went up to her studio. It was night, and the light shining through the ceiling windows was the ethereal glow from stars. The stars on Yedahn were brighter than Earth's, or maybe their atmosphere was clearer.

She'd made a home here for herself, one she was hoping to show to her parents soon. A long craft table stacked neatly with brushes, inks, and a piece in progress. The shelves of carefully organized supplies. In the corner a seating area for when she just wanted to sit and think.

In that same corner, a discreet wall inset datasphere console blinked, indicating a message in the inbox.

She approached. "Open and display unread message."

Coordinates flashed on screen. She had sixty seconds to commit them to memory, and like the handwritten note had instructed, the message self-destructed.

Come. Bring no one. Wear no devices. Their lives hinged on her cooperation.

Vivian wasn't stupid. As soon as she was in their power, the enemy wouldn't release Shira or Ori. But Tai'ri would come for her—she was the living breadcrumb that would lead to the end of this danger once and for all. They were fully bonded now. He would find her.

She continued to breathe evenly, allowing calm to flow through her. Spikes of anxiety here and there would be expected since he would know about Shira's kidnapping by now. He would anticipate her worry. But any sudden, prolonged distress would alert him before she was ready.

Vivian took a sheet of parchment paper and a black ink pen, and wrote down the coordinates. She withdrew the original note from her pocket and set it down as well.

"House, in two hours inform Banujani that there is a message for her on my workstation."

"Noted."

She had to trust they would come for her, and that they were professionals and knew her life, and Shira and Ori's depended on their stealth.

"I won't be taken again," she'd said to Vykhan.

"I believe you. I believe you will survive this."

Banujani stared past Tai'ri's shoulder as she made her report, expression blank, the tight skin around her eyes the only sign of her grim guilt. They stood in Vivian's studio where she'd been discovered missing. He couldn't drop everything and go after her—rash actions might endanger her life and prevent them from finding her forever.

But Tai'ri took the words like a blow to the stomach. No, knives, each one stabbing a rent into his chest. He delved down, down into his matebond, reaching for any sense of his mate. Too far . . . wherever she was, she was too far for him to sense anything other than that she was alive.

The only thing that kept him sane and Silent was the baby cradled in his arms, her small face nuzzling his chest in her sleep.

"Sir," Banujani said, voice gentle. "Call your mother."

One breath. Two. He couldn't find Vivian, rescue Vivian from their enemies, unless his daughter was safe. He kissed her tiny forehead.

"House, contact Agata."

His mother arrived and didn't ask questions, her expression serene as she took the baby.

She paused briefly before leaving, kissing Tai'ri's cheek. "Don't worry for your child, son. Do what you need to do."

She didn't ask where Vivian was, for which he was grateful. He wouldn't have been able to say the words through the stone of rage, fear and grief lodged in his gut.

"There is no time," Vykhan said once Agata and Mayleen were gone, accompanied by a squad of warriors.

Tai'ri met Vykhan's cool gaze and felt his lip draw up in a snarl. "You. You—"

Banujani grabbed his shoulder. "Tai. Anger won't help."

"He dangled my mate like *bait*."

Vykhan didn't move, hands clasped behind his back. "She will survive, and she has left a trail. If you are ready, Adyat will report."

Tai'ri tucked his rage away, called on Haeemah for control, and listened as Adyat's voice came through Vykhan's comm.

"Evvek ran the scenario as soon as Banujani reported Vivian missing," he said. "The main tracker in the transport she used was disabled. The embedded secondary tracker came online, and we believe was undetected—at least until the transport was destroyed."

"Last known location?" Vykhan asked.

Adyat rattled off the coordinates. Tai'ri stiffened. "They took her to Anthhori."

Vykhan went utterly still, eyes narrow and distant. "I will need to do something about that ship soon," he murmured.

"That ship is a scourge," Banujani growled.

"And the security is impenetrable," Tai'ri said, jaw aching.

"We have an advantage," Vykhan said, meeting his gaze. "Two. One, they do not know your bond is fully formed. Two, they do not know your mate is dangerous." Vykhan smiled. "Have faith. We hunt."

Vivian stepped out of the transport and looked around, pushing back the low-level emotional ache of already missing Mayleen. She couldn't allow fear to control her; fear of never seeing her daughter again, fear for the baby's distress in losing her mother.

The area defined the term ghost town. Abandoned construction, the floating streetlights dim, crackling in the evening sky.

A hand grabbed her shoulder. Vivian whirled, mind flashing back to Banujani's training. She grabbed the wrist and twisted. The man cursed, and a weapon was suddenly in her face.

"We said no resistance, Ms. Huang," he said, voice harsh and accented, though no anger appeared on his face. A professional, then. A hired thug.

She stepped back, lifting her hands slowly. "Apologies. I'm nervous."

"This is your only pass."

"Understood."

More men emerged from the shadows, one of them approaching the transport.

"Dismantle it," the one in front of her said.

Vivian suppressed a wince. She supposed she should have expected that. If Tai'ri recovered the vehicle, then they could determine her last location. Which was demonstrably not on their enemy's agenda.

The man was watching her. After a moment, he put the weapon away. "We thank you for your cooperation. Welcome to your shuttle to Anthhori."

34

Anthhori.

She'd heard about it, seen some news vids and read articles in various society blogs she'd perused to begin to immerse herself in the province's pop culture. A pleasure barge, a den of iniquity, a couple's retreat. A place where different species mingled, and the rules were made by those with power and the wealth to enforce it. The fact that it remained neutral territory meant Ibukay and her family had no jurisdiction over what went on there—but it also meant Tai'ri and Vykhan would be free to act with impunity in order to rescue her. The only rules they would have to follow was that of their conscience.

"When will I see Shira and Ori?" she asked as they disembarked into a long, neutral hallway.

Her captors ignored her question. They escorted her down the hall, unrestrained. It wasn't necessary.

She was here of her own free will and they probably thought there wasn't much a petite, slender, mostly untrained human could do against them anyway.

They were probably right. She knew what her job was. Get in, get to Shira and Ori, stay alive until the cavalry came.

"I thought this was a pleasure barge," she murmured as they walked down bland, quiet hallways.

"This is a private lower deck," her captor said.

She was surprised he deigned to reply, and tilted her head in thanks. No need to be rude.

"This is where your owner keeps his pets," he added, and Vivian downgraded her assessment of his professionalism.

Banujani's training must have gotten a better grip on her than she'd thought. Feeling slightly detached, she noted that she should be panicking. These clean, ruthlessly quiet halls reminded her so much of the pens, though of course in the pens space was a premium. She still didn't know what kind of building she'd been kept in. The bunker of an abandoned warehouse, perhaps. She'd been barely conscious during her rescue.

Her heartrate spiked, her breathing coming in quick pants, and she yanked her mind away from those thoughts. Just in time, as they stopped in front of a door. Her captor—perhaps she'd call him Roboghoul #1 for all the emotion he showed—placed a hand on the palmplate, and it slid open.

It was a cargo hold. The cargo were people.

When she didn't immediately enter, someone shoved. She stumbled once, then resumed control of her feet. A dozen people, all female from what she could tell, occupied the room. Her gaze took in the hard floors, blank walls. A water station was tucked into a corner and another narrow doorway led into toilet facilities. No privacy screen.

"Vivian!"

She spun. In the farthest corner from the door sat Shira, cradling Ori. "Shira."

She forced herself to remain calm, neutral. They had to know how important Shira was to her, but there was no need to reinforce that knowledge. Handing these people emotional leverage would only make the situation worse.

Vivian began to walk towards Shira, and Roboghoul grabbed her. Her muscles tensed and she gritted her teeth, then forced her body to relax as she gave him an inquiring look.

He pointed his chin at the various guards posted in the room. "No escape. No trouble."

"I understand." The *or else* in his tone was self-explanatory.

He let her go, and she went to Shira, kneeling down. "Are you okay?"

Shira's mouth thinned, and she snorted.

Vivian's lips quirked. "Fair enough."

"They feed us and there's plenty of water. They

haven't tried to take Ori away from me." Shira's steely tone couldn't quite hide the panic in her eyes. "What the *fuck* are you doing here?"

"Staging an intervention."

Shira gave her a look. "Funny." Ori rustled in her arms, nuzzling for her breasts, and she looked down. Vivian shifted her body to shield the woman as she placed the child on a nipple. "I will kill him before I let them have him."

"I don't think it will come to that. There are other players on the board."

"Is there a plan other than to sit here and wait to be rescued?"

Vivian grimaced.

"Great." Shira sighed. "In all the vids, the heroines are badass. They smuggle in weapons, dismantle the ship's systems, take down the evil guards with chewing gum and spit."

"Yes, my students on Earth used to try and get me to watch those too. I'm not much of a fantasy fiction reader, though."

Shira leaned her head against the wall, closing her eyes, lines of strain bracketing her mouth.

The same tension stiffened the back of Vivian's neck. Her breasts tingled, reminding her that at home Mayleen would be wanting to nurse. Had she done the right thing coming here? Was it wrong to place her friend above the well-being of her own baby?

But what kind of mother would she be if she didn't

teach her daughter even this early in life that there were just some evils you could not let come to pass?

The door slid open, and the two men who stepped inside drew a hiss from Shira.

Vivian glanced at Shira, observed the blatant hatred shining in the woman's eyes, and turned back to study the non-humans who clinically examined each of the huddled prisoners.

The first one was medium height, lean, with large uptilted eyes glowing with internal light and short, silky white locks that waved slightly. His deep, supernaturally smooth skin shimmered in places where the light caught chiseled bones, almost as if he was wearing cosmetics, but Vivian didn't think so.

The second stood slightly behind the first's shoulders, pale skin, the same large up tilted eyes, and wispy white hair.

Delicately pointed ears peeked through their hair.

"Are they elves?" Vivian asked in disbelief. They still told fairy tales on Earth, though children mostly learned about them in ancient history and literature classes.

"Don't say that where he can hear you," Shira said in a bare whisper, her lips against Vivian's ear. "They don't like that word. I was punished before. The pale-skinned one was one of my handlers. They're called Aeddannar."

Which meant he must be the broker who'd escaped, who'd made threats. Vivian understood the nature of the hatred now and felt it welling in her own chest. She'd never gotten or expected the opportunity to confront and punish those who had harmed her.

"This dark one must be a higher up," Shira said.

With that information, Vivian watched him covertly. He murmured to Roboghoul #1 on occasion as he toured the room, casually inspecting a person here and there. The pale one followed quietly, speaking when spoken to. The leader pointed to a short, blue-scaled person slumped in a corner, their silky one-shoulder tunic and pants wrinkled, narrow jaw slack and eyes closed.

Roboghoul motioned to one of his men, who went over and yanked the person up by an arm. Their eyes flew open, and they emitted a hissing shriek, speaking in a series of quick syllables. She heard the faint humming that indicated the language wasn't loaded to her translator.

"See the edge of its scales?" the dark Aeddannar man said. "That black inflammation is death. Process this one—we'll have to recoup the investment with their parts."

Vivian's breath caught, a chill of horror digging into her spine. This was so much worse than what she'd endured in the pens. But then she had been kept in a small cell alone and had had no one to talk to. She had no way of knowing if there were others who were treated like this rather than used for breeding stock.

Ori gurgled, and Shira immediately put him back

on the breast. But the sound drew the Aeddannars' gazes. When she met the eyes of the pale one, they were bright with malice.

They walked over unhurriedly and stopped a foot away, looking down. "There was no need to get my attention," the dark one said in a kind voice. "I am aware of your presence. Two of my loveliest investments. Both have caused me such loss and trouble in your own way, though you—" he locked gazes with Vivian "—the reports on you were exemplary. You really were a model acquisition, darling. A pity you didn't bring my infant."

It took her several seconds to realize that the man's possessive was directed at Mayleen. She tamped down her instinct to attack or even speak. Arguing with him that they were people and not his property would be pointless. She didn't know this man, had never seen him and was not aware of what his role in the trafficking was, but she saw the look in his eyes. The utter lack of empathy, of soul. He truly believed they were things to be bought and traded for profit. Her protestations would never change his mind.

"See," he said, glancing at Roboghoul #1. "She does not even speak. A perfectly behaved acquisition. *This* one—defiant, however. Impregnating her was difficult. She kept rejecting the mounts. I do prefer the surgical implantation but alas, budgetary considerations." He spread his hands.

Vivian allowed the words to crash over her head

like waves, meeting his gaze with an almost empty calm. Her marks throbbed, a low burn that broke through her narrow focus on the man in front of her.

"See how easy they are to manage?" he asked the pale one. "Perhaps now you understand why your punishment was so severe. I cannot tolerate incompetence."

A punishment, the pale one's eyes told Vivian, that would be taken out on her and Shira.

At her side, Shira shifted, breathing coming in fast, harsh gasps. Ori had quieted, resting in the comfort of his mother's arms.

The leader looked down at Ori contemplatively. "Take the infant."

"Happily," the pale one said.

Shira shouted, her entire body jerking. Vivian placed a hand on her arm, clamping down with strength she hadn't known she had.

She looked at the leader. "Human infants do not thrive when separated from their mothers. The nursing keeps them calm and impervious to illness, and gives them the ideal mix of fat and nutrients. It would jeopardize your investment." Later she would be amazed at how dispassionate she sounded. Later.

He tilted his head. "Hmm. That *has* been my observation. A pity you are fully human, and precious to the one who has caused me such a loss of profit. I am always looking for useful minds. But perhaps there is a way . . ."

"I would be best utilized to oversee the care and health of your current stock." She waved a hand at the others. "Communicating would be easier for me since I am one of them, and it would perhaps give you insight in how to increase your profit margins by ensuring optimal health and condition. The blue scaled one, for instance. That might have been prevented."

"True, true. Yes, there are always inefficiencies to any operation, areas that can be improved." His gaze sharpened, and Vivian saw the tinge of malice behind the relentlessly affable exterior as he looked at Shira. "You are lucky, pet, that I care more for my responsibility to my investors than I do about retaliation for the harm done me." He nodded at Vivian. "Do your job well, and there may be benefits."

She inclined her head, carefully taking her hand away from Shira's arm. "I understand."

He turned and began to walk away with his guards. "Of course, if your mate comes for you we will have to kill him, but that is not personal. Only business. I must recoup the damage done to my reputation. Taking you back should repair the breach, but if he were to come, even better."

"He will not live once he is here," the pale one said. "Do not allow yourself to hope."

"Tai'ri knows what he's doing, right?" Shira asked after they'd left the room with their escort.

"Don't worry. None of the guards I saw were a

match even for Yolu's training. He'll find us. Comfort your sweet baby."

"Mayleen..."

"Is safe, and with her family." By now, most likely. Tai'ri would have taken her to his mother. "All will be well." She repeated it to herself until she believed it then stood and began to move around the room to do the job that would buy Shira leniency.

Tai'ri hadn't known the true meaning of Silence until now.

He felt nothing, just breathed, each breath exhaled from a chest of ice. There was room for nothing but success, nothing but the utter conviction that superior strength, skill, and the rightness of his mission would weigh in his balance.

Vykhan and Banujani were at his side as they ghosted through the halls of this deck. Anthhori was never quiet, but today it was as if her bowels had emptied itself of the usual revelers in a sepulchral welcome.

They came to a corridor. Tai'ri gestured, and they went right. Vivian's trail went cold once the enemy had taken her into a transport up to the pleasure ship, and she wore no tracking device, but they had not counted on the strength of the bonding marks.

Tai'ri had delayed filing the paperwork officially

recognizing their bond, realizing it was just another avenue to track Vivian. The less information the enemy had, the better that lack could be used against them.

Evvek's voice spoke in his ear. "You have incoming. There's time to engage or take cover." Everyone heard the same words. He remained in their transport monitoring the corridors and feeding them information.

"If we engage now, they will either increase the guard around the women, or take them from their current location," Vykhan said. "We take cover and wait it out. Tai'ri?"

He felt along the bond. "She isn't moving. She isn't alarmed. Agreed."

Evvek gave instructions, and they hid.

35

Vivian convinced their captors that torturing them with twenty-four-hour light wasn't conducive to healthy stock. If they didn't sleep, they would fall into illness. The lights dimmed, and everyone was able to exhale as much as possible, and try to rest. A few moments of blissful unawareness were manna from the heavens, though Vivian could not sleep more than a few minutes.

Tai'ri was coming. The certainty of it settled into her bones. She felt his approaching presence. Her job was to stay alive and gather as much data as possible. She dug into her marks, scratching absently. They itched insanely, like fire ants crawling just underneath her skin. It must be a nasty side effect of the bond, of being separated from Tai'ri for so many hours.

He was coming. They just had to hold on.

"Mostly everyone here is humanoid," Vivian murmured.

She didn't know if it was morning, but after several hours the lights slowly brightened, and guards came in with a bag and tossed silver wrapped packages at everyone. Vivian grimaced. She'd eat the paste because she needed her strength, but she didn't have to like it.

The guard tossed one, and it landed against her chest. She stifled a hiss of pain. Her breasts were heavy with milk and sore. She'd have to do something soon. Vivian closed her eyes, desperately clinging to her calm. Grimly. She couldn't think of Mayleen. Couldn't.

After the guard left a shuffle of feet warned Vivian, and she opened her eyes as another of the captives inched over. This one was tall, oddly jointed and green skinned, her large eyes unblinking.

"No one who causes trouble survives," the alien said in a light, soprano tone. She whistled through her teeth. "Always punished." She tilted her head, and her large eyes half shut. "You think help is coming."

Vivian and Shira exchanged looks.

"My people have good hearing," she said, tapping the side of her head. "I've been listening. My name is Byeo-mi-cha'i, of the Hyunthu people."

It didn't surprise Vivian. When she'd made a tour of the room earlier and introduced herself—or tried— and spoken to each person for a few minutes, she'd noticed that when she returned to her corner, this green female continued to watch her and Shira.

"I think you may be mistaken," Vivian said carefully. She couldn't trust the female. For all Vivian knew, the guards could have planted her there as a spy. Though what the point of that would be, Vivian didn't know.

"Ah," the female said. "I have been here twelve cycles. Every four they take some of us and bring in more. Twice they have allowed potential buyers to come and examine us. Darosheiil—the Aeddannar—"

"Is that the dark one?" Shira interrupted. "The one who pretends to be the good cop?"

"Good cop?" The female paused, then whistled assent. "Yes, good cop. He thinks he is a businessman. I listen to him too." She didn't smile, but the shape of her face changed slightly.

"What day of the cycle are we on now?" Shira asked.

"Four. Today he will bring a new buyer."

There was no time left. But what could she do against six guards and with Shira and Ori hostages to her good behavior? She was one woman, barely trained even with access to the knowledge held in the bonding marks. Stay alive. That had been drilled into her head. Stay alive and wait for the professionals to get there. But if they didn't act and Tai'ri was too late, then keeping her head down and playing possum wouldn't matter, anyway.

Still . . . if this Darosheiil didn't try to sell her or Shira and Ori, that would buy more time.

"Alright," Vivian said. "I think we should keep our heads down, not draw attention to ourselves."

"You're hoping their buyers will pick someone else," Shira said.

"We need more time." That was all she was willing to say, but Shira understood.

"Right. But we need a Plan B, Viv. And when we get out of this alive, I'm taking you up on that offer to train with your guards."

The green female didn't interrupt the exchange, waiting patiently. Vivian decided to trust her. She had information they needed and if the female was a mole, well it wasn't like they weren't already screwed, anyway.

"Alright, let's plot."

The burn in her marks was a low, unbearable thrum. Anger, a sharp anticipatory taste of vengeance, filled her mouth. The emotions flowed through her, taking Vivian in their grip until her very vision sharpened, her muscles tensing with desire to do battle.

The posted guards lounged in their positions. There were three of them in the room, and other than discouraging talk they kept to themselves. When

Darosheiil returned, he would have another three with him. Six guards in total.

The marks flared, and Vivian bit back a cry of pain. Sudden certainty filled her. These feelings, these emotions weren't hers, though she was happy to embrace them.

One of the guards snapped to attention, and the others followed suit, their eyes with that half unfocused look from listening to someone speak. They must have comm implants. Their sudden tension could only mean one thing.

Tai'ri was here.

"Steady," Vivian murmured. Shira heard her, and she knew Byeo-mi-cha'i would as well.

The door slid open, and Darosheiil strode in, his energy less calm than his first visit. She shifted onto her knees, appearing at ease with her hands resting on her thighs. Shira cradled Ori to her chest in a makeshift sling that would hold the child still so she could use her hands.

Darosheiil came right to Vivian and Shira. "It seems you were juicer bait than I anticipated, my dear." Anger belied his casual tone. "My forces have taken quite the hit, among other things."

She said nothing, and he smiled. "Still no response?"

"You didn't ask a question." Vivian spoke with the same blank expression and soft tone, then shut up.

"True, true," Darosheiil said, pursing his lips as he

stared at her with those soulless eyes that pretended to be kind.

There was no time and baiting him to lash out would erase what little she had. She embraced the burn of the marks, gathered Tai'ri's emotions to her chest and sank into them. Sank into the muscle memory until the strange trance like euphoria began to flood her senses.

Breathe.

Remember her training. Open herself to her mate. Silence. Focus.

"He's through the first ring," the pale Aeddannar said, coming into the room abruptly. "Permit me to kill the female now and leave her body for him to find, with my own hands."

"This is not personal, Zhiannur," Darosheiil said coolly. "This is business. We do not act until the best advantage presents itself. We are not thugs to bloody our hands. These will do that kind of low work, when it is time." He gestured contemptuously to the impassive guards.

One of his guards murmured something, and he glanced over his shoulder, straightening. "Very well." Darosheiil turned and walked away. "This one we do not need, however. Kill the mother and take her child. Bring the other one."

Vivian sprang up, allowing the matebond fueled muscle memory to pilot her movements. Darosheiil streaked out of her path, moving faster than expected, but he wasn't her target.

"Stun only, do not kill!" Darosheiil exclaimed.

The first guard jerked, bringing up his weapon. Even then, the others didn't seem to take Vivian's threat seriously. Darosheiil would need a better quality mercenary in the future, if he had one.

She feigned left, grabbed the guard's wrist and twisted, pulling his weight forward to disarm him and take control of the weapon. His second of surprise was the advantage she needed, following the disarm up with a kick to the back of his knee. He collapsed to the ground and Vivian turned, firing. His body jerked and he went down, stunned into unconsciousness.

There was a moment of shocked silence. "Do your jobs," Darosheiil growled, his affable exterior vanished.

Byeo-mi-cha'i surged up from her huddle next to a guard. Vivian had seconds to observe that her long limbs must be dense with muscle because one punch and the guard next to her went down. Byeo-mi-cha'i retrieved his weapon, and chaos broke loose. Another attacked Vivian, and she snapped back into focus.

Shira's job was to remain out of the fight and protect Ori. The other females all had their tasks, and they knew they'd only get this one chance. The guards must have allowed their hushed conversations only because they had never fought back as a group.

Vivian shot her assailant, turned to find two more attacking. Byeo-mi-cha'i rapped instructions to three of the females who swarmed another guard. He was faster, shooting into the trio. There were screams, one woman collapsing to the ground, but the others grabbed his weapon arm, clinging for life as others jumped on his back and brought him down.

Inelegant, but effective.

Fire scored Vivian's torso, the reward for allowing herself to become distracted by her worry for the others. She engaged her assailant, reminding herself that her muscles might think they possessed Tai'ri's strength, but they didn't. She was still a short, slight woman who only recently began physical conditioning.

But still. Experience, even borrowed, counted.

"Vivian, behind you!" Shira screamed. Byeo-mi-cha'i whistled, a high-pitched shriek of fury.

"Comm for backup," a male voice snapped.

Vivian whirled, throwing herself to the side to evade the blaster shot and follow up kick which would have caved her head in if it connected.

"Alive, you idiot!" Darosheiil screamed again.

A blow from behind stunned Vivian. She collapsed to her knees, fighting the disorientation. Zhiannur darted forward, grabbing her by her hair and pulling her to her feet.

"You will pay for this," he hissed, and dimly she thought that the increasing glow of his eyes boded nothing good.

She snarled. "I won't be taken again."

He froze. He wasn't looking at her though, but over her shoulder.

"Release the female," a cool, peaceful voice said. "Death is your reward if you do not comply."

"A slow, painful death," Tai'ri growled.

She barely recognized his voice, clogged with rage and bloodlust. But she'd know him anywhere. Her marks flared, and she aimed a strike at Zhiannur's neck.

He gurgled, releasing her, and stumbled back. The enemy closest aimed his weapon, but dropped to the ground when a blast took him in the chest.

Darosheiil did not move, not even to raise his hands in surrender. He stared at Vykhan, expression fathomless.

"You overestimated your forces," Vykhan said. "I find that is a mistake your kind often makes. Curious."

Vivian looked around for Shira, finding her standing over an injured woman, a weapon clutched in her hand and her teeth bared in a snarl, her free arm clutched protectively over Ori.

"Vivian," Banujani said. "To us."

Warriors streaked past Vivian, taking out the rest of the enemy guards. One of Tai'ri's team stopped several feet from Shira, hands up, until the expression on her face faded and she blinked, arm lowering. He spoke in a low tone and she nodded, handing him the weapon.

Strong arms wrapped around her waist, jerking her backwards. Vivian knew it was Tai'ri and didn't react, though there was a fierce moment where she argued with the instinctive reaction of her muscles.

"Someone has learned some new tricks," her mate

said in her ear, his voice warm with approval and fierce with relief.

She turned in his arms. "Mayleen?"

Tai'ri pressed a kiss on her forehead. "Safe with mother. We'll be with her soon, and this will be just another day at the office—and now you know what my office is like."

"I knew you would come."

He stared down into her eyes. "I will always come."

Nothing could have intruded on that perfect moment of deep accord, their love and relief humming through their bond. Nothing.

. . . except for Banujani. She walked past them, saying over her shoulder, "Eh. I don't think you needed us, *aja'eko*. Next time we'll let you have at it and wait for the report."

Tai'ri snarled at his second-in-command.

"This feels too easy," Vivian said. Shira snorted.

A petite warrior wandered towards them and winked at Vivian. "We always only needed them to poke their heads out at the same time in the same place long enough so we could nab them," Eb said. "We've been herding them for months now. Our job is really very boring."

"That is true," Vykhan said, and Vivian glanced at him to see he stood next to Darosheiil, and the Aeddannar still did not move. "You did well. If you ever feel the need for more formal training, I invite you to join my morning circle."

"Run," someone yelled goodnaturedly, in a corner assisting one of the females.

Tai'ri sighed, running his hands up and down Vivian's arms. "I should get you home now. Mayleen will be missing you, and I won't be settled until you are safe." He glanced at Shira and smiled warmly. "I would feel better if you joined us in our home. Demonstrably your building's security is not what it should be."

"I've been asking her for weeks," Vivian said.

"I think I'll take you up on that now," Shira said.

Vivian laughed, and they went home.

EPILOGUE

"Here's to over a year in business," Shira said, lifting her glass in a toast. "And we haven't bit the dust yet."

Vivian threw back her shot, enjoying the burn of alcohol down her throat, and set it down with faint regret. "That's it for me. As soon as I get home Mayleen will yowl for boobs. She doesn't even bother to ask anymore, she just climbs into my lap and lifts my shirt up."

Shira sighed, set down her empty glass, and signaled for the bartender, her finger slightly wilted. "Something fruity and—" she grimaced "—nonalcoholic. For both of us."

The bartender nodded and moved away. "It won't be forever." Vivian heard the amusement in her voice. She'd never been much of a drinker, but Shira often mournfully recounted her 'boozy days.'

Shira swiveled in her seat, eyeing the dancefloor all the way up. Tiers of circular, translucent flooring with a central pillar soared to a ceiling twelve stories high. A telltale shimmer of light promised the protection of invisible barriers, but even thinking about daring the upper floors made Vivian dizzy.

She'd keep her feet firmly on the ground, thank you.

"I want to dance up there," Shira said, pointing.

"Of course you do."

Shira grinned at her. "Come on, let's expand our horizons. They don't have anything like this on Earth."

"Not yet, anyway. And we've been away a few years."

"Pleeease."

Vivian sighed, but slipped off her stool with a smile, pausing to reserve their spaces. The bartender would return with their drinks and finding the women gone, place them in protective shields.

They made their way to one of the lifts and emerged onto the eighth floor. This level boasted deep, booming drums and a masculine voice rasping to a fast beat.

Shira whooped and threw herself onto the floor, Vivian following more sedately.

Months of training now made her confident in her coordination, and she knew she looked good in the short, sleeveless sheath dress she wore. Electric blue with strategically sheer panels, it was deceptively simple and covertly sexy.

They attracted a few glances, some longer than others, and speculative. Beysikai province was one of the more diverse, with a robust interstellar immigration program, but single human women were still uncommon.

"This is great," Shira shouted over the music, her arms above her head as she swiveled her hips. Her golden-brown hair shone in wild waves against her deep pink halter top. "Girl, come on. Put some life into it."

"Why not for once," Vivian muttered, drawn into the music despite herself.

And after several moments found she *loved* it.

She threw back her head to watch the dancers above, grateful for the clever lighting which offered ladies in dresses some modesty, and lost herself in the rhythm of the dance until there was a slight transition in the music.

Vivian noticed movement out of the corner of her eyes and stiffened involuntarily, turning her head as a man detached himself from the crowd and glided over. He gave Vivian a brief glance, enough for her to register violet tinged eyes and a braid of silvery blue hair down his back. He wore gray; trousers, fitted t-shirt and a jacket, his skin a pale blue as if he didn't often see the light of day.

"Are you here alone?" he asked Shira, voice deep and smooth.

Vivian frowned, then realized the reason he sounded odd to her was because he spoke with a flawless Standard accent.

Shira scowled up at him. "I'm with my girlfriend; get lost."

He glanced at Vivian, eyebrow rising. His gaze flickered down to her arms. "The one with bonding marks?"

Shira rolled her eyes. "Not that kind of girlfriend." But she paused, eyeing him up and down, as if having second thoughts.

Vivian stifled her cough; he *was* hot. Shira would come to her senses soon.

"You can dance with me," Shira declared, "but watch the hands or I'll cut them off."

"Sure, sweetheart. I'll wait till you ask."

"Don't be an ass. Come on."

Shira glanced at Vivian, quirking her eyebrow, and Vivian shrugged. She was expecting company soon, anyway. He'd find her, she was certain of it.

Several minutes later, her faith was rewarded as strong arms slipped around her waist from behind.

For once the intense, edged mood he carried with him after work matched the atmosphere. Vivian turned in her mate's arms, enjoying the look of him, mussed dark hair and brilliant eyes. A slight, somber smile as he stared down at her.

"I like the dress," he said. "Is there any more of it?"

Vivian laughed. "Now, that wouldn't be any fun."

His gaze flickered as a dancer came a little too close. His head snapped around, and the man drifted away.

"It's a club, Tai'ri. People are going to get close."

He drew her even tighter into his hold as the beat of the music increased. Soon he was moving his hips, displaying an effortless command of rhythm she hadn't realized he possessed.

Her eyes widened. "You've been holding out on me! You can dance."

"We just haven't gone to a club like this before." Tai'ri lowered his head, his lips brushing her earlobe. "Wanted to keep you to myself as long as you would let me."

Which explained his odd scowl, but silent acceptance, when she'd told him she and Shira were going to a club for the first time. They'd been out, of course, but usually quieter places closer to home in case the toddlers got restless with their caregivers.

"I've got bonding marks," she said. "No one is going to flirt with me."

"You're human. They might try." His expression darkened. "Some people learn things the hard way."

Vivian just laughed again and laid her head on his chest. They danced, and a shiver ran through her body. Tai'ri's hands caressed up her back, light and possessive.

"If we go home now, I can take care of that for you," he purred.

"Shira is having too much fun." Vivian lifted her head and looked around. "Where *is* Shira?"

Tai'ri tensed. "You don't know?"

Vivian stopped dancing and turned in a slow circle, searching the crowd for a woman with honey gold skin in a sea of blues. "She found a dance partner. I didn't think she'd leave this level. She knows better."

"Let's go," he growled, taking her hand.

Vivian wasn't *too* worried—Shira had the same amount of training Vivian did, and would signal through the comm if something was wrong. But still, better be safe than sorry. Vivian initiated contact.

"Shira?"

It took another request, then Shira's voice came through. "Viv?" She cleared her throat.

"Where are you? Tai'ri and I are worried."

"Tai'ri is here?"

There was the murmur of a deep male voice.

"Who is that?" Tai'ri growled. "Shira?"

"I'm good, I'm good," Shira said. "I'll be back up in a moment."

She cut the comm. Vivian glanced at her mate, smirking. "I think we interrupted something."

Tai'ri shook his head. "I'm giving her five minutes."

"Don't be a spoilsport. Let's go get a drink and wait."

They made their way to the bar on this level,

ordered nonalcoholic shots, and lingered for several minutes before heading back out to the dancefloor again.

Vivian did her best to distract him, knowing Shira was up to absolutely no good.

He glared down at her. "I know what you're doing. Let's go find her. There was a male with her."

Vivian grabbed his arm. "She's a grown woman, Tai'ri."

He opened his mouth to protest, and she placed a finger over his lips. "No. She's in no danger. We'll wait for her." She stepped into his body, wrapping her arms around his neck. "Dance with me."

His expression shifted, going from outraged indignation to something hungry. Then he blinked and shook his head. "Fine, but if she isn't back in—"

"I'm here, hold your horses, Gramps."

Vivian snickered.

Shira appeared a second later, her dance partner at her back. "Tai'ri, just so there is no misunderstanding, this is—" she paused "—you know, I didn't get your name, but I don't think it matters. Future One Night Only, this is my guardian, Tai'ri. Is everyone happy, now? Can I go back to what I was doing?"

Vivian pursed her lips against a sly smile, and glanced at Tai'ri, who was staring at the man, expression completely blank. Vivian stilled, glancing between them.

But Tai'ri didn't move, and didn't say anything, just

nodded. The other man met his gaze, equally inscrutable.

Shira caught on as well. "Do you two know each other or something? You're doing the weird alpha stare down."

"He's never seen me before," Tai'ri said.

"Ooookay . . ." she paused, narrowing her eyes.

"It should be safe enough," Tai'ri added softly, gaze still on the man.

"That's great," Shira said. "Hey, Viv, you mind if I meet you at your place in an hour or two?"

"Sure. Make it two, girl. If that's all he has to spare. Have fun."

They shared a grin.

"Imma do my *best*."

As soon as the front door opened, Tai'ri pushed her against the wall and took her mouth in a hot, savage kiss. He tugged the halter of her dress and she ducked her head long enough for him to shove it down, exposing her breasts. She wore a bra that cupped and pushed up their still fuller than pre-pregnancy weight.

"This damn thing," he swore, unlatching the bra so she spilled free. "Better. I want a week of you to myself, naked. And if I catch you in clothes, you have to stop what you're doing then and there, and get on your knees."

She snorted with laughter. "Like you would *ever* take a week off of work."

"I'm not the only one with that problem," he retorted. His hand slid down her stomach, tangled in her curls and began toying with her clit.

"I'd take a week off faster than you would." She inhaled, gasping.

He narrowed his eyes at her and displayed his teeth. "Is that a dare, *yada'ami*? Please dare me."

His thumb flicked her clit, rubbing and kneading. She moaned. "Ibukay needs you right now. But maybe a weekend."

"I want that in writing."

She tangled her fingers in his hair, tilting her head up and sliding a leg around his waist. "And I want you in me."

He hoisted her up, shoving her skirt to her waist and grinding against her. His fingers pushed aside the scrap of her barely there panties, plunging inside.

She choked on a cry, bucking against him. He hooked his fingers and pistoned in and out, rubbing against her spot until she was writhing and crying out.

Vivian tugged at his pants, frantic for more, undoing the fastenings and reaching for his hardness. He filled her hand, hot and heavy, pulsing with heat and life.

"Stop playing," he hissed in her ear, teeth grazing her neck and nipping.

It was a command she was happy to obey. She positioned him at her entrance; he shifted, then surged in. It wasn't gentle; he fucked her against the wall with all the ruthless desire she'd spent weeks teasing out of him until he'd finally been convinced she could take all of him.

Vivian screamed, and he covered the sound with a kiss. Moments later he joined her, grinding deep inside as his hot seed filled her body.

"Fuck," she swore. Her legs slipped off his waist, but he held her up until she was steady. His seed and her juices slid down her thighs in rivulets.

Vivian blinked up at him. "I hope your cousin is asleep." They'd had a roster of Tai'ri's cousins who babysat Mayleen, and Ori as well when Shira went out with Vivian.

"So what if she did?" He sounded complacent. Then he scowled down at her. "I don't know what you and Daobah were talking about the other week, but she told the Matrons we're in our married sex phase now."

Vivian giggled. It never ceased to amaze her how open his family was about sex, though she supposed it came with their calling.

He helped her fix her dress, and Vivian kicked off her heels. They walked down the hall and toward their suite.

"House, Mayleen and Ori's status?" Vivian asked.

:*Mayleen and Ori are sleeping.*:

"We have time for a shower before Shira gets here," Tai'ri said. "Since she's busy."

Shower sex. Vivian dashed ahead of him to the bathroom.

Thank you for reading!
The next book in this series is **Warrior's Taken,** Shira's story.

EMMAALISYN.COM/WARRIORSTAKEN

WARRIORS OF YEDAHN

ARCHANS OF AILAUT

ABOUT THE AUTHOR

Emma Alisyn writes paranormal romance because teaching high school biology wasn't like how it is on television. Her lions, tigers, and bears will most interest readers who like their alphas strong, protective and smokin' hot; their heroines feisty, brainy and bootilicious; and their stories with lots of chemistry, tension and plenty of tender moments.

emmaalisyn.com

Made in the USA
Columbia, SC
08 October 2021